THE DARING GIRLS OF GUERNSEY

A NOVEL OF WORLD WAR II

GAYLE CALLEN

Published by Oliver Heber Books

OLIVER
HEBER
BOOKS

From *USA Today* bestselling author Gayle Callen comes a fascinating historical novel of three courageous young women who aid a desperate British spy during the German occupation of Guernsey Island in World War II.

In 1940, Germany seizes control of Guernsey without a fight – but not without resistance. Innocent young teacher Catherine is forced to house a German officer. Shrewd waitress Betty seeks to elude the persistent Nazi determined to conquer her. And courageous nurse Helen cares for her patients – both British and German – while hiding a British spy in her seaside cottage.

Their fight against the injustices being enacted on their island home brings the women, the spy, and their enemies together in one night that will change all of their lives forever. None of them could foresee that the battle they fought that night would reach across time to 1997, when the tragic fallout ensnares Helen once more.

To my sister, Connie Weiser, who read everything I wrote since I was thirteen years old and always kept my latest book on her nightstand. I miss you so much.

1

CHELSEA
ERIE, PA, 1997

"It's true, dear. Someone is trying to kill me. Oh, how lovely, you brought chocolates."

I gaped at my grandmother, Helen Coleridge, lying in her hospital bed. She looked smaller than the last time I'd seen her, with a cast on her leg and a bruise on the left side of her face. But behind wire-rimmed glasses, those green eyes still regarded me steadily...expectantly. Her wavy white hair was cut short, the laugh lines around her eyes and mouth were a little deeper. I handed her the box of chocolates, feeling bewildered and sad. Were my parents right—was Grandma starting to lose it?

She lifted the cover of the box and closed her eyes as she inhaled the scent of chocolate. "You Americans do know how to make chocolate, no matter what anyone says."

"Grandma, you're an American, too." Had she even forgotten that she'd left the UK behind after World War II? Not the UK, I quickly reminded myself. Grandma would always frown as she reminded me that Guernsey Island was a dependency of the Crown, not a part of the United Kingdom.

"I know I'm an American, Chelsea." Instead of eating a chocolate, she regarded me with eyes that turned from teasing to sober, even as a monitor continued to beep behind her head. "But I do wish your parents had kept my concerns to themselves. At twenty-two, you are too young to be involved."

For a woman everyone was worried was losing her mind, Grandma certainly remembered my age correctly. My tense shoulders loosened a bit, and I sat down on the edge of the bed. A nurse came in to check the monitor, and the beeping disappeared. Smiling, the nurse left with an apology.

"Grandma," I said, "I'm not too young. At my age you were living under German occupation."

She ignored that statement and ate a chocolate.

"My parents only told me because they're worried, and I pried it out of them." I leaned closer and lowered my voice, trying to keep my eyes from watering as I said gently, "You fell down the stairs. It can happen to anybody."

She gave me a smile. "Of course you're right."

She took another bite as I frowned in confusion. "So now you're just backing down? You told my parents you couldn't return to your house because someone was trying to kill you, that you needed help finding someplace else to live."

"That was a mistake, weakness on my part. I don't need anyone's help selling my house."

"Selling your house? You've lived there all your married life!"

"You're right, that will be too suspicious. And I certainly don't want to put you or your parents in danger."

In danger? I had to struggle to keep my lips from trembling, even as my eyes stung. But Grandma didn't sound like someone who was losing her mind. Shouldn't she sound vague, distracted? Instead, she was confident and calm, like always, no different than during our weekly phone chats. Erie PA and New York City were far enough apart to make it hard for me to visit. I went to audition after audition, trying for my big break, and she loved hearing about it.

Grandpa had died ten years before, and Grandma had retired from the nursing career she'd resumed when my mom was in school. She still enjoyed her garden and reading books and going on day trips with her church group.

But now she'd fallen down the stairs. And look at the bruise on her cheek! She didn't have a concussion, but surely something was rattled in there.

I reached for the frail hand that had come to rest on top of the closed box of chocolate. "Tell me why you think someone is trying to kill you."

I willed her to meet my eyes, even as she stared at the window shades or the bland painting on the wall, anywhere but at me.

"Will you pour me some water, Chelsea?"

I reached for the little plastic pitcher on her tray table and accidentally knocked it over. "Damn!"

Franticly, I moved two books and the box of tissues out of the way of the spreading puddle, revealing an envelope underneath. It was dripping wet and already sliced open, so I pulled the letter out and unfolded it to dry.

"Give me that," she said suddenly.

But it was too late. I read:

Catherine died. You're next.

A shiver of unease chilled me. No signature, just a newspaper clipping taped to it—an obituary.

"Grandma?" I said, surprised at how weak my voice sounded.

"Just a joke between friends," she assured me. "We're of the age that all our friends die, and we wonder who'll be next, that's all."

I threw some napkins onto the puddle and sat down on the edge of the bed. "You think someone pushed you down the stairs. Is this letter the reason you believe your fall wasn't an accident?"

She pursed her lips for a long moment, but I was going to be patient if it killed me.

"The letter isn't the initial reason, no," she finally said, her voice quiet but earnest. "I felt the hands on my back just before I fell."

I shuddered.

"I don't want to involve you, Chelsea, I've told you that."

"It's too late—I'm involved. I want to help. I'm not a child. Didn't you say I'm the exact age you were when the Germans landed on Guernsey Island all those years ago?"

She frowned. "You believe me?"

Her clear eyes searched mine. This wasn't a woman who made things up, and she wasn't losing her mind—I didn't need a letter to convince me of that.

"Of course I do! Tell me what's going on, please. I want to help."

She gave a long sigh and lowered her gaze to the letter. "That's the obituary of a dear friend of mine, Catherine Chastain. Though I moved away from Guernsey after the war, we always stayed in touch by letter and phone. We even visited each other several times. There's a bond you cannot break, after what we went through. She died last week, bless her soul. The obituary says she died at home surrounded by her family, which gave me peace. But after that letter? I don't know what to think."

"Would someone want to kill her? And kill you?"

She gave a tired smile. "They might. Things happened in the war, my dear. We all made choices in hopes of surviving, some of which we regretted. It's a long story, but one I've been waiting your entire life to tell you. I don't want to wait anymore, even though you might not like what you discover."

She looked at me with such intensity that I actually gulped.

"I want to hear it," I said.

I had a premonition that everything I thought I knew was about to change.

With a deep sigh, she leaned back against her pillow, her gaze wandering slowly to the window. "The sky looked just this overcast on the day the Nazis arrived on Guernsey Island."

2

HELEN

SAINT PETER PORT, GUERNSEY ISLAND, 1940

A t first, Helen Abernathy didn't recognize the sound of marching feet. She'd been focused on the overcast sky, wondering if she'd made a mistake leaving her umbrella at home while she shopped on High Street along with other women frantic to secure supplies in case the worst happened. The breeze was warm, the scent of jasmine soothing. Palm fronds swayed in the nearby park. For once there weren't German planes flying overhead on their way to bomb Britain. War encroached on their island like a tightening noose trapping them between Britain and France. France had fallen just a few weeks before, the only country between them and Hitler's Wehrmacht.

As she looked through a window at the long queue of women inside the grocer's, she heard that sound again, distant, like the drone of a bee you're wary of but can't see. She found herself touching her mother's brooch pinned just above her heart, as if to give herself comfort. It was a tiny sprig of flowers, and it never failed to cheer her as it reminded her of her parents, who'd gone to heaven just two years before.

But she didn't feel cheered today, not as that strange sound became louder and louder, until she thought the ground would begin to shake. Her heart pounded in matching tempo, and she gripped her purse to steady her trembling.

Around the bend in the street, between the two- and three-story stone buildings, a division of German troops marched toward them. Helen hadn't even known they'd landed on the island.

It felt as if the world around her stopped, everything out of focus except for the soldiers in grayish green jackets with black equipment belts around their waists, dark helmets protecting their heads, marching in perfect formation, legs extended forward with showy precision.

She'd known they would come—it was all anyone talked about, especially after the Luftwaffe had bombed Saint Peter Port harbor, killing dozens, destroying a long line of lorries brimming with tomatoes, their major export. Helen's seamstress had died while waiting for her husband's fishing boat to return to the harbor; farmers across the island had had their season's crop obliterated. Helen had rushed to the waterfront, hoping her nursing skills could help.

Tens of thousands had fled the Channel Islands both before the bombing and afterward, leaving Guernsey a shell of itself, stores abandoned, fields left fallow. Now it looked like their fears had been justified.

Helen stiffened as they came closer, their marching boots louder, the ground trembling before them. An old man stumbled back against the wall and gasped, and Helen imagined she saw his memories of the Great War flashing in his stunned eyes.

Everyone around her scattered out of the street, pressing back against the stone walls or fleeing inside as the

Germans approached, looking so tall and formidable. There were no smirks—it wasn't necessary, and the soldiers knew it. They'd conquered the islands without a battle, without a soldier lost.

They came abreast of her, six across in the narrow lane. She swallowed convulsively, trying to hide her emotions, praying that she could be brave. Her island had been invaded, and no one knew what would happen next. There were whispers of what the Germans had done to remote villages in Poland and Czechoslovakia, men killed, women raped. Guernsey had no defenses, no weapons, unless you counted kitchen knives or shotguns for hunting. What islander would be foolish enough to fight against the most powerful army on the continent?

Britain obviously did not consider the Channel Islands worth fighting for; they'd taken their weapons and left. Bitterness was like bile in her stomach. Ever since the bombing of Saint Peter Port, she'd woken up several times a night, convinced she'd heard that low threatening drone of approaching planes, but it had only been the sea crashing against the cliffs beneath her cottage.

The last of the German division passed by, their marching footsteps fading, and an eerie silence permeated the street. Then by ones and twos, islanders emerged from the shops and stared in fear at the backs of the German soldiers until they were out of sight. Several children ran to follow them, and Helen almost reached for one—but what was the point?

At least there'd be no more bombings now that the Germans had arrived, she thought with irony.

Their little island paradise was theirs no more.

~oOo~

Helen drove to her friend Catherine's house on the edge of town, realizing she'd forgotten to buy the wine she'd meant to bring in her shock at the German invasion. The Braun household was a second home to her, especially after Helen's parents had died. They were a real family, loving and bickering even as they welcomed her. She and Catherine had been the best of friends since childhood, roaming the seashore for shells all summer, and playing football with girls when the boys wouldn't let them. Catherine was everything Helen wasn't—red-headed, vivacious, and outgoing, the first to make a new friend, with the ability to see the best in everybody. Though Helen was used to living alone, it would be good to be among people almost like family to her after the day's frightening events.

No one answered her knock. After a minute, she tried again, but the curtains didn't even ripple. This wasn't like the Brauns, and the fear welled back up inside her so quickly. Mr. Braun was an electrician at the airport—had he been there when the Germans arrived? Had something happened to him?

She ran down the steps and around the side of the house to the garden, the favorite retreat of the family. She thought she'd try the back door, but to her surprise, she found the Brauns gathered near the lush June foliage beyond the swings. They looked around guiltily when they heard her coming, then sagged with relief.

Mr. Braun straightened slowly, stiffly, his usual cheerful grin absent. Dirt speckled his knees and hands. His eyes usually lit with gladness upon seeing her, as if she was one of his own children, but now he frowned and shook a finger at her.

"Helen Abernathy, what are you doing out on the roads this evening? Don't you know how dangerous it is?"

Behind him, Catherine winced and mouthed an apology, throwing her dirty hands wide. It wasn't a true conversation if Catherine's hands weren't moving constantly.

"I was invited to dinner," Helen said, dismayed. "What are you all *doing* back here? I was scared to death when no one answered my knock."

"Don't you know that the Germans have landed?" Mr. Braun continued with outrage. "They took command of the island as if they owned it! They sneered down at those of us just doing our job."

"I was on High Street when they marched by," Helen said.

With a gasp, Catherine started to cover her mouth with both hands, then seemed to notice the dirt. "They've left the airport and come to town?"

Mrs. Braun, short and plump, cried out softly and buried her face in her apron.

Her eight-year-old son Timmy gave his mum a worried glance, but when he looked at Helen, she saw the excitement he couldn't hide. "What did you see? What did they do?"

"They just—marched with precision," Helen said lamely. "I think they wanted to scare us, and it worked. But what are all of *you* doing right now?"

The Brauns exchanged nervous glances.

Catherine loudly whispered, "We're burying the silver. Want to help?"

Regardless of how overwhelmed she was feeling, Helen wanted to join in, anything to help them all believe they were doing *something* against the Germans. Timmy handed her a spare shovel, and she set to work alongside them. They didn't have all that much silver, but the ground was hard, and the light was failing. By the time they'd put several small boxes into the ground, replaced the dirt and the squares of grass, then leaned on their shovels in exhaustion, they could barely see each other.

"Come inside for supper," Mrs. Braun told Helen.

She was so hungry it was easy to agree.

The family trooped inside, but Catherine took Helen's arm and pulled her back, then burst into tears. Helen enfolded her in a hug, and they stood there, trying to find some comfort in their long friendship, the way they always knew what the other was thinking.

At last, Catherine's quiet sobs lessened, and she pulled back to tug a handkerchief out of her sleeve and blow her nose.

"Better?" Helen asked gently.

"No." But she was almost smiling as she spoke. "I'm glad you're here."

They sank down onto the swings they'd used since childhood and looked at each other.

"I didn't think the Germans would invade," Catherine said after a long silence. "Foolish of me, I know."

Helen sighed. "We certainly kept hoping we'd be spared."

"I feel so...selfish, as if it shouldn't happen to me, when it's happening to so many people in so many countries."

"You're not selfish."

"I am! I won't be able to receive letters from George—see how selfish I am?"

"You were dating—of course you're worried about him."

Catherine let out a sigh. "He was never going to love me, and I didn't love him. Even his last letter only seemed polite. But...oh, Helen, I just thought I'd live a normal life, get married, have children."

"You're going to do all of that."

"See how selfish I am? I'm upset a war interrupted all my grand plans."

Helen gave her friend an indulgent smile. Of the two of them, Catherine had always been the one to think about her wedding. She had a trousseau begun with pretty linens she'd embroidered; she had the music picked out for the church service. Weddings—marriage—were something Helen didn't let herself think about too much. She'd been focused on nursing, on supporting herself after her parents' deaths. And knowing her mother wouldn't be able to help her plan? She didn't even want to think about it.

"Ignore me," Catherine said. "I will get used to our new situation. Maybe it won't last long."

Helen doubted that, and she could tell by Catherine's distant gaze, that she didn't believe it either.

Soon they were called into dinner. Once the five of them were seated at the table, they all bowed their heads to say grace, and the war suddenly felt very real. No more *Help me keep my temper, Lord,* or *I had unkind thoughts about my teacher.* Now it was: *Let them treat us kindly, Lord. Keep us safe as the war comes to Guernsey.*

Into the reverent silence, Timmy's young voice piped up. "My brother will stop those Jerries! He's back from Dunkirk. Helen, did you hear how he was rescued?"

Helen nodded, and saw Mr. and Mrs. Braun exchange a glance full of fear, quickly hidden. Catherine's middle brother Richard had enlisted the moment he turned eighteen the previous year. Though his family was proud, Helen knew they never had a worry-free moment. Catherine often showed Helen his letters, with occasional lines blacked out, but full of patriotism and excitement. When Helen thought of Richard putting himself in danger every day, she could only remember him as a boy who'd tried to sneak a kiss from her when he turned sixteen. And now that boy was a soldier.

The British army hadn't tried to stop Hitler from taking the Channel Islands, and Helen felt another spasm of anger. No one had defended them, and they had to keep themselves safe.

How were they supposed to do that?

Most of the young men had gone, ten thousand of them from the islands. Helen and Catherine had each been dating men before the war started, but they had volunteered and shipped out. Their letters were less and less frequent. There'd been no love, no promises, and Saturday nights had been so quiet of late.

What would they be like now?

"This is all Chamberlain's fault," Mr. Braun said as he passed the potatoes.

"No war talk at dinner," Mrs. Braun said automatically.

Her husband gaped at her. "We've been *invaded*! Today!"

She blinked at him, and Helen saw that she was trembling.

"Of course I know that," Mrs. Braun murmured. "It's a silly rule anyway."

Mr. Braun covered her hand with his. "It's not. It's just... impractical now, my dear."

She nodded, biting her lip, even as she passed a platter of mutton.

"Take some, Mum," Catherine said quietly, pushing the platter back.

"Oh, of course." Mrs. Braun took a small slice and slid the platter back.

"A prime minister should look to his country's welfare," Mr. Braun said, as if he hadn't been interrupted. "Instead

Chamberlain practically welcomed Hitler to help himself to Austria, then much of Czechoslovakia."

"Dad, you know Chamberlain tried to negotiate peace between Hitler and the other countries," Catherine said.

"Pshaw. He believed everything Hitler told him and backed down."

"It's very easy to look back and see what should have been done," Catherine insisted. "At the time, no one wanted war. But now we have it. It seems our new prime minister, Mr. Churchill, sees the enemy for what he is."

"Perhaps, my girl, but I'll have to wait and see. He let our islands go quite easily—what else will be sacrificed?"

They ate in silence for long minutes.

At last Mr. Braun sighed. "Helen, I hope you've tried to prepare the best you can. My wife has been buying so much food."

"It's difficult to leave my patients," Helen said. "But I did manage to shop the shelves bare at the grocer's yesterday, thinking they'd be replenished. How long will that last with the Germans keeping British ships away?"

"Surely they have to feed their own men," Catherine said. "They won't let us all starve."

Her words fell into a heavy silence.

"Helen, you shouldn't live on your own so far from town," Mrs. Braun said, twisting a napkin in her hands.

Helen put on a bright smile. "But won't the town be where the Germans are? I won't let the Germans think they can bully us out of our homes." Quietly, she added, "And my home is...it's the only thing I have left of my parents. Why would they come to the boring countryside? I won't let the Germans take it from me, and they'll find that difficult to do if I'm living there."

Mrs. Braun looked at her husband, but he was staring

out the window as if he expected the Germans to storm the house. And he might very well be right, Helen thought. Fear shot through her belly, and for a moment, she feared she'd eaten too much and that her stomach would rebel.

But no. Her life was changing in ways she'd never imagined—she had to meet it head on. While Allied soldiers met Germans on the battlefield, it was up to civilians to do their part on the home front. While the rest of Britain put up blackout curtains and rationed food, Guernsey Island would be living side by side with the enemy.

3

BETTY

Betty stood at the serving station, menus in hand, finding herself reluctant to walk across the restaurant dining room. Not that she hadn't done it thousands of times in the four years she'd been working at the Guernsey Grand Hotel. But today was different. For several weeks, since half the island had evacuated, it had been hard for Betty to pay the rent on her flat, to purchase food for her mother, and she hadn't allowed herself to buy cigarettes.

But in just one day with the German occupying force, she'd already made the equivalent of a month's rent—it did not feel good to know that her well-being would now depend on Germans.

Dinner at the restaurant was filled with soldiers, many fresh from the horrors of the Eastern Front. They'd spoken accented English, telling her how beautiful she was, waxing poetic about the beaches and the picturesque town surrounding the harbor.

"The harbor you've just bombed where defenseless people died?" The words had slipped out of her without volition.

The two young German officers had stared up at her and actually blushed.

"It wasn't us," one had said.

"And it's war," the other said, almost gently. "We would never do anything to hurt a lovely lady such as yourself."

She'd wanted to scoff, but she was good at keeping her expression unemotional, her smile a mask hiding her thoughts. Germans were as blinded by her face, an accident of birth, as anyone else. Men were so predictable. And she knew how to make such predictability work for her.

Betty saw a customer's hand gesture at her with annoyance. She didn't even have to work hard to soothe the man's ego and tame his temper. She bent over him, smiling, giving him all her attention. He didn't even realize the methods she was using, the way he relaxed and expanded into her like a temperamental hothouse flower being watered.

Betty had all the motivation in the world to ensnare a man to do her bidding. She'd grown up with a mother who had no clue how to do such things, who'd let every man treat her like a servant. Betty's father had drained the vitality from his wife with his endless demands and taunts and even the back of his hand. Then he'd run out on both of them.

One bad man hadn't been enough for her mum, who continued on with a line of greedy, lazy men, looking in desperation for the one who would support her and her only child, never realizing that only a certain type of man was drawn to a woman so desperate for affection that she'd overlook any behavior. Mum had tried to protect Betty as best she could, sometimes forcing her to huddle silent in the closet for hours while the worst happened. Betty would cover her ears against her mother's muffled, pitiful cries and tell herself over and over that she'd never be like her mother, never.

German soldiers were another animal altogether. In just one day, she could already tell they were far more brazen and daring—they were winning the war; they'd conquered British territory. Right now, they were giddy with triumph, relieved to be on a lush island away from the fighting, trying to prove they were civilized men. How long would that last?

Already today, two Germans had offered to escort her out for an evening. She'd been able to dissuade them, but both had made it clear they'd ask again.

When at last the guests had departed and the dining room had been cleaned and ready for the next day's opening, Betty put on her coat, picked up her handbag and paused just inside the door leading to the rear of the hotel.

"Betty?"

She glanced over her shoulder and saw Margaret, one of the other waitresses.

"You don't have a car, do you?" Margaret asked.

Betty shook her head. "I don't live far. It's an easy walk."

"Not tonight, it isn't. Let me give you a ride."

Betty was about to refuse but she thought of the soldiers who'd seen no women during extended tours of war duty. They'd been nice in the restaurant. How would they behave at night on the streets?

She gave Margaret a polite smile. "Thank you, I accept your offer."

After a short car ride, they came to Betty's home on the upper floor of a flat off High Street, where the shadows were dark and long, as if no light would ever come to such a disreputable place. Margaret was too polite to say anything, although she bit her lip with worry as she looked out the car window.

Betty jingled her keys. "I'm ready. I'll be fine. Thanks,

again." She got out and hurried to the door, ignoring the distant sound of laughter and someone playing the piano.

The key let her into a dingy foyer where a bare bulb flickered overhead. A door led to the ground-floor flat, and a steep set of stairs disappeared up into the darkness. As usual, it smelled like mildew and something burnt.

Betty climbed up the stairs, but didn't hear the drone of the radio. Her mother normally liked to keep herself company with the BBC broadcast when Betty was working, but tonight the silence was almost eerie.

She let herself into the flat. The lights were out, and only a faint gleam from the streetlamp glowed in the window. "Mum?"

"Over here!" Her mother's voice was only a hiss.

Betty shut the door and heard, "Lock it!"

"I always do, Mum."

"I still can't believe you left me alone, today of all days."

Betty followed the sound of her mother's voice until she located her half hidden in the draperies as she stared out the window.

Her mother was one of those women who looked tired and defeated all the time, her face drooping as if she'd forgotten how to smile, her gray hair falling out of its bun.

If it had been up to Betty, they'd have evacuated the island weeks ago like so many of their neighbors. But her mother had this fixation that her father would someday return. She was afraid if they moved, he wouldn't be able to find them. It didn't matter that the man had beaten her and practically used her as a slave. Time had faded the worst memories, and all Mum seemed to remember was their early years, when he'd still been enjoying his life, his good job, and his pretty wife. But he'd been the kind of man who couldn't keep a job long, always convinced he knew better than the men in charge. One firing led to another, and he began to take out his anger on his wife.

"Those Germans," her mother said in a trembling voice. "You were out there"—she pointed frantically toward the window—"with *them*! Did any of them hurt you?"

"No, they behaved like gentlemen today."

"Like gentlemen?" Her mother's pale brown eyes were wide with confusion and fear. "They're *invaders*. What do they want here?"

"They're one step closer to England."

She pressed her trembling lips together. "I saw them on the streets below. I was so afraid..."

Pity rose up within her, and Betty put an arm around her mother. She seemed frailer, trembling.

"I know, Mum. But they're here now, and we can only do what we must to survive."

Her mother stared at her with desperation, as if trying to convince herself. "If we just behave, they might leave us alone?"

"I think so."

I hope so.

4

HELEN

Early the next morning, Helen stood at her kitchen window, a mug of tea cupped in her hands as she looked out onto the English Channel. Her little cottage was perched near the cliffs and, below, the water glistened with the touch of the sun. Birds called to each other; insects buzzed in time to the birdsong. Palm trees shaded her yard. It was an idyllic view, one that the British had flocked to every summer for their tropical holidays.

No one would be flocking there now. Helen had never questioned her decision to stay instead of evacuate. She had nowhere else to go, no place that mattered to her as much as this place.

Sipping her tea, she remembered how difficult it had been to fall asleep, what with the drone of airplanes high above the islands on their way to Britain. Catherine, spending the night in her guest bedroom, had surely felt the same, for although an early riser, she was still in bed. Her best friend had insisted Helen shouldn't be alone the first night after the invasion. But companionship couldn't make one safe. The bombing runs had been happening with more and more frequency, after all. At the beginning, she'd thought those planes were aimed at their island, and had lain in bed rigid with fear as she waited for explosions, but they'd only found a local target once, at the Saint Peter Port harbor. She couldn't imagine experiencing that kind of devastation and terror night after night.

It probably hadn't helped their sleep that the two of them had huddled around the radio listening to war news on the BBC, but had heard nothing about the Germans taking over the Channel Islands. Did Britain not know? How could that be?

Helen wandered through the parlor, looking at the desk where her mum had written her poetry and her father had graded science tests after teaching all day at Elizabeth College. She looked at a photograph of their small family, saw her mother's blond hair, her father's blue eyes, the traits she'd inherited. When she'd lost them both at once to pneumonia, it had sent her reeling, unable to fathom a life without them, unable to believe that her nursing skills had been useless. But gradually her memories had turned peaceful, surrounding her with a warm feeling of love. She never wanted to leave this cottage.

The sound of tires on gravel and the rumble of an engine startled her. For a moment she thought Catherine's father had come to take his daughter home. She glanced through the front window—and saw the German flag on the hood of the car. She froze, a sensation of vulnerability rising within her, even more intense than those days after she'd lost her parents. She touched her mother's flower brooch she always wore, remembering feeling helpless with grief and loneliness; now she was experiencing the helplessness of terror and fear of the future. She wanted to hide in the cellar, pretend it all might go away.

But it would not go away until Germany was defeated. She debated waking Catherine, wanting her to be prepared, but hoped there'd be no need to frighten her. When the inevitable knock came, she took a deep breath, straightened her shoulders, and went to answer it. Her hand shook on the doorknob, and she willed it into submission.

Standing on her stoop, two German soldiers looked at her. Their army jackets were wrapped in a bulky equipment belt, their helmets pulled low over their brows.

"*Frau*, is your husband here?" one of them asked in accented English.

"I am not m-married." She heard herself stutter, and knew she could not let fear incapacitate her. A good nurse was always in control of her emotions.

"Your father, then," he continued impatiently.

"My father is dead. I own this cottage, sir. What do you want?"

"The car is yours?" the other asked. When she nodded, he handed her a slip of paper. "We are requisitioning it for temporary use by the Reich."

"You cannot steal my only means of transportation," she insisted, forcing herself to sound stern. "I am a nurse, and my patients need me."

"We are not stealing the car," the first soldier said almost wearily, as if he'd repeated the same sentence several times already. "We are borrowing it for the duration. You will be compensated for any wear and tear. When the war is over, it will be returned."

"But—"

"The keys, *fraulein*."

They just stared at her, and she knew she'd never change their minds. She imagined people all over the island were losing their cars.

"I will be right back," she said tightly, then started to close the door.

A large male hand stopped the door. "Leave it."

She went to her desk in the parlor, dreading the sound of their boots tromping through her home as they searched it. But they waited on the stoop, right where she'd left them. She walked back to the door and held out the keys.

When he took them, he handed her a folded newspaper. "You should read this, *fraulein*. The rules that you must live under are written here."

She took the newspaper numbly.

He gave a precise bow. "*Danke*."

Her heart clenched with dismay as she watched the one soldier get in her car while the other got into the first car. Then they drove away. It was as if her freedom went with them, but of course, her freedom had truly left yesterday, when the Germans had arrived. Even now she could see several low-flying planes waiting to land at the airport and disgorge Germans like angry bees preparing for attack.

"Helen!"

She whirled around to see Catherine clutching her dressing gown together, her curls twisted with rags, tears streaming down her face.

"I heard them. I—I should have been here to support you. I—I couldn't make myself leave the bedroom." She gave a sob and briefly covered her mouth. "You were so brave, and I am such a coward."

Helen closed the door, dropped the newspaper on the hall table, and went to Catherine, enveloping her in a tight hug. They stood together a long moment, Catherine trembling with her quiet crying, Helen blinking back tears. She tried to tell herself that at least they'd only taken her car, not her cottage.

"I'm glad you stayed hidden," Helen said, pulling back and holding her friend by the upper arms. "They might have heard you and believed I'd lied about having no man about the cottage. They could have burst in and...made a mess of things." Or shot Catherine. Helen shuddered.

"You're just being kind to me." Catherine sniffed and wiped her eyes on the hem of her dressing gown. She looked past Helen. "Is that the newspaper?"

"Courtesy of the Germans. They left me a copy so I could read their rules."

Catherine lifted the paper and then headed for the kitchen, saying over her shoulder, "We need a cup of tea if we're to read what our future holds."

They didn't talk about the paper while they prepared breakfast, working silently together making tea, eggs, and toast, while the paper sat in the middle of the table like a death notice. At last they sat side by side at the dining room table, the paper spread out before them.

The Evening Press had a huge headline above the fold. "Orders of the Commandant of the German forces in occupation of the island of Guernsey."

Helen inhaled deeply. Catherine held a piece of toast in her hand, frozen. Their lives had changed for as long as the war would last. Germans on the streets were one thing—the rules they would now have to live by were even more sobering. They both read silently.

"There's a curfew!" Helen cried.

"We can't buy petrol or use cars!" Catherine said with a gasp, flinging her hands wide.

"We have to advance the clocks one hour to match Central European Time."

The change of time zone seemed so pointlessly stupid

that Helen snorted the tea as she sipped. Catherine stared at her with wide eyes and clapped a hand over her mouth.

Helen was hoarse as she practically wheezed, "Why do I feel like I want to laugh and cry at the same time?"

"We are...hysterical," Catherine said between giggles, holding her stomach. "But there's more to read."

And it sobered them. By special order of the bailiff, they were to offer no resistance to the Germans and obey their orders.

The two women sat back in their seats and looked at each other. "So that's it then," Helen said. "We are conquered, with no one to fight for us."

"What did you expect the bailiff to do?" Catherine mused. "He's an old, frail man. We have no soldiers."

"I know, it's just..." And then she looked at her watch. "Goodness! I'm going to be late! And without a car..." She jumped to her feet and headed for the stairs.

The telephone rang.

"Answer it, will you?" Helen called.

As she washed and dressed, she heard Catherine's muffled voice.

A few minutes later, Catherine called, "It was my father. He's coming to get me. Apparently, the schools are still open."

"I thought no one could drive," Helen said.

"I don't know, but he's coming. Maybe he can give you a ride to the hospital."

"No, thanks, I have an old bicycle. Might as well start using it today."

Fifteen minutes later, Helen had pulled the bicycle out of the garage, frowning at the approaching gray clouds. As if to complement the new state of her life, it began to rain while she rode to town.

The streets were unusually quiet. The people she *did* see didn't call out a greeting as they clutched their umbrellas low over their heads, walking quickly, furtively, as if hoping they wouldn't be seen.

The Germans on the street moved quickly as well, but with the open pride and precision of well-drilled men basking in their victory. When one whistled at her and elbowed his friends, she stared straight ahead, struggling to keep anger from her expression, and their laughter faded behind her as she rode away. How was she supposed to live her life normally?

Before her shift, Helen changed into a dry uniform—blue dress, dark stockings, white apron and cap—then met up with Bridgette, her closest friend at the hospital, in the nurses' lounge.

Bridgette, dark haired and plump, hugged Helen for a long time, her glasses digging into Helen's cheek, but she didn't protest. They weren't the only two women in the room needing each other's company.

At last, Bridgette broke away and chuckled nervously while wiping wetness from her cheeks. "I'm sorry. I've never been so frightened in my life. Mum didn't want me to come to work, but I couldn't do that to our patients. Dr. Caples says a third of the staff stayed home. I hope they don't get fired."

"I can't believe they would," Helen said.

"Did you see any Germans?" Bridgette asked, then hurried on without waiting for an answer. "We've been told to expect an officer to be assigned to our house—*living with us!*"

Helen opened her mouth—

"But that won't happen to you," Bridgette said. "You live in the country."

"The Germans came to my cottage this morning." Helen spoke in a rush before she could be interrupted again.

Bridgette's mouth dropped open, and for once she seemed speechless. Swallowing hard, she said, "You live alone! You must have been so frightened. What did they want?"

"My car."

"So *that's* why you were wet." Bridgette hesitated. "How did you bear it? Did they...barge right in?" She was looking Helen up and down as if searching for signs of bruises.

After Helen explained what happened, Bridgette gave a sigh of relief. "I'm so glad you're safe. You should move to town."

"I can't—I won't." It seemed like swearing a vow, as if remaining in her home was some kind of victory. Was it courage or stubbornness or recklessness? She didn't know.

As Bridgette shook her head in exasperation, the head nurse opened the door and leaned in.

"Ladies, your shift has begun. Keep calm and keep your spirits up. This occupation won't last forever."

As Helen made her rounds, the orderliness of the hospital and her routine eventually proved calming. Patients had to be bathed, surgical dressing changed, beds freshened. Helen could almost forget that the war had come to Guernsey—until the emergency ward doors were flung wide, and German soldiers carried in German patients on gurneys.

Bridgette, standing before an open supply cabinet, gave a startled cry. "Is there a battle somewhere on Guernsey?" she asked Helen.

"Surely we would have heard." Helen's mouth went dry with fear.

Who could possibly be fighting well-trained soldiers, when their own soldiers had shipped out just a month ago?

Her training overtook her fear, and she went to a moaning German patient with bandages on his leg that had begun to seep blood. He couldn't understand her, and she couldn't understand him—all she could do was calm him with her hands and her voice until at last he lay docile and let her use warm water to pry stiff bandages out of his wounds. She found sutures that had obviously been sewn days ago, but exertion had ruptured some of them.

Days ago?

She reported his condition to the head nurse, who'd make recommendations of patient priority to the doctor.

Helen caught Bridgette by the arm and whispered, "These are old wounds. They're bringing their wounded to Guernsey!"

They briefly sagged together in relief that there wasn't a skirmish on their island. But this would change their mission—they'd go from treating minor surgical patients to battlefield trauma recovery, the kind she'd only heard about in nursing school.

"Attention!" A German officer, badges of victory splashed across his chest, had just entered the ward, and now looked about with his fists on his hips. "I am *Herr Obersterstarzt* Fischer. These are my patients. All of their treatment will be coordinated through me. We will do things the proper way—the German way."

Bridgette and Helen glanced at each other, but didn't dare protest.

~oOo~

That night, Helen listened to the rain pounding on the

roof, trying to think of anything but the line at the grocer's she'd seen the day before, and wondering if food would become less plentiful if the Germans halted their trading with Britain.

And then she heard a sound.

She wasn't certain what it was—a branch falling? There wasn't much wind, just a drenching spring rain.

The sound echoed again. Was it a knock? Gooseflesh rose along her arms, even as she got out of bed and wrapped her dressing gown about her nightclothes.

She only had her father's old shotgun for defense.

After creeping downstairs, she stood in the front hall, listening. The absolute dark before dawn surrounded her, when only knowing her own cottage so well kept her from stumbling into something. She stood still and listened intently, until she heard the sound again, coming from the back of the house.

Taking her father's shotgun from the closet, she crept toward the back door off the kitchen. The sound happened again, definitely a knock, but a hesitant, quiet one. Could it be someone hurt?

She finally reached the door, head cocked, every hair on her body on end. The shotgun shook in her hand. She didn't ask who was there, not wanting to alert anyone to her presence. She reached slowly for the lock, and then the doorknob, and as she turned it, she sank to her knees beside the door, shotgun ready, knowing whoever came through wouldn't expect to find her in that position.

The door did not slam open. It was her heart doing all the slamming, rebounding so painfully she was afraid she'd actually faint. She didn't say anything—*couldn't* say anything, even as she wildly thought she was crazy for opening her door in the middle of the night.

"Hello?" It was a man's voice with a British accent.

"Who are you?" she hissed. "I have a gun aimed at the doorway."

"Helen?"

She stiffened. "Answer me!"

"It's Jack Dupuis. May I come in?"

She sank back on her haunches. Jack Dupuis? He'd left the island years before, searching for excitement and military adventures long before the war had even begun.

"Jack?" She repeated his name in bewilderment.

The door slowly opened, even as she scrambled to her feet. She kept the shotgun in her hands, but pointed away, unable to see anything.

She heard a click, then the light of an electric torch arched across her kitchen floor.

"Is anyone else home?" he whispered.

He was just a formless shadow against the dark rainy night.

"I live alone," she whispered back, and then realized she didn't have to whisper. Clearing her throat, she said, "Come in and shut the door. I'll turn on the light."

There was a small lamp on the table, and she switched it on, bathing the kitchen in a homey glow. She turned around —and gasped when she saw Jack. Rain ran from his dark, shapeless clothes, forming a puddle on her wooden floor. When he turned off the torch and set it on the table, she saw that his fingers and palms were bleeding.

The enormity of what was happening began to sink in. Jack was here, in her kitchen, on the island. Before the war, he'd come home for a funeral once, but she'd only seen him from a distance.

"What—how—" She couldn't even think of what to say.

Glancing at the window, he sank down into a wooden

chair. "I remember your place being remote, and I'm glad my memory served me well."

He remembered her home? She didn't think he'd ever been there.

"Jack, what is going on?" she demanded.

She hurried to the sink to pour a basin of warm water and gather soap and towels. She brought them back to the table and set them before him, but didn't know what else to do. She'd never imagined a person could look so exhausted and bruised, yet alert at the same time. His eyes seemed to alight on everything in her kitchen, from the oven to the sink to the cupboards, with a restlessness that was almost a little wild. He made no move to help himself, so at last she lifted one of his hands and put it in the basin. He didn't stop her and didn't help, so she used a cloth and scrubbed at the dirt encrusting his wounds. She put the clean hand on a towel, dumped and refilled the water, and put his other hand in to wash it. It was a strangely intimate act with a man she'd never let herself get close to.

When she tried to roll a bandage over his scrapes, he finally spoke. "No, that will hamper me."

"Hamper you how? What have you been doing and how did you get here?"

"A submarine dropped me off last night to do some reconnaissance."

She inhaled swiftly, but said nothing. Instead, she went to the oven and put a kettle on to boil.

"I've been hiding in the cave below your cliff." He looked at his hands. "It's harder to walk those cliff-side paths than I remember. I got off course in the dark and had to scale a pretty steep wall. I did try my parents' house first—I was hoping it was still abandoned after their evacuation. But I saw a German officer there."

She sank slowly into her chair across the table and just looked at him. Jack Dupuis and she had never had anything in common, had barely spoken to each other in secondary school. She'd been devoted to her books and studies, while he'd been devoted to...life. No room had ever seemed big enough to contain him. Guernsey was too confining—he'd wanted to see the world. He dated girls who matched him in attractiveness, not girls like her.

"The cave," she finally said. "*My* cave? There's nothing there but stone and sea water."

"I know. Believe me, I don't mean to stay long."

She noticed how his cheeks had gotten leaner, how he'd become a man when she'd once thought him that already. He'd had sandy-haired good looks when most of the island boys were dark-haired. She was so busy staring at him that it took her teapot whistling to bring her out of her stupor.

After pouring the boiling water into the jug where ground coffee already waited, she said, "You need a change of clothes. I have some of my father's in the attic."

She hurried upstairs, found some clothes, and laid them out in the guest bedroom.

On her return, she poured him a cup of coffee, her mind buzzing, her thoughts out of order. She'd never felt like this before. She'd always prided herself on her calm head, her nurse's training, but now Jack Dupuis was here in her kitchen after all these years.

And he was hiding from the Germans.

A shot of fear went through her—but it was strangely mixed up with excitement. A British soldier—Jack!—sat at her kitchen table after sneaking onto the island. She could barely look at him as he sipped his coffee and watched her, one corner of his mouth turned up with faint amusement.

And it suddenly bothered her. "This isn't funny," she

said.

His smile disappeared. "The situation is not. But you... I've upset your evening, and watching you unsure of yourself is so surprising that I'm amused."

She frowned, putting her hands on her hips as she looked at him. "What are you saying? You don't know anything about me. It's not as if we socialized."

"That's true enough, for many reasons." He suddenly shivered.

"We can talk later," she said. "Come upstairs and try the clothes I laid out."

He stood up, his face becoming part of the shadows as he moved away from the light. "I *should* say no. I resisted coming here."

"Then why did you come?"

He turned his head away. "I don't really know; realization that I couldn't just stay in a cave for days or weeks, perhaps."

She felt strangely disappointed. "And you couldn't have. You'd have caught your death."

His smile was faint and ironic. "I believe I've experienced worse than a cold these last few years."

He followed her upstairs and into a small unused bedroom, then looked at her father's clothes. "I was sorry to hear that your parents had died. I couldn't get leave to attend the funeral."

Startled, she stared up into Jack's eyes. "I did receive your letter. Thank you."

She'd been surprised and touched that he'd thought of her, even writing about her father's kindness in helping him repair his bicycle when he was a child.

"Please get changed," she said. "You can bring down your clothes in the morning, if you'd like."

"Would you happen to have something to eat?"

She clapped a hand to her forehead. "Of course. I'll have something ready when you come down. The bathroom is next door."

She hurried back down the stairs and into her kitchen, still feeling as if it was a dream. After bringing the leftover soup out of the larder, she lit the burner above the oven.

Jack came down almost too quickly, his hair toweled, the trousers and buttoned-down shirt loose on him. Taking another sip of his coffee, which was surely cold now, he didn't complain. She felt him watching her as she stirred the soup.

"So you know why I'm here," he said, "but why are *you* here? I was told the island knew weeks in advance that an invasion could happen. Tens of thousands of people fled. Not you."

She wanted to be offended—what business was it of his? But...he was concerned, and she was touched.

"I couldn't leave the only things I had left of my parents."

He folded his arms over his chest and waited.

"That's it—the entire truth. This is all I have in the world, Jack. But is there any strategy for the Channel Islands?"

"I'm to study what the Germans are doing in case they're planning to use the islands as a base of invasion."

She ladled him a bowl of soup, and he began to devour it. He was taking so many risks—traveling to the islands under the watchful eyes of German guns, spying. She looked at his lean face, his haunted but determined eyes, and felt a deeper admiration and respect—and envy. She was doing nothing to fight Hitler, just sitting on the island, trying to pretend life was normal, feeling helpless.

But tonight, she was hiding a spy.

"I remember Richard Braun telling me that nursing was your profession," Jack said.

"It is." He had talked about her with Catherine's brother?

"Do you think you'll work for the Germans?" he asked.

"I've already treated German soldiers today. What other choice do we have? Stop feeding our families or paying rent?"

"Will that be difficult?" he asked with sympathy.

"I don't ask a sick person who they are. I treat anyone who's ill because I took a vow to do so. I've learned to be as efficient and unemotional as I can be. It's my job."

"I imagine some would not see it your way."

"I can't imagine people would show condemnation. Everyone here is just trying to survive until the war is over."

With a nod, he took another spoonful of soup.

"What will you do now?" she asked.

"Go back to the cave during the day, and scout at night."

"You don't need to be uncomfortable in the cave. Stay here."

He frowned. "That's impossible. I won't put you in that kind of danger."

"You don't think I'm in danger now?"

"Helen—"

"In twenty-four hours, I've already seen people skittering out of the way of German soldiers, praying for help that probably won't come. But now you're here."

"I'm not the help you need to save the whole island," he said with a sarcastic tilt to his mouth.

She leaned over, hands braced on the table. "But you're trying to help us by bringing about the end of the war. That's the only way we're going to survive. I want to help. Did you know that there's another way out of that cave?"

5

HELEN

Helen could see Jack's confusion, his eagerness, his doubt.

"What are you saying?" he asked. "I explored the entire cave. There's no magical back door."

"Did you look up?"

She watched his expression change from bafflement to understanding.

"There's an entrance to the cave beneath your cottage?" He was whispering, as if they shared the world's best secret.

"I'll show you."

She walked to the closed cellar door, opened it, and switched on the electric light. The wooden stairs creaked as she descended, and the scent of damp earth grew stronger with every step down. There were neat stacks of wooden crates, several broken chairs, and a tall set of shelves that filled one wall. Every inch of shelf space was filled with her canned vegetables and fruit. She prayed her supply would be enough. Who knew what the Germans intended to do to them?

Jack's gaze raked the floor, intent and focused. Once, he'd been full of life and joy, a young man who never sat still, who exuded charisma. Now he was serious and sober —a spy. His intensity in the small darkly shadowed cellar was almost intimidating.

In the far corner, she pushed aside a stack of crates. A door was flush with the wooden floor.

He gave a low whistle. "Some kind of soldier I am. I never even looked."

"It would have done you no good," she said, gesturing to the bolt that locked the door closed. "You can't get in from the cave unless this is unbolted, and you have a ladder."

"Can you show me how it works?"

"The bolt?" she asked, amused.

He gave her an impatient look, and she chuckled. With two hands, she gripped the bolt and pulled hard.

"Let me—" he began.

She shook her head. "No, I can do this. I've never let the hinges get rusted."

His slow smile took on a wicked edge. "Good girl."

His praise made her face heat, but she ignored it. The bolt shot back, and she put her fingers in the steel loop and pulled up. Soundlessly, the trap door lifted.

A damp coldness rose up from the depths, swirling about them, bringing the smell of the sea.

Helen stared down into the black hole. "My dad used to say that we had smugglers in our family last century."

"No doubt about it," he murmured. He pulled out his electric torch. "How do you get down?"

She gestured to the ladder leaning against the wall. "The old-fashioned way. Unless you want to swing down a rope."

They continued to look down in silence for a long moment.

"You don't need to go down there tonight," she said quietly. "You could sleep in a comfortable bed. It is hardly neglecting your duty to get warm and rested and fed."

He hesitated. "All right, I'll take you up on your offer—just for tonight."

He closed the trap door, and the sound had a strange feeling of finality to it. She'd made this offer, and she certainly wouldn't change her mind.

But a long-ago part of her, innocent of war, remembered how disreputable it would be to sleep in the same house as a man unrelated to her.

But that life didn't exist anymore—that girl had faded away beneath the onslaught of fear. She could play a small part in the war effort by helping Jack—that's all it was, she told herself.

She would not remember how he'd once occupied her thoughts. None of that girlish silliness mattered anymore. Doing her part for the war effort was far more important.

"I don't want to hear about 'just for tonight,'" she said, echoing his words.

"It would be far too dangerous to stay in one place for long."

"Every day we're all in danger. I'm several miles outside Saint Peter Port. Why would the Germans come here? If you're careful during the day, you'll be fine here."

"We'll discuss this another time," he said.

"I've always managed to get by, living on my own, and I'll continue to do so. Your mission is critical."

She headed up the two flights of stairs, knowing he followed her. She opened the door to her old bedroom. "You can sleep here."

He moved past her, and suddenly the room seemed too

small. He took up all the space with his broad shoulders and his rangy height.

Jack let out a deep breath as he turned back to her. "It's been a long time since I slept in such a peaceful place."

"I'm glad it's peaceful." She hesitated. "What will you do next?"

He gave a crooked smile. "Sleep."

"What will you do *tomorrow*?"

"You know I won't involve you," he said. "I'm already putting you in enough danger."

"Stop saying that. You can't keep me from danger—I'll be brushing shoulders with the enemy every day." She hesitated. "Will I see you in the morning?"

"I don't know."

"At least you're honest about that."

"Thank you. Good night, Helen."

She closed the bedroom door behind her and went back down to the kitchen to clean up, feeling so wide awake that it might be hours before she slept. Thank goodness she didn't have to work in the morning.

But when she retired to her own room, she was very aware that she wasn't alone in her little cottage. She lay awake in the darkness, listening, but heard nothing. He must be exhausted from coming ashore and hiding out in that inhospitable cave.

Doubt assailed her. Had someone seen him lurking on her property? Were the Germans even now lying in wait?

She took a deep breath, forcing herself to relax, letting the calm swell up in her as if she bobbed on the ocean in the summer sun. She was now trapped on the island. Someone had to stop the Germans. Perhaps it would be Jack.

When she awoke in the morning, his bedroom was empty, the bed so neat it was as if no one had slept in it, the house strangely silent, the ladder to the cave undisturbed. She stared out the kitchen window, her fingers absently touching her mother's brooch, as she heated water for her tea and wondered what he was doing. Would she see him again?

6

CATHERINE

As Catherine and Timmy walked home from school, cars constantly drove past with German officers riding in them. She'd told her father what had happened to Helen's car, and he was bracing himself for the same, even as he'd driven to the airport to work.

Her mother was waiting as they walked up onto the veranda, then pulled them inside and closed the door forcefully.

"I never thought about you walking home!" Mum said shrilly, clutching Timmy to her.

He pushed his head out of her chest. "Mum! I can't breathe!"

She let him go with obvious reluctance.

"The Germans invaded our school!" he practically shouted.

With a gasp, Mum grabbed hold of him again.

"They didn't invade," Catherine insisted when her mother turned wide, terrified eyes to her. "They came to inspect."

When Timmy struggled, Mum let him go.

"What do they need with a school?" Mum whispered.

Catherine could see the dread overtaking her unnaturally pale mother. She hadn't eaten much at dinner the previous night either.

"I'm sure they just want to see everything on the island, so there are no surprises," Catherine said calmly.

"Don't speak to me like that." Her voice was sharp. "I'm not some doddering old biddy who needs to be placated."

Catherine glanced pointedly at Timmy, who was looking from Catherine to their mother with fascination.

"Go wash up, Timmy," Catherine said, giving her brother a push down the hall.

He grumbled, but did as she asked.

"I'm sorry," Mum said.

Catherine put her arms around her. "No need to be," she whispered. How could she tell her mother that she spent her day rationalizing anything the Germans did, making herself breathe deeply instead of panic. After seeing the German officers file into school, she wished she never had to leave her house again. Last night, she'd opened her trousseau chest and pretended she was living another life, that George had come home from the war and they'd fallen in love. But it was just a dream.

She gave her mother one last squeeze, inhaling deeply and smelling flour and spices, the scents of her childhood. "You smell like lunch. What did you make?"

Mum seemed reluctant as she stepped away from the embrace. "Shepherd's pie. Now you go wash up, too."

When they were seated at the kitchen table, just the three of them, there was a sudden heavy knock at the front door. Her mother's face went slack and white with dread, and Catherine's stomach seemed to turn over.

Timmy started to stand up.

Mum caught his arm. "No."

"We have to answer the door," Catherine said, hating that her voice trembled. Her own fears could not be allowed to frighten her brother. "It might very well be neighbors."

Her mother took her hand. "I'll come with you. Timothy, stay here."

For once, he didn't protest, just watched them leave the kitchen, his eyes wide.

In the front hall, Catherine and her mum exchanged a nod, then Catherine opened the door. A German officer stood there. Catherine's mouth dropped open in shock, and she wondered if she'd spend until the end of the war startled and afraid every time she saw a German.

She gave her mother's trembling hand a squeeze and collected herself. She spoke English and prayed that he did, too, because she'd rather not explain that she also spoke German. "May I help you?"

He pulled off his cap, bowed, and held out a slip of paper. "I have been assigned to live here," he said brusquely but politely. "Here are my orders. You will be paid."

Catherine numbly took the paper, but couldn't stop looking at his face. Then he reached for the small leather suitcase, picked it up, and waited to be invited in.

"There must be some mistake," Mum whispered, clutching her hands together at her chest.

"No mistake," he said. "It is awkward for everyone, *ja*? I am *Leutnant*—Lieutenant Schafer."

Though Catherine wanted to slam the door shut, she took her mother's arm and gave her a gentle tug out of the way. "Come in, please," she said, her voice hoarse.

He stepped into their front hall as if he was their own private German invasion, his uniform giving him a sinister air. Catherine had been looking at that uniform in movie news reels as the Wehrmacht swept across Europe, rolling back civilization with every country that was toppled.

Their home, their place of refuge, would be peaceful no more.

"You have a free bedroom, *ja*? Records say your son"—he looked at her mother—"is gone."

Enlisted, Catherine thought, *to fight you*.

"He's coming back," Mum insisted faintly.

"But not right now. I see his room, *ja*?"

"Please follow me." Catherine headed up the steep, narrow staircase, feeling the German too close behind. She glanced back and saw Mum taking hold of Timmy, whispering something before sending him away and following them up.

Catherine opened the first door on the left. The air didn't smell stale, since Mum cleaned it regularly, lovingly, but it was warm and stuffy.

Lieutenant Schafer looked at the narrow bed, the chest of drawers with model airplanes and seashells on top, the small desk where several books were stacked, and the closed wardrobe. School certificates were framed on the wall, along with a photo of Richard and his mates on a fishing boat.

"My brother left behind clothes." Catherine opened the wardrobe and removed several suitcases they'd stored inside. "Please give us some time to make room."

He put his suitcase in the corner. "I must return to my post. I will be back this evening."

He marched into the hall and down the stairs. Catherine and her mother didn't move until they heard the front door close.

And then Mum began to cry, walking about the room aimlessly, touching first the bed, the books on the desk, then a seashell. Helplessness brought tears to Catherine's eyes, too.

"How can they do this?" Mum finally said in a loud voice, as if shouting to the world. "They've bombed us and killed people, they've invaded our island, and now they're forcing us to house them like they're family?"

Timmy ducked his head into the door, his face pale. "Mum? Are you all right?"

Their mother stared at him blank-faced for a moment, and then her complexion turned splotchy with color. "Oh, Timmy, I'm sorry. I'm just angry and frightened all at the same time. I've never felt like this before."

Timmy took a step into the room hesitantly. "I can help."

Mum wiped a hand across her eyes and gave a wobbly smile. "I know. And I love you for it. Why don't you find a crate in the cellar and pack Richard's books and models?"

Timmy ran out with youthful enthusiasm, and Catherine put a hand on her mother's arm. Mum shook her off and opened a suitcase on the bed. Catherine could practically hear her teeth grinding as she began to open drawers.

"Mum, it will be okay," Catherine said.

"I am not a fool, and I don't want to be placated. I've been frightened to death of what might happen, and now this—this villain!—will live among us. We'll have to watch what we say. We'll have no peace, no solace away from the war..." She bowed her head and her tears fell onto the suitcase.

Catherine hugged her from behind.

Her mother was trembling, but at last she patted her daughter's hand. "I'm sorry to be so weak-willed. It's not what a mother wants her child to see."

"Weak-willed? No!" Catherine echoed, aghast. "How else should a person act when the enemy has invaded her home?

You're doing everything you have to to keep your family safe. But we have each other, and I've always known that's what makes us strong."

Mum stared at Catherine, blinking back tears, her lips at last forming a trembling smile. "I don't know if I've ever heard a lovelier sentiment, and today of all days, it was much needed. Thank you, my dear."

Before they could become as weepy as wet handkerchiefs, Timmy burst back into the room, dropped a wooden crate onto the floor, and put his hands on his hips as he looked around.

"Where should I start?" he asked.

"I think the top of the chest of drawers," Mum said.

"I'll make it bare for him," Timmy continued. "Maybe he'll set his gun there. Do you think he'll let me hold it?"

Catherine and her mother exchanged stricken looks.

7

CHELSEA

I watched Grandma sleep for what seemed like hours, trying to reconcile the story of her and her friends as young women my own age and what they'd had to deal with.

When I heard voices in the hall, my mother a little loud with worry, my dad trying to quiet her down, I went to the doorway to meet them.

"She's asleep," I murmured, finger to my lips. "I need to talk to you guys."

"There's a waiting room down the hall where we can speak as loud as we want," Dad said, eyeing Mom with amusement.

She rolled her eyes, but it was all good-natured. My parents had a strong relationship that I envied. They'd met in college, Dad the classic "boy from the wrong side of the tracks," and Mom the child of a doctor and nurse.

We walked together into the waiting room, bare except for some chairs and bland prints on the walls.

Dad gave me a sober look. "How's Grandma?"

"The same," I said, "trying not to make a big deal of things."

Mom gave me a concerned look. "Did she say…"

"That someone was trying to kill her? Yep. And I believe her. She has proof that something else is going on. Someone sent her an obituary about her friend from Guernsey, along with an unsigned note." I held it up and read it out loud. "'Catherine died. You're next.' Seems like a threat to me."

My father took the note and studied it.

"She started telling me about her friendship with Catherine," I continued, "all about Guernsey Island during World War II. Now that she's been threatened, she's ready to talk."

Mom and Dad exchanged a glance I couldn't read. Maybe they knew what secrets Grandma wanted to tell me, but I couldn't worry about that right now.

"We need to call the police," I insisted.

Dad sighed. "I called Bill, my cousin's friend who's a cop. He said there was nothing much he could do. There's your grandma's age, and the fact that there are no witnesses. Even if I show him the letter, it's only pointing out that Grandma will die next. What are the police going to do, head across the Atlantic to Guernsey and look for the anonymous person who wrote the obvious?"

I understood how difficult it would be to move forward on such skimpy information. We needed more details. Back in Grandma's room, we found her awake. She tried to distract us by talking about the latest show she was watching, *Buffy the Vampire Slayer*. Nobody was having it.

"I told Mom and Dad about the letter," I said. "I'm sorry, but they needed to know so that we can keep you safe."

Grandma took a deep breath, then nodded. "We need to

find out how Catherine died. Then we'll know if someone is just playing a prank."

"Let me help with that," I interrupted. "You need to relax and recover. I'll call Catherine's children. Or maybe the town clerk—wonder if they have them in England."

"The Channel Islands," she pointed out. "Not England."

I smiled. Same old Grandma.

"I have Catherine's address at home," she continued. "Can you hand me my pocketbook?"

I found it on a chair beside the bed and gave it over.

After reaching inside, she pulled out her keys and handed them to me. "Thank you for your help, Chelsea. Placing overseas calls in the hospital is such a nuisance— and so expensive! As for my address book, it's in the top left-hand drawer of the desk."

She was trusting me to help her and keep her safe. The enormity of that suddenly hit me. My parents were studying me, too, with the same skepticism they never bothered to hide whenever I was in the middle of a school assignment that I was neglecting. They'd had every right to be skeptical then. But now? This was Grandma we were talking about, and I loved her and wanted to help.

Mom and Dad each leaned down to kiss Grandma's cheek.

"We'll see you tomorrow," Dad said, giving her hand a squeeze.

She gave him her beautiful, patient smile. "I'll be here— where else would I be?"

My parents moved toward the door.

I leaned down to kiss Grandma and whispered, "I'll figure this out, I promise."

"Thank you. But there's one other thing I need you to

do." She pitched her voice even lower. "There's a handgun in my desk. Can you bring it to me, Chelsea, dear?"

My mouth fell open, and I stared at her. She just gave me the sweetest smile, then covered her lips with one finger, obviously asking for my silence.

My grandma had a gun?

8

HELEN

Helen walked her bicycle back to the garage as dusk settled eerily around her cottage. Her stomach gave a little growl, as it often did, even after a meal. By the looseness of her skirt, she knew she'd have to move the waistband button soon.

Walking to the cottage, her thoughts dwelled on a recent awkward dinner with the Brauns. It was almost physically painful not to tell Catherine about Jack. But how could she put the Brauns in danger? They were already surrounded by it, with Lieutenant Schafer in their home. The lieutenant's appearance reminded Helen that Jack's life was now in her hands.

She knew if the Germans found out, she could be sent to a German prison camp. But somehow that didn't matter as much as helping Jack.

Where was he?

She could hear the distant sounds of waves crashing against her cliff, but little else. Even the birds seemed subdued as she approached her dark cottage.

Weeks went by between his visits, and sometimes she

only knew he'd been around because he'd taken a clean set of clothes and left dirty ones behind. And now every hour she was home, the time crept by as she waited for the sound of his approach, or a note left for her, but there was usually nothing.

And then the same thought would start to nag her: had he left the island?

To her relief, she found a neatly piled set of dirty clothes in the bedroom he sometimes used. It hadn't been there earlier. Running down to the basement, she opened the trap door and heard the distant roar of the waves echoing to the back of the cave.

"Jack?" Her voice seemed to die amid the water crashing.

What if he was injured down there?

She reached for the ladder against the wall and began to extend it down into the darkness. She grew more unbalanced the farther it slid, but at last it bumped against the floor of the cave where she settled it on the uneven surface. Grabbing her electric torch, she stepped onto a rung and started down.

It had been many years since she'd explored the cave; even when the Germans had come, and she'd known it might be a last-ditch retreat, she still hadn't gone down.

Each rung descended brought cool damp air swirling around her legs. The temperature dropped steadily. Part way down, she turned on her torch and swept it across the cave, but all she saw was shadowy rock, with the darkness receding where the cave took a turn toward the channel. There was nothing below, so she finished her descent and crept slowly toward the mouth of the cave. Since the floor was slippery, she watched her step, listening intently. For all she knew, the cave had been discovered, and Jack hadn't been foolish enough to return.

She turned off her torch before leaning slowly around the corner. There was no one in the cave. With a sigh of relief, she walked closer to the mouth. As dusk approached, the channel looked slate gray with impending storms. Out there somewhere were German boats and planes keeping everyone on Guernsey prisoner.

Did the Germans have Jack?

Or—was he gone? Perhaps a submarine had come for him. Wouldn't he have left a note or...something?

But no, he wouldn't risk his assignment that way. She might never know what happened, and suddenly that seemed unbearable.

She stood for long minutes in the mouth of the cave, which dropped away at her feet down an incline toward the rocky shore. She hugged herself in the gloom. Across the expanse of the channel, France seemed so far away, though just thirty miles. But the channel represented a line of war that could not be easily crossed. Their strange imprisonment seemed endless. Germans were everywhere: at dance parties, across the aisle at the cinema, in the grocer's. Jack's arrival had made her think of the forbidden—of resisting, of spying, of overthrowing.

But she was just one woman.

That night as she lay in bed, restless, she heard the engine of a lorry moving steadily closer. The only people who drove anymore were Germans, or those given permission. She held her breath, imagining them coming for Jack —coming for her because they knew she'd helped him.

And strangely, such thoughts made her stiffen her resolve. She was no meek rabbit.

At last, the rumble of the lorry faded away, back toward Saint Peter Port.

~oOo~

Two nights later, Helen was awakened by a faint knocking at her bedroom door. She bolted upright in bed, the room stuffy with summer heat, the darkness complete.

But she wasn't afraid as she put a thin dressing gown on over her nightdress. Germans would break down the front door, not quietly knock.

Upon opening the door, she wasn't surprised to see Jack, his clothes as ragged and filthy as his face. The smile he gave her gleamed white and tired in the shadows.

He lifted up his dirty hands, and she thought she spotted blood.

"Guess I need to wash up," he said hoarsely.

She gestured him toward the bathroom, laid out clean clothes, and then went downstairs to heat up a meal.

He ate the small amount of stewed swedes and onions with the heavy bread made of corn she'd gleaned herself, as if it was a feast. She watched him quietly, feeling a weird sort of pride that she could do even this small thing for him. He was clean again, his hair wet and slicked back, shadows beneath his eyes.

"How did you hurt your hands?" she asked when he was nearly done.

He glanced up at her, but didn't put his fork down. "Climbing the cliff side above the cave. They saw me, and I was leading them away. I didn't want them to know about the cave."

Her stomach dropped with anxiety for him, but she forced herself to calmly say, "Thank you."

He gestured toward his plate and gave her a smile of wry amusement. "Thank *you*. And thank you for my clean clothing. I do believe there was a torn seam or two that is now miraculously mended."

"Nothing miraculous. I have to repair my clothing all the time. We can buy little new anymore, so everything will have to be mended until it's so threadbare it falls apart. Don't even talk to me about shoes."

He smiled, but kept eating.

Her attempt at light-heartedness faded. "I thought you'd left the island, or...something worse."

He set down his fork. His blue eyes were still alight with mischief, she thought, but his expression was solemn.

"I don't believe they're coming for me anymore. They think I'm lost to them."

"What will you do?"

"Keep doing my job and try to find a way to get my information off the island."

"And while you're doing that, you're done trying to skulk about my cave, barely escaping Germans. You need to stay here, hidden during the day. As I've told you, no one comes here. You'll be safe."

"Helen—"

"How do you think I felt, knowing you were out there somewhere? Why is it okay for you to defend our country, but not me?"

He blinked at her for a moment. "Because I'm a soldier," he said, as if it was the most obvious thing in the world.

And something buried rose inside her, tightening her throat, bringing tears to her eyes. "You don't think I can fight for my country, too? You don't think that after months of being held captive, I want to do something—*need* to do something?"

"Helen—"

"I know I'm not a trained soldier; I know you don't want

to have to worry about me. But it's too late. *You* came to *me*. You needed my help. And you're going to get it."

"Helen—"

"Stop trying to interrupt me!"

"Stop interrupting *me*, so you can hear me say thank you, I accept, and I promise I'll keep you safe."

She blinked at him, her mind whirling.

"I'll lie low," he went on. "I won't leave the cottage during the day; I won't risk the enemy finding a reason to search your home."

She saw the frustration he couldn't quite hide. He was back on the island for who knew how long, the place he'd always been so desperate to leave. He saw relying on her and her home a weakness, a risk. She had to make him see that he was wrong, that she could be of help.

"I'm glad, Jack," she said quietly. "It's been—terrible wondering if you were dead or alive."

"It could be terrible knowing I'm here, putting you at risk. You might spend your work day worried to come home. Helen, you have to promise to tell me if this is too much for you."

She leaned toward him, that strange excitement rising within her again. It could not be Jack making her feel this way—it was what he represented, her chance to do something more.

"It won't be too much for me," she said slowly, clearly. "It will be what motivates me, what gives me hope."

He studied her across the table. She didn't look away.

His lip quirked. "I give you hope?"

She blushed. "Keeping you safe, knowing it will help Britain, gives me hope."

"And that's all it is?"

Suddenly there was an interesting tension rising

between them. Was he flirting with her? Now? Helen straightened and gave him a serious frown. "Don't do that."

"Do what?"

"Act like this isn't serious."

"I've never been more serious."

But his eyes almost sparkled. Was he enjoying bantering with her? She didn't know what to think—it was too confusing.

9

BETTY

He was looking at her again.

Betty was used to the frank gazes of German soldiers. She looked straight ahead as she walked through the restaurant, threading between tables, calmly dodging the occasional reaching hand. But this officer was new, shadows of fatigue beneath his eyes, like so many had when they came from the Eastern Front. He had short blond hair, a meticulous uniform, and a smile that seemed polite but... knowing. She made sure she didn't wait on his table.

The next time he showed up at the restaurant, it was between meals, when she was the only waitress on duty. He studied her with one eyebrow arched, smiling again, as if daring her to ignore him.

"Good afternoon," she said, striving to sound cool but polite.

"*Fraulein*." He gave a brief bow of his head.

She handed him a menu. "Would you like something to drink while you make your choice?"

"Coffee. Thank you."

A restaurant that catered to Germans still managed to

find real coffee, so she nodded, left to pour him a cup, and returned with it balanced on a saucer. After placing it on the table, she gave him an expectant look.

"You don't need to write this down?" he asked, his amusement making her want to grind her teeth.

"The menu is limited at this time of day, sir."

"Franz."

"Pardon me?" She frowned.

He chuckled. "My name is Franz."

"My employer wouldn't appreciate such familiarity, Lieutenant..." she trailed off.

"Captain. But call me Franz. I insist. I believe your employer would not mind." He gave her another patient, knowing smile.

And he was right. The Germans were the hotel's only clientele. "Very well. May I take your order?"

"Franz."

She inhaled and said quietly, "Franz."

His smile widened to a grin. "You see, that was not difficult. I'll have the lamb stew."

With a nod, she took the menu and left. Only when she was in the kitchen did she realize she was trembling.

The cook, a stooped man in his fifties, gave her an inscrutable look and turned away. Betty knew that look—it was war, and people were too worried about themselves to risk angering Germans, even on behalf of a friend. And she and the cook weren't friends—they weren't enemies either, just fellow survivors. After placing the order, she returned to the captain's table with bread and butter.

"Your island is beautiful," he said, as she tried to make her escape.

Pausing, she nodded.

He cocked his head. "You don't like to speak much—ah,

but your employer doesn't like familiarity. We've already established that that won't be a problem between us. What is your name, *fraulein*?"

"Betty."

"A good name. I am new to the island, just assigned here. Would you be willing to show me about?"

He wasn't the first to ask her out since the Germans had invaded, but they'd all accepted her refusal, since there were other foolish women desperate for the attention. Betty hadn't imagined there would be so many women who didn't care what others thought of them, as long as they had lipstick and chocolates and car rides.

"I cannot, Captain," she said.

The cook called her name and she escaped. He handed her a bowl, glanced past her toward the dining room, and turned away. His own daughter was safely married, Betty knew.

She took the lamb stew to the captain's table.

"Ah." He looked as pleased as if she'd brought him a seven-course meal.

To her surprise, he did not ask her out again that day. She wanted to feel relieved, but was far too cynical. As she suspected, he visited on another afternoon when she was alone in the dining room, almost as if he'd asked her work schedule. While she served him, he asked her out again, and once more she politely said no.

He studied her, still smiling. "No?" he repeated.

"No, Captain."

"Franz."

"Franz."

"Why not? Are you married?" He pointedly looked at her ring finger.

"No." She wished she could lie, but he could ask anyone about her.

"Are you seeing a particular young man?"

She hesitated a fraction too long. "Yes."

He chuckled. "What is his name?"

"Alfred."

"A lucky man."

He took the rejection in stride and left her the same handsome tip he had the first time.

A week later, Betty turned off High Street, several tins of meat her reward for hours of queuing. She was paying more attention to her food than the big draft horse trying to maneuver the narrow streets while pulling a cart heaped with potatoes. She jumped out of the way, catching herself against the stone wall of a building, her tins spilling onto the pavement.

A boy tried to get the attention of the farmer, begging for a tossed potato. The horse reared up, the boy cowered, hands over his head, frozen in place. Betty screamed and scrambled forward, even as she knew she would be too late.

Suddenly, a German officer darted into the street and pulled the boy back to safety. The farmer got the horse under control, and it moved past Betty, who was still breathing hard. When the cart was gone, she was able to see the other side of the street again. The officer was talking to the boy, a hand on his shoulder.

Then the officer looked directly at her, and she recognized the captain who'd been asking her out. Was he following her?

The boy gave another nod and raced away, disappearing amidst the shoppers. Betty stooped to pick up her tins, and when she straightened, the captain was standing right in front of her. A chill swept over her, even though the sun shone.

"Betty," he said, touching the brim of his hat.

"Captain."

"Franz."

"Franz." She hesitated. "Thank you for saving the boy's life."

He gave a self-deprecating shrug. "Anyone would do so. Children are the future, after all."

She nodded, but was already wondering how she could escape.

"Running into each other on the street is not a coincidence," the captain said. "I have been very curious about you, Betty."

She inhaled sharply, even as her narrowed eyes met his. "You followed me?"

He chuckled. "You should be flattered."

"I am not." She stopped breathing altogether when she realized how she'd spoken to a German officer.

The captain's smile didn't fade. "You are so confident and brave. I like that about you."

The stares of passing islanders stung like daggers; they didn't dare whisper too close to the captain, but she saw heads come together when they were far enough away. Her face burned with embarrassment and fear.

"I think we should start with a cup of coffee," he said, "just a brief conversation."

"No, thank you." She started to walk past him.

He did not touch her, but she couldn't miss his words.

"I won't keep you long from your mother."

She froze.

"I understand the two of you live alone."

Slowly, she looked up at him. "You are talking to people about me?"

He briefly looked away, as if pretending embarrassment. "I followed you. I know it was not a nice thing to do. I cannot stop thinking about you, Betty, and I was curious."

Light-headed, she forced herself to take a slow deep breath, even as a band of fear seemed to choke her.

"I can see you're upset," he continued, "but you needn't be. I was just curious. I understand your mother is not in the best health. It is wonderful that she has you to care for her in these difficult times. Let us have coffee rather than discuss this on the street."

A wave of inevitability washed over her. At least that was better than feeling panicked, a weakness she despised.

"Very well," she said coolly. "There's a café off High Street."

His face brightened as if she'd given him the best news —it felt...unreal. But it was her life now, and she would find some way to keep control. She couldn't tell herself the war might end any day; that would be foolish. But she would outlast the war—she would outlast the captain.

~oOo~

But two months later, as the Christmas holiday approached, Captain Lunenborg showed no signs of being put off. She'd met him for the occasional meal off High Street, spoken to him when she worked at the restaurant, but had avoided anything more. He liked to talk about himself, and she let him, managing to offer little more than details about her work at the restaurant, as if that was all she was, all she wanted. He occasionally held her hand or kissed her cheek at the end of the evening, always in the shadows, which she reluctantly appreciated.

Yet he was being particularly persistent about a Christmas party he was attending. She'd heard about those parties, with officers escorting islanders. There were plenty of women who didn't care what others thought of them, who wanted to attend German parties, dress up prettily, laugh gaily. They were missing the young men who'd left to fight for Britain. But with few parties, no one to dance with unless it was other women, and now the scarcity of food and new clothing—all these things had made some foolish young women desperate or lonely or just bored.

But the captain wasn't taking no for an answer. Soon he began to speak about the party as if she'd agreed to go. Continuing to contradict him seemed...dangerous. He hadn't brought up her mother again since she'd begun to accept his dinner requests, but Mum's safety was always on Betty's mind.

When the Christmas party was only a few days away, the captain took her out for tea and asked her what she planned to wear.

Betty stared into his eyes. "I've told you I don't wish to attend."

He smiled with lazy confidence. "And I've told you that my friends wish to meet you. Should I pick you up so you can introduce me to your mother?"

She held his gaze, even as she knew she'd been defeated. "That won't be necessary," she said coolly.

His smile widened. "My car will be waiting at the corner at eight o'clock."

The night of the party, she lied to her mother about attending the cinema with friends. As she walked down her street toward the waiting car, the brisk wind off the channel made her clutch her coat beneath her chin. The driver saw her and stepped out to open the door. As she ducked inside, the captain waited, smiling, always smiling.

The party was in the lobby of the Guernsey Grand Hotel, and Betty's stomach clenched with dread as they walked up the front walkway instead of the employee entrance at the rear. None of the staff had mentioned the party to her, which could only mean they knew about her relationship with Captain Lunenborg. The hotel was on high ground, overlooking the harbor and the channel with distant views of the other islands that seemed to hover over the horizon. It rose up, five stories of stone, and had weathered the storms of the channel for at least a hundred years.

Inside the main lobby with its marble floors, dark wood wainscoting on the lower half of walls, and large Guernsey landscape paintings above, the captain waved to a friend seated at a small table in the corner, then led Betty past decorative evergreen branches and plenty of red ribbon.

Another woman sat at the table and gave Betty a faint, timid smile. The captain introduced her to Lieutenant Hamachers, who introduced her to Lucy. Blond and apple-cheeked, she seemed very young. Soon the two men went off to drink and smoke, leaving the women alone.

Lucy gestured to Betty. "I love your dress."

Betty glanced down at the burgundy silk she'd pulled from the back of her closet. "Thank you. I like yours, too."

The girl blushed. So, so young.

"Where are you from?" Betty asked. "I've never seen you before."

"I live on a farm on the north side of the island," Lucy said. "Too busy with chores to come to town much now that I'm out of school."

"But you must have met the lieutenant somehow," Betty answered dryly.

"Oh, yes, I was at the store with my mum once."

"That's all it takes. I'm sorry."

Lucy shrugged, not looking at all discomfited. "I'm not. I milked cows for my lazy brother, and milked cows when my father drank too much. Now he doesn't dare overwork me."

Betty lit a cigarette. "Good for you—I guess."

"Not just good for me," the girl said earnestly. "My brother broke curfew and would have gone to prison but for Lieutenant Hamachers. Now he just paid a fine. Not that he's speaking to me." Lucy's expression turned downcast, her large, fringed eyes lowering with sadness. "Does your family still speak to you?"

Betty hadn't been able to discuss her new life with anyone else, and her tongue loosened. "My mum's all I have left, and she doesn't know." She hesitated. "Do you wish your family didn't know?"

"There'd be no way to hide it," Lucy said. "The lieutenant has to come fetch me. My parents tolerate him, of course, but...things will be different later."

"Later?"

"When we marry." Lucy's innocent smile turned dreamy. "After the war, he plans to stay here to be with me."

Betty could only blink her confusion and skepticism.

Lucy leaned across the table. "I know what you're thinking, but we love each other. And when the baby comes—" She covered her mouth at the slip, but her smile didn't dim. "I shouldn't have said that, but you won't tell anyone."

"I won't." Betty's stomach roiled, but she had to ignore it as the men returned.

Lucy's whole expression lit from within when the Lieutenant bent to gently kiss her cheek. Betty hadn't realized how young he was either, with his lovelorn brown eyes. If he hadn't been wearing a hated uniform, they might have been any enraptured couple.

Captain Lunenborg watched her with amusement as if he could read every thought in her head. She hated that he was so confident he knew her, that he could outwit her. When they played cards after dinner, Lucy and her lieutenant were hopelessly outmatched as Betty and the captain competed at whist, trying to win every trump. It felt petty, but Betty couldn't stop herself.

To her surprise, the officers and their dates played hide and seek like giggling children, drunk on champagne. Lieutenant Hamachers treated Lucy like she was made of spun glass. Betty couldn't take her eyes off them in morbid fascination.

"Do you want to play?" Captain Lunenborg whispered near her ear. "You seem quite intrigued."

She stiffened. "I am not. And I do not wish to play a child's game during a war."

She held her body so stiff she ached, but the captain only chuckled and didn't force the issue. He tapped his foot as the band began to play again. Lucy and her beau sat back down, laughing, breathless, eyes shining with Christmas joy. When the captain urged Betty to the dancefloor, she went just to get away.

The first dance was a waltz, and he held her too close. Her face heated with resentment. Someone had opened the French doors onto the terrace, and she was almost relieved when the captain whirled her outside into the cool night air.

Lanterns hung from the trees along with Christmas decorations. It could have been a magical place with the right man. And the captain wanted to be that man, she knew. He slid his arms tighter around her and stopped dancing.

"Betty."

She met his gaze. He leaned down and kissed her. She wasn't shocked by his behavior and had been expecting it. The pressure of his warm lips wasn't demanding.

He finally lifted his head and stared down at her. "It's a start," he murmured.

10

HELEN

Jack showed up for dinner unexpectedly one evening, surprising her by coming out of the hall shadows as she made coffee. Even though he'd promised to spend the days at her cottage, he was often gone by the time she came home from the hospital.

"Good evening," he said. "Sorry if I startled you."

She attempted a calm smile. "Not at all. Will you be joining me?"

He hesitated, then nodded.

Something tight eased inside her chest, but she didn't want to examine it too closely.

She poured coffee through a strainer into a cup, then pushed it toward him as she gave an apologetic smile. "It's made of acorns."

"What?" he asked, his eyes narrowed with confusion.

"You haven't seen me hunt for acorns? I roast and grind them. The island children hunt for them as well and sell them to the shops."

"I don't recall that being a local delicacy," he said wryly.

"It is now. I kept my old tea packets for as long as I could, drying them and rebrewing them over and over, but when the flavor was gone, I had to try something else. I like acorns better than brambles."

"Brambles?"

"Bramble tea."

"I'm sorry I didn't realize the food scarcity had gotten so bad."

Was he blushing? She found that rather sweet.

"German rules are so strict with our fishermen to prevent any escape, that most of them can't make a living. We're surrounded by water, with barely any fish available at the market. But you have more important things to worry about."

She didn't want to burden him with how her life had changed. She'd spent months co-existing with the enemy, watching Lieutenant Schafer encroach on Catherine's family day by day, watching Germans swarm the shops and her neighbors forced to wait on them. Helplessness had been making her feel small and insignificant, just a survivor finding ways to work and yet hunt for ever-shrinking supplies of food on store shelves.

She got up to stir the soup, feeling embarrassed that soup was a regular way she made her foodstuffs last. She winced at how watery it was with just a few floating vegetables. Any flavor of meat came from the small piece of beef that she'd used because it was too tough to chew. She brought him a bowl, another for herself, and sat down.

He sipped a spoonful and smacked his lips.

She rolled her eyes. "No need to pretend it's a decent meal."

"I'm not pretending how grateful I am."

She gave an unladylike snort. "Don't get your hopes up for large meals."

"Anything is better than scavenging." He eyed her. "My excellent spying ability has ferreted out that people are looking thin. The Germans are rationing?"

"Quite a bit. But the BBC says it's the same for our people on the mainland. I imagine I wouldn't enjoy eating my fill every night knowing others are hungry."

He arched a dark brow. "So you'd forgo food for patriotism?"

Her face grew hot. "Well..."

"Do you wish you would have evacuated before the war like so many of your neighbors?" he asked gently.

"Not at all. I've seen what happens if a house is unoccupied—the Germans take it over. They have no respect. I heard some of them use china for target practice, although most of them have been civilized."

"Civilized?" he echoed.

"I know. I remember everything we heard before the war about the Germans taking over Eastern Europe. But here...they seem to want to be different. Early on, before the beaches were mined, they even swam in their bathing trunks, trying to prove they were just like us—maybe trying to prove it to themselves as much as us. They would wait patiently for their turn on the tennis courts, even as islanders would deliberately lose points to make games last. There haven't been atrocities committed against the islanders, although I can't say the same about the poor prisoners they've brought in to work."

He sobered. "I've seen them. They're building their artillery batteries and bunkers on the coast. They're pitiful, ragged creatures, these workers, these slaves."

"I see them from a distance, and I'm horrified at what they're enduring. It's hard to feel justified complaining that it's difficult to get food. But I never imagined how it would feel to live with such restricted freedom, to know you can be punished for breaking their rules. It's a struggle not to feel this looming sense of dread all the time."

"What's the punishment for breaking the Germans' rules?"

"They put people in jail here on the island. But the jail is small, and sometimes people have to wait until someone else is finished before serving their sentence."

"Are you saying people take turns in jail?" he asked, eyes wide with amusement and disbelief.

"Yes, for breaking curfew, stealing furniture from an abandoned house to use as firewood, and other minor offenses. Remember Sam Babineaux? He was caught milking a farmer's cow in the dead of night."

"People steal milk from their neighbors?"

"The Black Market makes everyone a little crazy, even as some can't live without it. Many farmers are getting rich selling their goods to Black Marketeers, so the desperate islanders feel justified in doing a bit of stealing. The worst offenders—they're sent to French jails or shipped to Germany. Some return, some don't."

"Being sent to Germany..." He sighed. "We've heard terrible stories of what they do to prisoners, especially Jews."

"Most of the Jewish islanders evacuated before the war, though a handful remained behind. Eventually the Germans demanded they register."

Jack frowned. "The first step."

"Yes. Not long afterward, they were arrested and sent away. Three Jewish women. It was...terrible. To be deemed a danger just because of your ancestry, your religion..." She shuddered, then tried to look at him with hope. "Do you think this will end soon?"

His expression was grim. "No. It's not going well for us. You've probably guessed that from the BBC coverage."

The stark truth of that was frightening. In her day-to-day life, she never let herself think of the future, of when life might return to normal. Anything to not be afraid all the time. But to hear there was a chance the Allies could lose?

Jack was studying her face. "Perhaps I was too blunt."

She shook her head. "No, I don't want to be lied to. I listen to the BBC every night, so I do know some of the terrible things that have been happening. But about German plans for the island, you must know more than me. What have you found out—if you can tell me?" She held her breath, remembering how he'd shut down any of her questions in the past.

"Probably nothing you don't know. I've tried to study the daily activities at the airfield and memorize the gun placements on the cliffs and beaches."

"They're working on that all the time. They even built a railway from one end of the island to the other to move the equipment they needed to build those massive gun batteries and bunkers, used the railway once or twice, then started tearing sections up and going a different way. Insane."

As she spoke, she felt a small feeling of accomplishment, as if in telling Jack she was helping the war effort, even in some small way.

She thought of the occasional rumor, how some seemed to eat better than others. She wanted to believe that their gardens were just more prolific, that they had savings to spend on the Black Market, because otherwise, it meant they were earning their extra food, their privilege, another way, that they were currying favor with their oppressors, or even worse, turning on their fellow islanders.

She'd seen an ugly side to people she hadn't imagined existed, especially toward the women who dated Germans.

She thought of Betty, who she suspected of falling into that trap, but didn't know what to do about it, or if she could even help.

It was so easy to be depressed at what was happening. When was the last time she'd even wanted to laugh? She felt so different now, a shadow of the woman she used to be.

Jack finished his bowl of soup and did not ask for another. She knew he was still hungry—he had to be, but understood what the occupation had done to the food supply. She had to bring more into the household.

"Would you like to listen to the BBC tonight?" she asked hopefully.

He shook his head. "I will help with the dishes, and then I have to go."

He didn't explain, and she didn't ask. She handed him a kitchen towel and they stood side by side at the sink. They had a strange relationship, roommates who didn't question each other too closely, for fear of...what? Knowing each other too intimately? What would that lead to—not that Jack seemed like he would risk it.

When he said good-night and disappeared into the shadows of the hall, she listened for the creek of the stairs then the floorboards of his bedroom. She knew he would change into dark clothing and leave her—she'd watched from the crack of her bedroom door more than once. She tried not to think about what he was doing, how dangerous his mission was, because then her mind would be restless with worry and fear for hours on end. She was grateful he was doing something to end the war, when she herself was helpless with frustration.

~oOo~

The next morning, after her breakfast of tea and porridge, where she automatically looked for any maggot husks, she dressed in ripped trousers and a stained blouse, her gardening clothes. She opened the front door, ready to toil beneath the overcast sky in her vegetable garden, but something fluttered at her feet, as if it had been wedged into the doorframe.

Frowning, she bent to pick it up and saw that it was piece of paper with typed paragraphs and narrow margins. Across the header was the acronym *G.U.N.S.,* and below, *Guernsey's Underground News Service.*

She stared in disbelief, having never heard of such a thing. She looked out the door again but saw no one. Back inside, she stood near the light from the window to read. It was a summary of the BBC news broadcast from the night before. Helen still had a radio, although she knew many didn't. More than once, the Germans had confiscated radios as punishment before giving them back. Perhaps someone had typed this up to reassure people that they'd always have access to news of the world?

She was hiding a spy, and now someone had thought she'd want to read an illegal newsleaf. It seemed wildly improbable that they were connected.

Or was someone testing her, to see if she'd turn in either the newsleaf—or Jack?

11

BETTY

The car moved smoothly through the streets of Saint Peter Port, German flags flying from the bonnet. Betty rode as she always did, face forward, never openly looking out the window. She knew what she'd see, after all—expressions of scorn or anger, and very rarely, pity. It was that last look that could make her eyes sting just a little.

She drew deeply on her cigarette, then tapped the ash out the window, staring at the back of her driver's head as they sped toward the park, where the evening's football match was scheduled. At least the Germans had let them have the occasional sporting event, anything to distract them from how the rationing had escalated, and that the slaves—what else to call them?—from the mainland were growing so skeletal it was a wonder they could build a German bunker at all.

At the edge of the park, Arthur, the driver, pulled to the kerb and glanced back at Betty. With Franz, he was polite and deferent, a good soldier in the German army, but to her, he wouldn't speak at all. After all, Betty was just the woman Franz was "seeing." And that was putting it politely.

Arthur didn't get out to open the door for her, and although he hoped to irritate her, she was fine with that. It called less attention to her. She'd developed other ways to call less attention to herself—wearing her plainest hat, her oldest coat. Franz kept offering to buy her a new coat, but she refused, saying she had to live in Saint Peter Port with all her old neighbors. There weren't many new clothes to buy on the island anyway. People were patching everything they had, including shoes. Women were even starting to do without hats, which were so expensive and hard to repair. She wasn't wearing one today, not even a scarf tied beneath her chin, the fallback when your hats were too tattered to wear anymore.

Franz told her she could live with him at the hotel, but she kept putting him off. She wasn't sure how long his patience would last.

The car sped away quickly the instant she closed the door. She never had a chance to tell the driver when and where to pick her up, and she was certain that was on purpose. She could walk home; the town wasn't that big. Taking a deep breath, she crushed out her cigarette beneath the toe of her shoe and turned to the football stands.

Soon she was swept up in the queuing crowd. She thought she'd succeeded in anonymity, but heard a low hiss of "Jerrybag." She stiffened but didn't look behind her. Others glanced at her; most had the decency to look away with indifference or embarrassment.

That word...it was a terrible thing to call a woman who consorted with the Nazis.

Betty walked along the path between the raised rows of benches. No one spoke to her, many refused to meet her gaze. She'd known most of them her whole life: her neighbors or her customers at the restaurant. The island was small, after all, and Saint Peter Port even smaller. But now she was an outsider.

Why was she torturing herself like this?

She clenched her jaw. Because even someone like her deserved some time under the sun, watching her fellow islanders pretend nothing was wrong as they kicked a ball around.

She noticed Helen and Catherine in the front row, saw their surprise, Catherine's hesitant smile, Helen's nod of recognition. They'd never been close friends of hers—Betty didn't see the point of close girlfriends. Even as a child, she knew women were jealous of her, or talked behind her back. Not that she could accuse these two women of that. They'd always been nice, if distant. Betty's stomach unknotted a bit; her humiliation sank back into the dark where she forced it to slumber uneasily. She told herself their opinion of her didn't matter. They were living a different life, with careers people appreciated, their self-respect intact.

In the back row, she sat alone on her bench, setting her handbag to the side, though it had been difficult to unclench her hands. She watched the match, and in a few minutes her shoulders lowered, her upper back eased, and she let herself become involved in the spectacle of players on the field laughing in triumph, the spectators cheering when a goal was scored. It was a short return to her youth, when she'd insisted that the boys let her play. Though they'd tried to band together to keep a girl away, they'd backed down in the face of her belief in herself, her belief that they wouldn't say no to her. Boys didn't say no to her —then.

Half-time came so quickly that she was disappointed. There was no food stand to buy treats, no ice cream to eat.

She needed a smoke.

And then Betty saw Catherine marching toward her with determination, a frowning Helen trailing behind. Catherine gave her a cheerful smile as she sat down on the bench next to Betty. Helen sat on Catherine's other side, her fingers clutching her handbag. Betty could sympathize.

"Hello, Betty," Catherine said, as if greeting a student on the first day of school.

"Hello," Betty replied.

Catherine looked around and exhaled a little too loudly. "It's a beautiful day for a football match, isn't it?"

"It is," Betty answered.

What were they about? She saw Catherine's foot touch Helen's.

"Hello, Betty," Helen said quietly, seriously.

Betty bit back a knowing smile and gave a brief nod. She'd of course seen the women since the occupation had begun. They'd tried to talk to her more than once, but she had rebuffed them. She was not about to explain what she was going through. They'd come to the restaurant occasionally, and she'd seen them at church, even though she was about as welcome there as the black plague.

A middle-aged woman wearing a dark hat decorated with sadly wilting feathers kept glancing over her shoulder at them. Betty met her gaze and smiled. With a huff, the woman turned forward again.

"Don't mind her," Helen said. "That's Mrs. Raikes, the post master's wife. She thinks her husband's position makes her superior to everyone else."

"He doesn't have much of a job lately, does he," Catherine added, shaking her head. "Not many letters allowed through nowadays."

The three of them sat quietly, pondering the sad truth of how cut off they really were. No letters, no telephone calls with the outside world. Was this rare quiet feeling they shared...camaraderie? Betty couldn't let herself risk that kind of hurt.

"Well, of course she's looking back here," Betty said. "You two are sitting with a Jerrybag."

Catherine inhaled sharply.

Helen gave Betty a concerned look. "Don't say that."

"Why not? You're thinking it." Betty knew her voice sounded light and amused—she'd had so much practice.

"We're not thinking it," Catherine scolded.

"Yes, Teacher." Betty chuckled, although she'd never felt less amused.

"You're just trying to get us to leave," Helen said. "And we're not going."

"Such bravery," Betty mocked.

"Don't be like this." Catherine touched her hand. "Don't push us away. This is not the time to be distant with each other."

"Because there's a war, we're supposed to be noble patriots?" Betty laughed.

Mrs. Raikes gave them another lethal glare over her shoulder as if she was staring down the barrel of a rifle.

"Tell that to people like her." Betty gave a wave, and Mrs. Raikes whirled around.

"We don't care about her," Helen said.

"You should," Betty said with a quiet fierceness she didn't know she was feeling. "If the rest of this town turns on you, you won't like how it feels, and I don't want to be the cause of it." Her throat went tight, making it hard to breathe calmly, making her eyes sting. Then she realized that she was fighting tears. She hadn't let herself cry in... years. And she wasn't going to start now. She took a deep breath.

"Betty, you're pushing us away again," Catherine said, the scold back in her voice.

"For your own good."

"We know what's good for us," Helen added.

"Then what do you want?" Betty asked impatiently.

Mrs. Raikes leaned toward her closest neighbor, Madame Caron, the grocer's wife, and whispered something. The two of them sent twin glares of disapproval toward the back bench.

Wasn't half-time over yet? Betty thought in desperation.

Catherine seemed to force a smile. "We just wanted to tell you that we came to your play last week and you were wonderful in it."

Betty blinked in surprise. Where once she'd often had the lead in the community theater productions, now she had walk-on parts, often in costume and make-up as the director tried to keep her hidden. Betty knew she should stop torturing the acting community with her presence. A long time ago, she'd felt the freedom to become different people, had shared that joy with her fellow actors.

Before she could stop herself, bitter words spilled out. "You know the only reason they let me act is because of whom I associate with."

"Is that the reason you associate with him?" Helen asked pointedly.

Catherine gave another gasp, another kick of her foot at Helen's leg, and Betty found herself reluctantly amused again.

"I imagine I'd get better parts were I single," Betty said, letting her breath out tiredly.

After hesitating, Catherine asked, "Then why aren't you? We all have Germans in our lives. My father works for the Germans at the airport."

"I nurse wounded Germans every day," Helen said bitterly.

"I even have to teach German in school." Catherine flung her hands wide. "The headmaster revealed my skill to them, and now they want every child to be a good German citizen."

There was a long pause, and Betty knew they were all thinking of their lives under German rule. "We aren't citizens, but prisoners of war," she whispered.

"We're not allowed letters from my brother anymore." Catherine's voice cracked. "We've had just one since the Germans arrived—we don't know if he's alive or dead." She glanced at Betty. "Are you longing for letters from the outside world?"

"My father never wrote when letters could *get* through." Betty heard herself admit something so personal, and she didn't know who she was anymore. "There's nothing for me to miss."

"Don't you miss your old life?" Helen asked. "Why are you doing this?"

Again with the probing questions that were none of their business. The football match began, distracting the two nosy, middle-aged women in front of them. A goal was scored quickly, the cheers rose, but Betty missed the brief feeling of camaraderie that had deserted her.

Helen reached across Catherine, and now it was her turn to touch Betty's arm. It had been so long since someone touched her out of friendship.

"What do you need that man for?" Helen asked.

"Do you think I have a choice?" Betty's voice broke. She pushed Helen's hand away. All these emotions were rising up inside her, breaking through the barriers she'd erected to get through her day, to put up with her mother, to deal with Franz.

Helen and Catherine stared at her with big innocent eyes, tears brimming. Betty felt so old compared to them, used up, although she wasn't yet twenty-five.

"Enjoy the rest of the match," she said and, picking up her handbag, she strode away before their shock and sympathy really made her cry.

12

CATHERINE

Catherine couldn't speak for a long time after Betty fled. The emotion in her stiff back and marching feet had been powerful and obvious.

Was Betty really being *forced* to accompany that German officer around town?

No, that couldn't be what she'd meant. She'd said she had no choice, not that she was being forced. There was a wide difference between those two.

Wasn't there?

Catherine wanted desperately to talk to Helen, but her friend was frozen, eyes on the football match though she obviously wasn't watching.

When the match was over, Catherine and Helen rode their bicycles back to Catherine's house. One of the Germans' many rules was that bicyclists could not ride side-by-side, a silly rule, but one could spend a night in jail for breaking it. So Catherine focused on Helen's back as they rode, thinking of all the things she wanted to say.

But at home, Mum was bringing in the laundry from the clothesline, so Catherine and Helen assisted her, carrying in

the wicker baskets piled with fresh laundry. Mum immediately went to the oven to stir something that smelled
surprisingly good. Not that she wasn't an excellent cook, but
it was more and more difficult to find decent ingredients.
Helen had dinner with them so often, unable to take time
off from the hospital to queue at stores, that she usually gave
most of her ration coupons to Mum.

Helen continued to seem preoccupied at dinner, barely
realizing she was being asked to pass the boiled cabbage.
Flushing red, she did so, then cleared her throat. But before
she could speak, the front door opened and slammed. A
visible shudder ran through all of them. There was only one
person who would enter their home without knocking. As if
given a signal, everyone lowered their gazes to their plates.

When they heard more than one voice, Catherine
winced. Lieutenant Schafer had taken to inviting fellow
soldiers over whenever he wanted. She heard them enter
the kitchen. Once, he would have waited politely at the
door; he'd long since lost that impulse.

"What is there to eat?" he demanded.

Once, he would have brought food to share, as a supple-
ment to the meager "rent" they were offered.

But islanders weren't the only ones low on food. Lieutenant Schafer had lost weight as they had, and with it, his
sense of decency. Catherine glanced at them furtively. At
first, she didn't recognize the other soldier, who held his cap
in his hands, twisting it. He was stocky and dark-haired,
with a pale complexion that easily showed his red cheeks.
His gaze moved over Catherine, then returned in a startled
manner to her face. She froze, shocked and confused. She'd
met him before, but he hadn't been wearing a German
uniform.

Dad said, "We have little food, as you can see. Surely they could have served you dinner at the barracks."

The silence thickened and chilled. Even Timmy seemed to hunch into himself. Catherine tried to look away from the newcomer, but couldn't escape his surprised stare.

"But they did not feed us," Lieutenant Schafer said between gritted teeth.

He took a plate from the cupboard and began to help himself to the boiled potatoes and green peas. His friend seemed frozen, wide-eyed, his flush encompassing his whole face as his expression turned beseeching to Catherine.

"This is purchased with our rations," Dad said, his outrage too near the surface.

"You let *her* eat." Lieutenant Schafer gestured with a fork in Helen's direction, so close to her head that she jerked back.

"She gives me her ration coupons," Mum said, her voice trembling.

Catherine barely resisted gaping at her mother. Mum had actually spoken to the German soldier without being forced. But then Helen was like a second daughter to her.

"I am paying rent," Lieutenant Schafer pointed out, sounding aggrieved.

Dad didn't make the mistake of pointing out how little he was actually paying.

"I protect your home while I'm here," Lieutenant Schafer continued.

Catherine bit her lip before asking from whom he was protecting them—his fellow soldiers? The one he'd brought seemed horribly uncomfortable intruding on a family dinner. And would the lieutenant really go against them if they came storming in to search, or would he step back and let it happen? Catherine suspected the latter.

"And we're appreciative," Dad said calmly. "We've always been polite to you, and you have been the same. Why are things changing? Is something happening in the war that we should know about?"

Lieutenant Schafer didn't answer. He usually took his meals in his room, as uncomfortable with the Brauns as they were with him, but now he hesitated.

The second officer began to speak in German. "Herman, let's leave."

Even his voice was familiar, Catherine thought. But where did she know him from?

"No."

Lieutenant Schafer spoke with belligerence, like one of Catherine's students when he knew he was in the wrong.

Dad rose to his feet and gestured to his chair. Without thanking him, Lieutenant Schafer sat down. He took the last piece of bread and ate with a gusto Catherine wasn't used to seeing. Was hunger making him so angry?

"Coffee," he said, between bites.

His friend winced.

Catherine found herself playing the hostess, however unwillingly. To the second soldier, she said, "Would you like something, sir?"

"Sergeant Doepgen, *fraulein*," he said, still red-faced. "Thank you, but I am not hungry."

His stomach loudly growled, but they all ignored it. *Doepgen*, Catherine mused silently. It did not strike a chord of familiarity within her. But the sergeant kept looking at her as if he, too, felt the strange "connection"—a word she did not wish to associate with a Nazi.

Mum rose and went to the oven. Catherine watched her

hands shake as she poured the coffee pot. Would the lieutenant notice it was parsnip coffee? Mum tried to lift the cup and saucer, and the shaking was so violent that the rattling threatened to tip over. Catherine took a step toward her, but Helen beat her there, taking the cup and saucer and giving Mum an encouraging smile.

Mum smiled back tremulously and sank back against the counter.

Helen set the saucer down near Lieutenant Schafer. He looked from the cup up her arm and into her face as if he hadn't seen her before. For a long moment, no one said anything. Helen's expression turned from impassive to concerned as she straightened and stepped back. Lieutenant Schafer watched her narrow-eyed, and Catherine felt a shiver of unease. She put her hand on Timmy's shoulder, prepared to yank him out of the room. Sergeant Doepgen frowned intently, as if trying to signal his friend, who was ignoring him.

Helen just blinked at the lieutenant, saying nothing, but not backing down either. Catherine had never felt more admiring of her friend, whereas her own soul cowered inside her. This German soldier knew she had a brother fighting in the war. If Richard was captured, the Germans could make him pay for any supposed acts of rebellion the Braun family showed—even if none of it was true.

At last Lieutenant Schafer looked away and continued eating, taking sips of the coffee in between. He glanced up in annoyance. "Stop watching me eat. It's as bad as being with the prisoners in the labor camp."

He flushed, as if he knew he'd said too much. It took everything in Catherine not to say, *Of course they watch you eat—you're starving them!* How did an entire nation succumb to such evil?

Dad sat down in Timmy's chair, taking Timmy onto his knee. Eyeing the soldier, Timmy started to eat, a hungry boy who wasn't getting enough to keep growing at a healthy pace.

Though her legs were shaking, Catherine forced herself to sit back down. Helen followed, and lastly, Mum. Beneath the table, Catherine squeezed Mum's hand. Sergeant Doepgen stared down at his feet.

Without another word, Lieutenant Schafer pushed away his plate, stomped from the room and up the stairs, the abnormally loud sounds echoing through the small house. His friend quickly followed.

Catherine looked at her family for a moment, uncertain what to do. She wanted to ask if anyone else recognized Sergeant Doepgen, but it seemed too ridiculous to mention. Then Helen took a bite of what now must be cold food.

"Helen," Mum said, "let me warm your plate."

"No, ma'am, it's fine." She straightened and looked at Mum. "It reminds me of something I've been meaning to tell you. I can see now that I'm making the right decision, that you don't need the added work." She took a deep breath. "Mrs. Braun, I won't be imposing on you to queue for my rations anymore."

Everyone turned to look at her, even Timmy, who gnawed a practically bare mutton bone now that he was back in his own chair.

"Helen, dear, it is no problem," Mum said, her forehead wrinkled in obvious concern.

"Thank you, but...I feel like I need to be an adult about this. I need to support myself and prove that I can."

"This is a time of war," Dad said. "We all should be helping each other."

"And you have been!" Helen reached across the table

and squeezed Mum's hand. "I just...need to prove to myself that I can do this."

Helen's manner seemed...odd. Was it because of Betty saying all her choices had been taken away, and Helen realized she still had some, even under an occupation?

Or was it all about Lieutenant Schafer, and how his very presence was growing more ominous by the day. Who knew how many men he'd invite to dinner? Maybe the next one would have no qualms about taking their food.

And the way the lieutenant had looked at Helen—Catherine shuddered. He was obviously taking out his frustration on their family, and it could get worse. Catherine felt a sense of both helplessness and anger. She was no longer living her own life, and now her best friend was being driven away.

After supper, the two young women went outside to talk, settling on their childhood swings, side by side, feet dragging gently in the dirt. Helen watched her own feet make circles beneath her.

Catherine took a deep breath. "You don't want to be here because of Lieutenant Schafer."

Helen's head came up quickly, her eyes wide. "No! I'm no coward."

"Of course you're not a coward," Catherine said. "I just meant, why would you want to be here with—him?"

"That's not what I'm thinking, I swear. I'll still visit. It's just that—"

As Helen paused, Catherine could swear she wasn't quite meeting her gaze as if she was hiding something.

"—that I feel like I'm using you and your mother, rather than standing on my own."

"Helen—"

"Please, I've made up my mind, and I frankly feel

terrible about it. I never meant to hurt your mum's feelings —or yours. I just need to do this, to prove something to myself."

Catherine let it go, trusting that Helen would reveal the truth in her own time.

"About Betty," Helen continued at last. "What do you think she meant, that she had no choice?"

They swung slowly, clutching the chains of the swings as if they could be young girls again.

"Maybe she means that she has to work at the hotel and be nice to the Germans," Catherine said, "in order to earn her living. She has her mother to support, after all."

Helen shook her head. "That wasn't what she meant. Did you see her expression?"

Catherine had, and it still made her heart give a pang of pain and sympathy. "But not having any choice—do you think he...forced her?" Nausea bubbled in her stomach as her imagination failed her.

Helen grimaced. "Maybe. Or did he persuade her enough that she felt she had no choice but to give in. The thing is—what are we going to do about it?"

"Do?" Catherine echoed, throwing her hands wide. "What *can* we do?"

Helen smiled. "I can judge your level of emotion by how much you wave your hands around."

Catherine snorted and linked her fingers in her lap. Sometimes it was the only way she could keep from looking like she was conducting an orchestra.

Helen's smile faded. "We need to figure out a way to help her. It's not as if she has any reason to trust us. We've never been intimate friends. But we grew up with her, and she's obviously suffering. I hate to admit it, but I thought she was enjoying the power of being a...a German's girlfriend."

She'd almost said Jerrybag—Catherine could tell by the way she blushed.

Helen continued, "I think we need to find a way to convince her that we care, so that she'll tell us what's happening and accept an offer of help."

"You are a good person," Catherine said quietly, "and very brave."

The back door opened, and Lieutenant Schafer stepped out on the veranda, a pack of cigarettes in his hand, trailed by Sergeant Doepgen. The men paused on seeing the two of them, then without breaking eye contact, Lieutenant Schafer lit a cigarette and inhaled deeply. His friend did the same, but looked anywhere except at the women.

Catherine wanted to stare right back at them, but inside she crumbled, and her gaze dropped as she succumbed to the fear that always seemed to paralyze her. And then suddenly she remembered where she'd seen Sergeant Doepgen.

"What is it?" Helen asked. "I know when you're upset."

Startled, Catherine looked up. "I—I've met Sergeant Doepgen before," she whispered, "before the war."

Helen's mouth dropped open, and she stole a furtive glance at the Germans. "Where?"

"At a wedding in Germany five years ago—my father's cousin got married. I was seventeen, and I met—*Lukas,* that was his name," she said in a rush. "Lukas Doepgen. He was related to the bride, and I to the groom." Catherine remembered the thrill she'd felt when the handsome young man had asked her to dance. The adults had looked on approvingly, and she'd glowed with the knowledge that he wanted to be with her, to touch her.

And now he was her enemy.

Nothing made sense anymore.

"I don't remember you talking about him," Helen said.

Catherine shrugged, knowing her face had to be red. "How do you talk about an infatuation that could go nowhere? It seemed a secret dream when we danced. Later that night we sat outside under the moon and talked about school and family, and how our lives were different in some ways, the same in others. He stole a kiss, and then he never wrote, though he'd asked for my address."

"Ah," Helen murmured, nodding.

"I was so embarrassed and upset that I didn't want to talk about it." Her glance stole to the two soldiers. "And now here he is. I'm afraid this connection will remind neighbors that we have distant family in Germany, that we've visited. I don't want anyone to find out."

She sighed, and the two women continued to swing gently in silence.

"What will you do?" Helen asked softly. "He keeps looking your way."

"I don't know. Maybe he can't remember where he knows me from. Maybe he'll just ignore me." So many maybes, Catherine thought. "Let's not talk about it anymore."

"I don't think it's that easy to ignore the Germans. Lieutenant Schafer seems much angrier today."

"It's been building for a long time. I'm afraid of where it might lead."

"Don't think about it," Helen whispered, her eyes narrowed. "We can't let ourselves think about anything but taking our country back and winning this war—whatever it takes."

Catherine wondered again if there was something her dear friend was keeping from her.

But why would she do that?

Catherine sighed. "What can we do about Betty?"

"All we can do is be her friend. Let's invite her out."

Catherine's spirits lifted. "I'd like that. I'd like to do *something*."

Helen was staring hard at Lieutenant Schafer, who continued to puff on his cigarette, glance at them, and look away.

"Let's go to her flat and visit her mum early Sunday afternoon, after church," Catherine said. "Betty might be there then."

Helen nodded. "It's a plan."

Lieutenant Schafer continued watching them without bothering to hide it, even though his friend kept trying to get his attention. Catherine shivered, and thought it could easily be her instead of Betty.

13

CATHERINE

Catherine wound her arm through Helen's as she looked up at the shabby two-story stone building where Betty lived.

Helen gave Catherine's arm a squeeze. "Not a pretty neighborhood, is it?"

"They don't have much. Betty's father ran off," Catherine murmured. "But Betty was always a confident girl. I always believed there was nothing she couldn't accomplish when she set her mind to it."

Helen banged the door knocker, and minutes passed before they heard the slow tread of feet coming down the stairs.

From the other side of the peeling wooden door, a cautious voice asked, "Who's there?"

"Mrs. Markham?" Helen called in a cheerful voice. "It's Helen Abernathy and Catherine Braun. We're friends of Betty's."

They heard the door being unlocked, and then a diminutive woman with drawn features behind round spectacles peered out at them. Catherine forced her smile to remain, even as sympathy stung her eyes.

Mrs. Markham squinted as she regarded them. "You're... Mary's daughter?"

Catherine brightened. "I am!"

Mrs. Markham opened the door wider, her smile hesitant. "It is good to see a friendly face." She looked past the two women with a quick, frightened glance. "Please come in. It's not safe on the streets with all these"—she dropped her voice to a hoarse whisper—"Germans."

Catherine followed Mrs. Markham, who turned and started a slow ascent of the stairs which squeaked beneath her slight weight. She heard Helen close the door and follow them.

Inside the flat, Catherine kept her expression pleasant, even though she wanted to wince with sadness at the drab furnishings, the lack of light with the curtains drawn, the stale smell of cigarette smoke. Mrs. Markham asked if they'd like tea, and when they politely declined, she seemed relieved.

Helen was her usual unsubtle self. "Does sunlight bother your eyes, Mrs. Markham?"

The old lady slowly sank onto a worn chair, where the stuffing had obviously been mended many times, a full ashtray on the nearby table. "No, but I cannot bear to see what has happened to our lovely town. The Germans frighten me so. Betty keeps telling me that I shouldn't let them, that I should go out, but...I cannot. I haven't left this flat, not even to see Betty star in one of her plays."

She didn't meet their gazes, obviously ashamed, and Helen and Catherine glanced at each other in surprise and sadness.

"I tell Betty not to risk drawing attention to herself," Mrs.

Markham whispered, hands spread wide. "Some German officer might be tempted by her beauty."

Apparently Mrs. Markham had no idea about Betty's suitor, Catherine thought. "If it makes you feel better, Betty played an elderly woman in the last play."

"So she told me," she said wanly, then continued in a surprisingly resolute voice. "I'm a coward to hide here, I know. But I remember what they did in the Great War. I remember the boy I loved, his lungs scarred, his refusal to see me again. He left the island and left me behind. My husband—Betty's father—did the same. But though I'm afraid, I don't leave when things are difficult."

She lifted her gaze with a flash of defiance, and Catherine saw a hint of Betty's spirit.

Helen sat down on the sofa opposite Mrs. Markham's chair, not bothering to hide her surprised admiration. "We can certainly understand not leaving the island, can't we, Catherine?"

Catherine took her seat next to Helen. "We can. My family chose not to leave, but my mother didn't seem to realize what having Germans walking our streets would truly mean. She didn't leave our house for several months after the they arrived."

Mrs. Markham flushed. "You're both like Betty, so brave, able to go out and live your lives as best you can."

"We don't have a choice," Helen said. "We have to eat and pay our rent."

"And Betty works so hard at that," Mrs. Markham said. "I wish she could have found a position that didn't involve waiting on Germans."

"We all wish that," Catherine said. "Is she coming home soon?"

"She's at the restaurant, I think," Mrs. Markham said, a

frown wrinkling her forehead. "Although we usually spend Sunday afternoon together."

Helen bit her lip before saying, "Maybe she's out with friends."

Mrs. Markham shook her head. "These days Betty works far too much. She says so many of her old friends evacuated before the Germans arrived." She sighed. "Betty wanted us to go as well, but I just...couldn't."

Mrs. Markham sipped her tea, and Catherine glanced surreptitiously around the little parlor. Certainly the Markhams didn't seem to be living in a better style due to Betty's connection with the German officer. Perhaps there was more food in their cupboards; did Betty feel like she had to feed her mother?

The front door suddenly opened. Betty entered and turned to bolt the door automatically. She wore a tight skirt, her dark hair curled just so around her face, emulating the style of the American movie star Hedy Lamarr. Helen liked to say that Betty had a rare beauty—if only she didn't know it.

Betty set her handbag on a side table, took a step farther into the room, and came to a sudden stop upon seeing guests. Her eyes flashed with anger, but then it was gone as she gave her mother a faint smile.

"Hello, Mum, how nice of you to entertain my guests. I'm sorry I was delayed."

Mrs. Markham smiled with happiness. "I'm so glad you're doing something with the girls. You need that, Betty."

"You need that, too, Mum. Mrs. Thornton asks about you all the time."

Mrs. Markham's smile turned wistful and sad. "I know."

"I could invite her to visit."

It was obvious Betty had made that offer many times.

Mrs. Markham hesitated, then gave a nod. "That would be fine, Betty. You do that."

Betty blinked as if stunned, then turned a more resolute expression on Catherine and Helen. "Let me change, and I'll be right with you."

Catherine wanted to wince at the bright, too pleasant sound of Betty's voice. Instead she answered Mrs. Markham's questions about her students, while Helen fingered her flower brooch nervously.

When Betty swept out of her room, she was wearing a smart printed silk dress, once a brilliant shade of green, now faded. Mrs. Markham lifted her cheek for Betty's kiss and waved them all off.

Helen and Catherine followed Betty, who marched down the stairs as if at the head of a brigade of soldiers.

As they paused while Betty lit a cigarette, Catherine glanced farther down the lane and realized there was a queue of people in the distance.

"I didn't think there were any shops this way," she said.

Betty blew out a stream of smoke. "There aren't. That's the soup kitchen. The Germans don't feed their prisoners enough, so islanders are trying to help. The Germans don't bother keeping them penned up, since this is an island, so they're free to roam, as long as they work every day and spend nights at the prison camp."

Catherine put a hand to her mouth, taking a few steps toward them. She could see that some had tied sacks onto their feet, or had cords wrapped around their shoes to keep them together. They were thin and filthy, and she knew they'd gotten that way helping to dig the cliff-side gun embrasures that would be guarding their island from the Allies.

Catherine kept walking toward them, not knowing what

she intended, even as Helen called her name. Two laughing Germans strode toward her on the pavement, a third man behind. When they saw her, one drew his gun and drunkenly aimed it at her chest. She froze, and the sounds of the street seemed to disappear.

"Stop this at once!" said the third German.

His voice was faintly familiar, but she could give it no other thought.

"We're having fun," said the aggressor, the muzzle of his gun weaving circles in front of Catherine.

She wanted to pray, but couldn't remember the words. Her entire world shrank to that dark muzzle that could end her life.

And then it was gone, plucked out of the man's hands by Sergeant Doepgen, Lieutenant Schafer's friend—the man with whom Catherine had once shared an evening.

Helen put an arm around her shoulders and whispered, "Breathe."

Catherine did so, taking in a deep inhalation even as her head spun.

Sergeant Doepgen gave her a concerned look, then said to the others, "Put your guns away and have some coffee. It's Sunday afternoon, for God's sake."

The first two men just laughed and walked past them down the street, giving Betty looks that were almost an assault themselves.

"*Fraulein* Braun." Sergeant Doepgen's voice was sober. "I am so sorry. Are you well?"

She nodded, still trembling.

"We have some place we have to be," Betty said coolly.

Sergeant Doepgen gave a brisk nod. "I will escort you to High Street, in case those fools are still nearby. How terrible of them to frighten women."

Helen turned Catherine's shoulders until she was facing the right direction, and then she remembered how to walk.

"You have textbooks, *Fraulein* Braun," the sergeant said. "You are a teacher?"

She cleared her throat. "Yes."

"It is a strange coincidence, but I am, too."

Catherine finally looked up into his eyes. They were brown and kind, and for just a moment, she remembered a time before the war, when she would have loved talking to a man who understood her profession—especially a man who'd once been drawn to her even in a crowd.

To her shame, her eyes began to sting with tears.

He seemed to realize he was only upsetting her. They'd arrived on High Street, and he tipped his cap. "Good day, ladies." He turned and walked away.

Betty started to stride the opposite way, and Catherine had to pick up her pace to keep up with her.

"Happy now?" Betty demanded, her smile fake, her gaze straight forward. "It was your idea to visit. Does my neighborhood meet your expectations? We have a soup kitchen, slaves, *and* Germans."

"We have no expectations," Helen said dryly.

Helen was looking at Catherine with such concern, that she began to feel foolish. She could not let every confrontation with a German overwhelm her.

But a soldier had pointed his gun at her chest. A drunken twitch of his finger, and...

Forcing herself to stop shaking, Catherine looked at Betty. "What did you expect us to do after what you said about dating a German, that you had no choice? I didn't know if your mother was ill, or you were desperate for money."

"You think I would see a man for money?" Betty practically hissed.

"Your mother seems relatively fine," Helen said, "but sad and afraid."

"My problems are none of your business," Betty said.

"Problems are better when they're shared with friends," Helen countered.

"So now you're my friends?"

"We want to be," Catherine said quietly.

Betty stopped walking and looked from Catherine to Helen, taking a puff of her cigarette.

"You revealed your problem to us," Helen added. "You don't say something like that unless you mean to. I can't believe *you* say anything by accident."

Betty blinked and just looked at them. They were stopped in the middle of the walkway, and several people passed them, including a German officer. Catherine shivered, but this was a different man, who only touched his hat to Betty as he went by.

Catherine watched the subtle way she stiffened, saw her expression grow impassive, her eyes cold, and then her shoulders briefly sagged.

"Friends, you say?" Betty murmured. "I don't really know what that means."

Catherine's heart gave a little squeeze of sadness. "Everybody needs friends, especially now. I don't know what I would have done without Helen."

"You have your entire family," Betty said with a trace of bitterness.

"But I don't," Helen shot back.

Betty inhaled sharply. "I spoke without thinking. I'm sorry."

Helen gave a crooked smile. "It's all right. I was sorry to

hear that your mother is so frightened that she hasn't left your flat."

In unison, they all started walking again, trying to be casual as they strolled down High Street, passing empty storefronts or queues of islanders desperate for goods.

Betty sighed. "I've tried everything, and nothing works. She didn't have many friends to begin with, and most have fallen away or evacuated."

"You obviously take good care of her," Catherine said. "She's lucky to have you."

Betty remained silent for a long moment. "You're wondering *how* I take care of her."

"I'm not." Catherine said earnestly. "You work at the restaurant, and I assume that since the hotel is full, so is the restaurant."

"It is. I don't upset anyone; I just do my work, and that's how I support my mother."

Catherine wanted to elbow Helen to say something, but Helen walked with her head lowered, her hands behind her back, listening. Betty glanced at Helen.

Helen lifted her head. "I am bothered that you think our motives are worse than concern for your welfare."

"And this concern is because you're my friend now." Betty's voice could have been sarcastic, but there was a faint amusement laced in her words.

The two of them shared an actual smile.

Relief and hope warmed Catherine, who said impulsively, "Let's go to the tea shop." Maybe they could pretend that nothing had changed, that they didn't confront death on every corner, that old admirers didn't become Nazis.

Soon they were sharing good-natured complaints over the lack of real tea, and debating the use of parsnips or acorns for a hot beverage. It was small talk, and often awkward, but Catherine couldn't help thinking it was a beginning.

Not that Betty was the type who would open up about what was troubling her. Their conversation didn't touch on her German boyfriend, and neither of them tried to probe deeper.

A German soldier came into the tea shop, and all half dozen customers grew quiet, including Betty. When the soldier saw her, he smiled and gave her a nod.

She looked away, and that was the end of their easy conversation.

Catherine knew winning Betty's trust would be a challenge. Although the following week they attended a variety show together, and the week after that had dinner at Helen's house—where Helen, strangely, was the awkward one—Betty never once brought up the man she was dating.

14

BETTY

Though Betty read men better than she did women, anyone with eyes could see the tension between Helen and Catherine at dinner. Catherine wore an air of wounded bewilderment, and Helen was tense and easily startled in her own home.

At first, Betty tried to ignore the unseen drama. She didn't like people prying into her business, so why would she do it to others? The three of them made dinner together, stretching the potatoes as far as they would go and adding peas. Catherine talked about the garden she was tending with her students, and Helen mentioned the stand-off between German and Guernsey doctors over a tricky patient diagnosis.

Betty didn't have much to say, and wished she could go outside for a smoke. She certainly didn't want to tell them about her personal life and see their pity.

When they began to eat, a silence descended over them, at first the natural silence of hungry people grateful for food. Helen must have braved the mined beach, because Betty tasted the faintest hint of crabs in the soup. Or perhaps she had money for the Black Market. But gradually tension resurfaced like the rise of a whale at sea.

Catherine heaved a sigh and put her spoon down. "Helen, what's going on? I'm very concerned."

Betty looked back and forth between them with interest. She knew how men handled problems—usually with an open discussion or a fight, and then it was over. But women...she'd watched the drama in school, and lately among the restaurant staff. The lying, the wounded feelings, the grudges held. She'd be disappointed if Helen and Catherine did the same thing.

Instead of pretending she didn't know what Catherine was talking about, Helen set down her fork and met her friend's determined gaze. "I didn't want to worry you. I thought I could deal with it on my own, but apparently I'm not good at hiding anything from you."

Betty turned to look at Catherine, like this was a tennis match, and the ball had just been hit across the net.

"You know I'll help you through anything," Catherine said, reaching across the table to give Helen's hand a squeeze.

"Should I leave the room?" Betty asked dryly.

To her surprise, they both turned to look at her and said, "No!" simultaneously.

"You're our friend, and I trust you," Helen said, before rising and leaving the room.

Betty and Catherine exchanged a confused glance.

Helen returned with a typed piece of paper and, moving aside the teapot, set it on the table between them. Betty saw *G.U.N.S.* across the top, along with *Guernsey Underground News Service*.

"This is typed news directly from the BBC broadcast of the night before," Helen said. "Someone put it in my door. I don't know if I was an accidental recipient, because I haven't received another. But then again they haven't confiscated our radios recently."

"This is forbidden," Catherine whispered, reaching out her hand to touch it, then pulling back as if it was electrified.

"I didn't want to tell you and involve you in the *crime*," Helen said, exaggerating the word. "But now you know."

"It's wonderful that someone is trying to keep us informed about the world outside our island." Catherine tentatively picked up the newsleaf. "So a person listened to the broadcast and typed out the news? Do they retype it many times? It doesn't seem printed in a press."

"Looks like a single copy," Helen said, "and someone— maybe a lot of someones—retyped it."

"I wonder how many people are involved?" Betty mused.

"It amazes me that someone was brave enough to do something like this." Helen reached to touch the flower brooch on her blouse. "We could be brave, too. We should do something."

"Like what?" Betty asked.

"I don't know," Helen said. "The Victory campaign really annoyed the Germans while it lasted."

Betty thought of the chalked "Vs" that had appeared all over town. It made her smile every time she saw one, and she'd added her own "V" on the occasional late-night walk home from the hotel.

"Timmy cut a 'V' out of cloth and pinned it under his lapel," Catherine said. "When Mum found out I thought she'd take a broom to his behind. But I think she was secretly proud."

"But the Germans counteracted with their own 'V is for

Victory' propaganda," Betty pointed out. "Took the wind out of our sails."

"I have an idea," Helen began slowly. "We all know Germans. Maybe we can keep our ears open."

"You have just suggested spying on the Germans," Betty said.

Catherine chewed her lip, her gaze lowered.

Helen nodded. "Maybe I am."

There was a slight challenge to her voice that Betty admired. "To what end?"

Helen glanced away with a sigh. "I don't know. We're trapped here, which means any information we might gather has nowhere to go. But I just...*need* to do something."

"Stop this insanity." Catherine looked intently at Helen. "We're just women—captured women. Bad things could happen to us or to our families."

Helen nodded, but Betty didn't think she was giving up so easily. When Helen glanced at her, Betty gave her a smile.

15

HELEN

Helen thought it was very strange to have a man living in her home. Jack prowled her cottage during the day, desperate for something to do when he wasn't sleeping, before a night adventure took him away. She found a loose doorknob repaired; he cleaned out the boiler ash and sifted for usable pieces of wood to burn again, since nothing could be wasted during the occupation.

Every evening, they sat together at nine to listen to the BBC. Helen hadn't realized how easy it would be to talk to Jack. He'd spent some time in London when he was on leave, and now told her stories of London during the Blitz, air raids every night, never knowing if your house would collapse around you while you waited in shelters.

The BBC news ended and a band concert began, and still Helen and Jack sat in opposite chairs. His fingers drummed restlessly on the chair arm, and his frustration was a palpable tension that felt like it could explode.

"Jack," she said quietly.

He glanced up. His intense blue eyes met hers, and she

felt her breath catch. But she forced down her unthinking reaction to him. She wasn't a schoolgirl any longer.

"Yes?" he asked.

"Did you ever get married?"

He sat back and cocked his head. "I left here to join the army and have been a soldier ever since. No time for a wife."

Something eased inside her. She was such a fool—a lonely fool.

"I've gone out with a pretty girl now and again," he continued, "but I couldn't give her the life she wants—especially not during a war."

"What about your brother? Didn't he join up, too?"

Jack nodded, his expression giving way to sadness. "He's in a London hospital right now, recovering."

She gasped. "What happened?"

"Lost an arm in Egypt during the North African campaign."

Helen covered her mouth with one hand. "That is so tragic."

"He's alive," Jack said firmly.

"Will he be able to return to fishing after the war?"

"I think he'll find a way because he's smart and quick-witted. But he thinks our family business is lost to him. Whatever he does, he'll survive, unlike so many of our friends who've died."

She knew them all, had gone to many memorial services since the dead could not be returned for burial.

"But what about you?" he asked. "Did you ever marry?"

She gave a very unladylike snort. "Do you see a man around here, even in pictures?"

He smiled back at her. "I had to ask."

"I was dating someone when the war started."

"Do I know him?"

She shook her head. "He was an incomer from Scotland, who managed one of the hotels. We had fun together for a few months, and then he joined up, just like most of the other young men."

"Must have been lonely for you girls."

She shrugged. "Our dating life wasn't a consideration. We knew what was important."

"I bet other young ladies didn't see it the same way."

She stiffened. "What do you mean?"

"I've been spying; I've seen our island girls with the Nazis."

"Don't judge them all." She couldn't help thinking of Betty, and wondering if she looked happy and lively when she was with her German officer.

"Have you dated a Nazi?" Jack asked.

"Of course not!"

"You put up with being lonely. It's a shame others couldn't."

"Every story is different, Jack."

He regarded her curiously. "You sound like you're sticking up for them."

"Not most of them, no. Boredom is a poor reason to conspire with the enemy. I'm ashamed that some of my fellow islanders need parties and doting men to feel alive, even if those men are trying to kill their friends and family."

"They probably try not to look too closely at it."

"Now you're the one who sounds sympathetic."

He shook his head. "No, but no one is perfect."

The sound of an approaching lorry made their conversation die. Once, Helen never gave a thought to the rare lorry passing by her cottage. She'd always assumed one of the neighboring farms had a delivery. But the Germans had made her far more skittish.

And Jack was no fool after weeks of hiding. They shared a tense silence, waiting for the lorry to rumble past.

She could tell when it turned down the drive toward her cottage.

As they both jumped to their feet, Helen said, "Take the radio down to the cave with you. I usually hide it when I hear them coming."

Jack scooped up the polished wooden box and rose. "How can I leave you to face them alone?"

His gaze kept going to the window, where they caught a glimpse of headlamps.

"Don't be foolish," she said, coming around the table and leading the way to the cellar stairs. "I have been dealing with Germans every day. Much as I hate and despise them, I know how they treat us. It will be fine."

"It's late, and they're coming here for a reason. Do not underestimate them. They treat the islanders decently almost on a whim. It will not last if the war turns against them."

"Then I'll have to deal with that when it happens. But for now, I'm not going to watch you get captured and know I did nothing to stop it. And there is my radio to hide," she added, trying to lift the mood.

She opened the cellar door, clicked on the overhead bulb, and hurried down. Jack put the radio into her hands while he cleared stacks of crates off the trap door and opened it. The darkness yawned beneath them, and the salty damp smell of the sea rushed in to fill the room. The tide must be high, lapping at the mouth of the cave.

After sliding the ladder down into the hole, Jack stepped onto the first rung. Helen bent over to hand him the radio, and their gazes met.

"Helen—"

"I'll be fine," she said.

"Don't do anything foolish. Give them what they want. And leave a light crate on the trap door so I can push it open if you don't return quickly."

He started down into the blackness, reaching for the electric torch she handed to him. After he pulled the ladder down with him, she closed the trap door.

Helen hurried back upstairs and took out the older, unreliable crystal wireless set she kept just in case of confiscation. She barely had time to place it on her father's desk when someone banged on the door.

In the front hall, she took a few deep breaths before calling, "Who is it?"

"Open the door!" a man said in a heavy German accent.

She unlocked and opened it. Two soldiers pushed past her. One of their rifles brushed against her, and she recoiled in distaste. She didn't recognize them from past encounters, but then again, there were thousands and thousands of Germans on the island.

She kept telling herself not to be worried, but the reassurances weren't helping, and her fear of being alone with them began to feel like it was choking her. But if she was going to find some way to fight back, she had to learn to control these useless emotions.

She followed them into the kitchen, where they began to slam open cabinets.

"If you tell me what you're looking for, I can help," she said.

Her mother's favorite teapot crashed to the floor. Tears rushed to her eyes.

"Your radio," one said. "We are confiscating it."

"But why? What are we being punished for this time?"

"It's not your concern. Where is it?"

"It's in the parlor," she said as they opened the cabinet where her mother's china was kept.

They didn't let her lead the way but pushed past her, a broad shoulder shoving against her chest, touching her unnecessarily. She knew it was an attempt to make her afraid, and it worked.

In the parlor, one of the soldiers focused in on the desk, where she'd placed the old wireless set. But the other soldier walked around looking at the mementoes on table-tops—her father's pocket watch, a ceramic flower she'd made in grammar school—and then the books lining the shelves.

The soldier gave her a look as if there were a set number of books, and she'd gone well over the limit.

"My father was a professor at Elizabeth College," she said, trying to sound nonchalant. "My mother used to write poetry. They liked to read."

Helen had already hidden any title on the Germans' banned book list after Catherine had warned her. She had no idea what they had against authors like F. Scott Fitzgerald or Ernest Hemingway.

When one soldier would have continued examining the books, the other brusquely said, "Let's go—*schnell*. We're wasting time."

Helen tried not to let her breath out in a thankful rush. The soldier turned from her books and gave her a cold stare from beneath the lid of his helmet. It was not difficult to appear meek and terrified. The first soldier gave her a written receipt—so orderly, those Germans.

When she'd closed the door behind them and locked it —like that would matter to them if they wanted to get back into the cottage—she stood looking out the narrow window until they'd gotten in their lorry and driven down the dirt lane. Only when they were out of sight, heading for the main road, did she lean her back against the wall and sag with relief.

She couldn't seem to stop trembling. She saw Germans every day and was used to the sight of their gray-green uniforms and that evil spider insignia, the swastika. But it was always in a public setting or in hospital rooms with patients. The few times they'd come to her cottage had seemed vastly different to a woman living alone.

But she wasn't alone.

She took off at a run for the cellar stairs, her feet pounding hard down each wooden step. She shoved aside the crate and raised the trap door. It was pitch dark below and totally quiet.

"Jack!"

He stepped into the square block of light caught by the open trap door. "Helen."

He said her name in a strange tone of voice, part relief, part...something else. She shook that thought away.

After he threaded the ladder up through the door, she stepped onto a rung and started down. It wasn't as if she could escape the invasion of her home.

"What's going on?" he asked. "Are they still in the house?"

She reached the bottom and turned around to find him standing right in front of her. "No, they're gone."

He loomed above her in the gloom, just the two of them alone in the dark. Her fear began to melt away, leaving her body so swiftly she felt weak. She wanted to sway into his embrace, let his arms circle her and protect her.

But she shook such thoughts away—she wasn't going to be that kind of woman, not when she wanted to help him fight the Germans.

"I just wanted to see where you hid the radio," she said. "It's going to have to stay down here from now on, unless we're listening to it. They're confiscating all the radios, and for the first time I had the sense that it wasn't a temporary punishment."

He didn't move at first, just stood before her as if he could sense her conflicted emotions. She wanted him to treat her like a woman—she wanted him to treat her like a colleague. This wasn't the time for silly, contradictory emotions, she kept telling herself.

At last he stepped back and, she followed him to a depression in the rock wall. Using the electric torch, he showed her how the radio was hidden, covered by canvas to protect it from moisture.

She looked up into his shadowy face. "Jack, it's not enough for me just to hide you here. I want to do more for the war effort. Look at this." She pulled the crumpled newsleaf out of her pocket. "Others are doing their part."

He took the paper from her hand and shown the torch on it, while she explained how she'd received it.

"This is far too dangerous," Jack said. "Don't you see that?"

"I don't care about that. What does protecting myself mean when we could be under German occupation for the rest of our lives?"

He remained silent, as if he didn't want to give her any kind of encouragement. She knew the war effort was going badly, but standing here in near darkness seemed so different than sitting beside the radio in her lighted parlor.

"If only I spoke German and could eavesdrop on the men around me," she said with frustration.

"You mean as they discuss medical cases?" he said with faint sarcasm.

"Or maybe they're discussing something else. I'll never know."

"I'm glad you don't speak German," he said. "You might do something foolish."

She stiffened, hating that he downplayed her help. "Catherine speaks German."

"And Catherine is sensibly too frightened to do anything with that skill."

"So I'm not sensible."

"I didn't say that." He spread his arms wide with exasperation. The torch beam darted randomly all over the walls.

She turned and started back up the ladder. He followed behind her, shaking the ladder with his weight, following too close.

"You don't think *I'm* frustrated?" he demanded as she stepped off the ladder into the cellar. "I came here on an assignment, and lately all I can do is watch for Germans coming down the main road each day and time their movements—as if that would tell our generals anything."

She wouldn't soften; she wouldn't feel sorry for him. "Good night, Jack."

He didn't say anything as she marched up the cellar stairs. She was tempted to slam the door behind her, but in the end, she left it open and retreated to her bedroom. Inside, she angrily wiped away tears of frustration, until she remembered that she, Catherine, and Betty didn't need his permission to do anything. They would make a plan.

16

CATHERINE

Well into the summer holiday, Catherine and her brother Timmy went out to their garden to take care of their pet rabbits. She'd never imagined owning rabbits, let alone feeling so indebted to them, but it had become a way to bring meat to the family during these times of deprivation. The key was to not get too attached to the animals as pets, but just to think of them as a food source, she always reminded Timmy, though she was also trying to convince herself. The first few times they'd eaten one of the rabbits, Catherine had returned from school to find the rabbit already prepared—which had helped. Her mother was a peach. But Catherine had still fought back tears while remaining grateful to have the food.

She helped feed the rabbits on occasion, even though their care was Timmy's main chore. It gave her a way to feel close to her brother, who was fourteen years younger. She was concerned that so many children seemed to be running wild on the island, since adults either worked or stood in queues for rationed food. She'd heard stories of Germans randomly offering food to children, like the milk they supplied the schools, and wanted to make sure Timmy felt close enough to tell her anything suspicious. She couldn't believe that the German army who'd committed such atrocities in Eastern Europe could be offering food without a sinister motive.

"What do you think of Sam here?" Timmy asked, opening the cage door and lifting Sam out by the scruff of the neck.

"He's getting big."

He cuddled the rabbit in his arms and nosed his white and black fur.

"Timmy—"

"I know, I know, don't get close to the rabbits. I'm eating them with no problem, aren't I? But they deserve some loving for their sacrifice."

"That sounds reasonable." She hoped. "And Sam looks like he's thriving."

"Sometimes hunting through hedgerows for plants isn't enough. I'm finding the best hay for him. Mr. Arcand let me scour his fields last week after a haymaking. But I have a treat for Sam today." Timmy reached into his pocket and pulled out a single squashed cabbage leaf.

Catherine opened her mouth to protest that he shouldn't take food meant for the family, then changed her mind. The fond look on Timmy's face when he fed Sam, the only pet he was allowed to have—the pet that he would have to eat. His childhood was being taken away. He'd confessed to her that he couldn't remember what a banana tasted like. Would he forget the good times before the war?

Children ran everywhere on their small island, watching the Germans build their fortifications through guarded fences, forgetting that the soldiers were an invading force to be frightened of. The children were used to following the

German lorries laden with produce, hoping to pick up anything that fell. The soldiers often tossed extra potatoes to the children, like warped Pied Pipers.

Sure enough, a division of soldiers went marching past their house, their uniforms pressed, their weapons shiny.

"Catherine, there's John—may I join him?" Timmy asked, excitement in his eyes.

She turned and saw a half dozen boys following the soldiers, mimicking their marching, even as some of the Germans turned their heads to watch and smile. She shivered. She didn't want to think of the soldiers as human, though they were barely a few years older than Timmy.

"What about the rabbits?" she asked.

He looked so crestfallen that she relented almost at once, knowing how hard he worked to help their household survive.

"I'll finish," she said. "But be home for tea. You know how Mum gets."

He gave her a quick hug around the waist. "Thanks! You're the best sister."

She didn't feel like the best sister, she thought, watching as he put one hand on the stone half wall and vaulted it.

Did the best sister do more against the Nazis, or do nothing and keep her brother safe?

Lieutenant Schafer came out of the back door and lit up a cigarette, as he often did. His frequent sidekick, Sergeant Doepgen, was with him again. She felt uncomfortable with both of them in different ways. Lieutenant Schafer watched her as she fed hay to each of the six rabbits. Though she felt his stare in the center of her back, her strategy was to ignore him.

The sergeant was different. If it wasn't for the uniform he wore, she could almost forget he was the enemy—and that was dangerous. More than once he'd started conversations about teaching, and she'd found herself answering without remembering what they truly were to each other. He told her about his parents and his little brother, who was only a year older than Timmy. They never spent time alone, and she wasn't able to ask if he remembered her. Did she want him to? She felt like a Jerrybag, like a woman who wished the war wasn't happening, who could just find a husband and start a family. The shame overwhelmed her sometimes.

But now Sergeant Doepgen stood behind Lieutenant Schafer, who was angry again, as he was more and more. She knew the Germans had considered Guernsey as a stepping off point for an invasion of Britain. It had never happened and probably wouldn't, now that the Americans had joined the war effort. According to the BBC, Germany was taking heavy bombing campaigns every night, targeting their manufacturing.

But listening to the BBC was no longer an option. Lieutenant Schafer had made sure his fellow officers knew about their radio, and it had been confiscated. The only way they'd even heard about the bombing of Germany was through the mysterious newsleafs Helen recently started receiving again. Catherine read the newsleaf several times, and repeated it back to her parents, who were shocked and amazed at the bravery of fellow islanders.

And then she heard Lieutenant Schafer coming toward her, and the hairs on her neck rose. She was still such a coward.

"*Fraulein* Braun," he said in an angry tone.

Her trembling hands made it difficult to close the last rabbit cage.

"Yes, Lieutenant?" She turned to face him, linking her hands together before they betrayed her fear. Lately she sensed he *needed* to see fear to remind himself of German superiority, since it was no longer so certain they could win a war against the Allies.

He took a puff of his cigarette, eyeing the rabbit cages. "They look fat and healthy."

"My brother collects hay from the fields for them." She tried to think of how Betty would answer, what Betty would say.

She didn't know *what* Betty said to that German officer who escorted her to movies and parties. She still had not trusted them enough to confide anything.

"Give me one," Lieutenant Schafer said.

She frowned. "What? You want to hold a rabbit?"

"I want to feed my men."

Her mouth opened but she could think of nothing to say. She was at war with herself, wishing she could fight back, but knowing that her brother Richard could come into German hands at any time and pay for her mistakes. She glanced at Sergeant Doepgen, who wore his usual uncomfortable expression. Why was he even friends with Lieutenant Schafer? "But—"

"But what?" Lieutenant Schafer blew a puff of smoke into her face and smiled smugly.

She turned her head and coughed, eyes stinging as she looked back at him.

"But what?" he repeated, taking a step closer.

"Do you intend to hurt me to steal a rabbit?" Catherine couldn't believe the words that came out of her mouth.

He seemed surprised, too. "You're like a little rabbit who's showing some spirit." He reached past her and opened a cage, pulling out Timmy's favorite rabbit, Sam.

They'd eat him someday, she knew, but she found herself pleading. "Oh, not that one, please. My brother—"

Sam the rabbit squeaked and struggled to get away. Lieutenant Schafer twisted its neck in his two fists. The audible crack made her jerk, and tears came to her eyes. Poor Sam, she thought, looking at his lifeless body.

Sergeant Doepgen's expressive face had gone slack, as if he too couldn't believe what was happening. He gave Catherine a look, perhaps with regret, but she really couldn't know. Grabbing the lieutenant's arm, the sergeant pulled him toward the requisitioned car. Lieutenant Schafer threw Sam's lifeless body onto the floor of the back seat and they drove away.

Catherine sank down onto a garden bench and burst into tears. She wasn't sure how long she sat there, quaking among the cabbage plants, shoulders hunched, reliving the lieutenant's menace and her own cowardice. Why was he behaving like this? At the beginning he'd seemed as awkward as the Braun family about the living arrangements, apologetic even, but the war had changed him, though he hadn't seen any military combat on Guernsey. She imagined you couldn't be a Nazi for long without being infected by their beliefs.

But was it worse that Sergeant Doepgen tried to be nice, when he was her enemy? Wasn't that the real mask?

At last she wiped her face with her apron and stood back up. She noticed her next-door neighbor, Mr. Russell, a dapper, mustached man in his thirties, watching her with interest. He and his wife and young son had moved to the island only a year before the occupation, drawn to the tropical breezes and endless beaches, Dad had said after his first conversation with Mr. Russell.

The couple wasn't very friendly, which had been obvious when Catherine had brought a cake her mother had baked, along with an invitation to a private dance. They'd politely but coolly turned down the invitation and taken the cake with barely a thank-you. They'd made no offer in return, and resisted all small talk when Mum was hanging laundry. Gradually, the Brauns had become used to exchanging only polite nods.

But now Mr. Russell was watching her, had perhaps seen and heard everything. Catherine didn't blame him for not interfering—he would have risked his and his family's safety. But he didn't come over to the half wall separating their gardens and ask if she was all right. Instead, he turned away and hurried into his house.

Her mind sifted through everything she knew about the Russells. Their clothes weren't as patched and worn as everyone else's on the island—except for the Germans, with their access to their supply chains on the continent. Somehow, the Russells still had money, or at least plenty of clothes to wear, and access to buy expensive goods. Just because they were luckier than most people on the island didn't mean there was any reason for Catherine's suspicions, but a quiet feeling of unease persisted.

17

BETTY

Summer passed into autumn and the beginning of winter, and Betty knew Guernsey Island life was changing in one major way: everyone on the island had to register and was assigned identity cards to carry. All the cameras had been temporarily requisitioned in order to get the massive job done. The Germans had delighted in stopping whoever they wanted, to scrutinize both the photo i.d. as well as the islander. Betty knew it couldn't be a good thing that the Germans could now demand you produce proof you belonged there.

But those identity cards led to a terrible outcome—two thousand of their fellow islanders, those who hadn't been born on the island, were deported to France, with their final destination Germany. Several of Betty's regular customers were suddenly just gone. Mum told her about seeing three of their neighbors walk away with a suitcase, heading for the pier. Many of the farm workers had to leave, and the thought of less food being harvested the following year sent a chill throughout the island.

Without ready access to the BBC, the underground

newsleaf, G.U.N.S., was proving invaluable. She learned that the United States had joined in bombing missions in Europe. British clergy and some politicians were holding public meetings professing outrage about the Nazi persecution of Jews. The United States was beginning to turn the tide in far off Pacific islands like Guadalcanal. And Germany itself was feeling the sting as its most famous leader, Lieutenant General Rommel, was trapped in Tunisia, and the forces who'd capture Stalingrad were now surrounded by the Red Army.

In a closer call, Sark, their neighboring island to the east, was attacked by British commandos rattling the Nazis, though they only captured one German soldier. Betty didn't know if she should pray that the British attacked Guernsey or not, because people would certainly die.

But was it better to be a prisoner of the island? Or to be dating a German officer?

On a late, cold December Saturday afternoon, Betty was waiting tables when she saw Helen and Catherine come in. They were wrapped up in their fading coats and darned mittens, like so many on the island.

They both smiled as Betty approached them, and Betty couldn't help feeling a warming of her cold heart. She didn't want to like them, but they'd been trying so hard these last months to prove their friendship. And their need to do something against the German occupation certainly matched her own.

"Hello, ladies," she said, before leading them to a table. "Come here to warm up, did you?"

Catherine blushed, but Helen just laughed and said good-naturedly, "That might have been one reason."

They weren't the only customers to warm up at the hotel and save on their own dwindling supply of fuel.

"The other reason was to see you." Catherine sat down and put a hand on Betty's arm. "You didn't come to Helen's for dinner the other night."

Betty looked away and forced a smile. "So busy. You know how it is. What can I get you?"

She brought them coffee while they looked over the sparse menu, and when they only ordered a sandwich to split between them, she brought a whole sandwich for each.

"Betty, no, this isn't what we ordered," Catherine protested.

Betty shrugged. "No one will know that if you keep your voice down."

Catherine's shoulders sank as she looked around.

"How's your mother?" Helen asked.

Betty shook her head. "The same. She won't leave the flat—and now it's too cold to, the perfect excuse. But at least our neighbor has been visiting occasionally. That lifts Mum's spirits. And your mother came, too," Betty said to Catherine.

"She mentioned having a lovely talk. Although I can't decide if it's good for them to confide their fear to each other as a means of letting it go, or if they just might make each other worse."

"It can't get worse," Betty said dryly. "I'm hoping the fact that your mother was once just as reclusive will make Mum realize she could get out more. If it weren't for dusting, she'd have little movement at all."

They all nodded in commiseration.

Catherine took a deep breath. "Ladies, can I ask your opinion?"

Betty glanced around the dining room, but no one seemed to be looking for her. She perched on the edge of a chair.

"Is everything all right at home?" Helen asked.

"Yes. It's not that. But...it's Sergeant Doepgen." She glanced at Helen. "He's that friend of Lieutenant Schafer, the one who drove off those drunken Germans on the street a few months ago?" To Betty, she added, "I think I met him at a wedding in Germany before the war, but we have not discussed if this was so. He...keeps bringing food to our home. I tell myself he feels guilty for how Lieutenant Schafer treats us, but I'm worried it's...more than that."

Betty had the strangest feeling that Helen was trying not to look at her. "You think he's interested in you?" she asked.

Helen gaped in surprise, but Catherine blushed as she said, "Yes, I'm worried about it. Now the Germans know I can understand them, so they all watch me more carefully, but his attention feels like he's trying to pretend the war isn't happening, that we're fellow teachers discussing our profession."

Helen arched an eyebrow. "When his profession is now killing people?"

"He says he's not on the front lines, that he's a medic."

"Uh huh," Betty said, feeling old and cynical.

"I tell myself he just feels bad for letting Lieutenant Schafer kill Timmy's rabbit, or that he wishes to remember an easier time before the war, but..."

"But you think he wants something more?" Betty asked quietly.

Catherine bit her lip and nodded. "I don't know what to do. I don't want to offend him, to risk angering him—not that I've seen him angry even once—but I also don't want to give him the wrong idea. But once or twice, I find myself forgetting what he is, and we just talk about students and it all seems so normal and—then I come to my senses, and I'm horrified. What should I do?"

Helen said nothing right away, and Betty knew they were waiting on her—the one with the experience.

She sighed. "I tried avoiding any kind of discussion—and it obviously didn't work for me. But your German doesn't seem the same as Franz."

Catherine's face went red, and she stiffly said, "He's not my German!" Her eyes widened and she hunched her shoulders, throwing a furtive glance around the dining room, as if realizing someone might be eavesdropping.

But it was the middle of the afternoon, and few customers were about.

Betty softened her tone. "I know. I only meant to distinguish the two men, not to accuse you of anything."

Catherine's eyes began to glisten with tears. "This is all just so...awful." She pulled a handkerchief out of her sleeve and dabbed her eyes. "So you think I should just avoid talking to him as much as possible?"

"It's worth a try. Unless you *want* to talk to him," Betty added. "I know an island girl in love with a German. She's had his baby by now, swears they're going to get married."

"That's not me!" Catherine's voice grew shrill. "I desperately want to marry someday, to have everything my parents have, but not like this."

"Then stop talking to him," Helen said. "He seems decent. He'll take the hint."

"Betty!"

At the sound of a male voice calling her name, Betty felt a chill of recognition and a sense of impending fate. Her life with Franz and her friendships were about to collide. She was embarrassed and ashamed, two emotions she hadn't thought herself capable of feeling anymore. She needed a cigarette.

Franz stopped beside her, his hat beneath his arm as he

gave a short bow to Helen and Catherine. "Betty, *meine liebste*, am I finally to meet your friends?"

Franz liked to behave as if he was courting her, so polite and jovial, but she often felt like a bone fought over by dogs, the way he showed her off to his fellow officers. When he touched her shoulder, all friendly and intimate, she stepped away.

He spoke to Helen and Catherine. "I am Captain Franz Lunenborg, a friend of Betty's. And who might you ladies be?"

"I'm Helen Abernathy and this is Catherine Braun."

Betty's spirits rose a bit at her polite but cool response.

"We have seen each other before," Helen continued, "at the German hospital. You visited one of your injured men."

Franz's smile widened, and not for the first time, Betty wondered how he could have no problem forcing his attentions on her, knowing she couldn't refuse?

But Betty had so far refused the final thing he'd wanted. She didn't care if everyone thought she traded sex for car rides, parties, and nice dinners—she knew she hadn't. In his mind, he was trying to pretend he was courting a woman; her refusal to give in played along with that scenario...for now.

Franz reached for Helen's hand and bowed over it again. "How foolish of me not to recognize you, *Fraulein* Abernathy."

"I was wearing my uniform," she said. "Perhaps that made a difference."

"I'm sure it was simply concern for my men that distracted me," he answered.

Betty rolled her eyes behind his back. Catherine saw and pressed her lips together in obvious dismay, and Helen's eyes briefly sparkled.

It was foolish to make fun of him, Betty knew, with Germans at every table. But as usual, they were engrossed in themselves and their conversations, convinced as a people and a nation that they were more important than anyone else.

Franz turned to Betty as if to include her in the conversation. He always made it a point to be above reproach where politeness was concerned. Sometimes she wondered if somewhere deep inside him he knew what his country was doing was wrong, and was determined to do his part to show that Germans weren't monsters. But that would make him far more sympathetic.

That kind of man wouldn't force his attentions where he wasn't wanted.

"And how do you girls know each other?"

Betty flinched inside, wanting to tell him they were not silly girls but women. But she'd grown very good at hiding her thoughts after a lifetime of practice. "We went to school together here on the island."

"Ah, schoolfriends." He nodded. "The ones who know you the best."

Betty didn't let them get to know her. It had always been hard to get to know anyone, to risk others knowing your pain, your secrets. It was just easier to be alone. Only lately had she felt truly lonely.

"Tell me something I don't know about Betty," Franz said, sliding an arm around her waist.

In her mind, Betty retreated as she always did with his public familiarities, ignoring the sideways looks from the rest of the staff, the jealousy from a few German officers, the pity Catherine couldn't hide.

Helen cocked her head and eyed Franz. "I know what a proud woman she is."

Franz only gave Betty a grin. "She is that. Look at how she performs on the stage—she has much talent to be proud of. Please, do tell me more."

He pointedly looked at Catherine, who wet her lips. "She—she takes very good care of her mother."

"I have not met *Frau* Markham yet," he said, giving Betty a reproachful look.

"I've told you," Betty said coolly, "she is frightened to death of Germans. You'll give her a heart attack just walking through the door."

"I don't think I believe you," Franz said.

Oh, he thought he was so amusing, full of warmth and teasing. Betty's stomach clenched tighter.

"She's hasn't left the flat since you Germans arrived," Betty continued. "You don't need more proof than that."

Franz gave an exaggerated sigh. "I'll convince you yet to introduce us." He gave Betty's waist a squeeze and let go. "I'll leave you ladies to your gossip. Until tonight, Betty." He kissed her cheek and walked away.

Betty was frozen for a moment, then shook him off. "May I warm up your coffee, ladies?"

Catherine's moist eyes were too full of compassion. It was easier to meet Helen's gaze, for her jaw was rigid and her eyes flashed anger at Franz's back.

Helen said the last thing expected. "Betty, you need to come to my house next Sunday. That's your day off, right? We're forming a play-reading group."

Betty frowned, sensing Helen's urgency, which seemed so out of proportion for the topic.

"We hated to bother you at work," Catherine said, "but you seemed unhappy when we visited your mother."

Betty sighed. "I didn't know you as well then. I've apologized, haven't I?"

"Then come," Helen said with quiet insistence.

Betty gave in. "Very well."

Helen glanced once again at Franz, who was settling into a corner table with another officer. "What does he do on the island?"

"He has something to do with the munitions stockpile on the island."

Helen's face lit up with the excitement of a Christmas celebration. "Perfect!"

"What?" Betty asked, turning to Catherine.

"Never mind," Catherine said, picking up her sandwich. "Helen, just eat and leave poor Betty alone."

Betty went to take care of another table, but couldn't get their invitation out of her mind. Their unusual behavior didn't help matters. As she approached them with the bill, she had every intention of asking more questions, but Franz intercepted her just before she reached their table.

"Betty, I'm going to drive you home after your shift today," he said.

Betty knew that Helen and Catherine could hear every word. Heat burned in her face and to the tips of her ears. "Franz, I've told you several times what I think about that. I have to live in that neighborhood."

"Nonsense, we Germans are half the island's population now. People are used to seeing us. If it helps, my driver will drop us off a block away. I have a gift for your mother, and I insist on delivering it and paying my respects."

She knew he wasn't going to back down, and she could hardly protest in such a public place. He'd planned that, she could see by the hint of amusement in his eyes.

Giving a cold nod, she moved past him to Helen and Catherine's table. She placed the bill down with precision when she wanted to slam it hard. She refused to meet their gazes and see their pity.

Franz was waiting for her three hours later when she left the restaurant by the kitchen entrance. He opened the rear door for her while the driver waited inside. As usual, Arthur didn't look at Betty.

After they were dropped off on High Street, Franz took her arm for the short walk down her dark street. She stepped gingerly through the slush, but he held on even tighter. Although there was no car to attract neighbors' attention, Betty knew many of them would see Franz anyway.

At her door, Franz was particularly amused as she searched for her key in her handbag, then took off her gloves to continue the search.

"Come, come, Betty, you don't think this is going to change my mind, do you?"

She looked pointedly at the box he carried under his arm. "Not one bit."

He chuckled, and she found the key. She didn't care what he thought of the dark hall or the creaking stairs.

After unlocking the door to their flat, she called, "Mum, I've brought a visitor."

"Hello, dear," Mum called from the little kitchen.

Franz pressed in behind Betty, and she was forced to step farther inside.

"What meat did they have at the butcher's?" Mum came out of the kitchen, wiping her hands on a ragged towel.

And then she saw Franz. Her face went so white, Betty started toward her, but her mother clutched a corner of the wall to brace herself.

"What is happening?" Mum asked in a high, hoarse voice. "What have we done?"

Franz stepped up to Betty's side, and she knew he was taking in the shabby rooms, their obvious poverty exacerbated by the war. She could see his mind work, how he thought he could use this in leverage over her.

"Mum, we haven't done anything," Betty said softly, trying to smile. "Please don't panic. You know what the doctor would say."

But Mum was staring wild-eyed at Franz. The stupid man held out the box.

"*Frau* Markham, I am Captain Franz Lunenborg, a friend of Betty's. I've brought you a gift."

Betty took her mother's arm. Mum didn't look at the gift, only stared at Franz's face as if he would change into a monster. Of course, he already was one.

"Sit down, Mum," Betty said, taking the box and putting it on the sofa next to her mother. Her mother was shaking so badly that Betty's fury rose at Franz and even herself. She hadn't done enough to protect her.

Franz sat down in the chair opposite the sofa, the chair where the stuffing was coming out. "Why don't you open my gift, *Frau* Markham?"

Betty sat beside her mother and put the box in her lap. It was a colorful tin, probably from France. Betty had seen such boxes a lifetime ago.

Mum's fingers were shaking so badly, she couldn't begin to untie the string. Betty did it for her and lifted the lid. Inside were French chocolates. For a moment, Betty stared at those chocolates, and they conjured an image of long ago, when one of her mother's male friends had tried to ingratiate himself with Betty. A child then, she'd been thrilled with the gift, her mother not so much. Betty understood why even more now.

Mum couldn't stop looking at Franz's face with dread. She didn't care about the chocolates. Betty felt proud of her.

"Now we know each other," Franz said, almost conspiratorially. "When you see me in the streets, you don't have to be a ghost, pretending not to notice me."

Mum licked her dry lips. "A—a ghost?"

"It is what we call islanders who act like we're not here, as if we'll go away."

Franz's tone of voice said that was just plain silly, that of course Germans were *never* going away. Betty felt a stab of despair but she buried it beneath her rising anger, the anger she couldn't show.

"I'm glad we've met," Franz continued.

He looked at Betty with satisfaction. It was a threat, and they both knew it. He was inching his way into her life, and there was nothing she could do about it. He wanted to sleep with her, for her to give in and accept the inevitable.

"We don't have any tea to offer you," Betty said. "But thank you for the chocolate."

Franz clapped his hands to his thighs as he rose, then put his hat smartly beneath his arm. "I have no time for tea, so it is just as well. It was good to meet you, *Frau* Markham. No need to escort me to the door, Betty."

And then he was gone. Giant tears tracked down her mother's face as she stared at the door.

"Mum—"

"Oh, Betty!" Mum stared as if she didn't know her, then turned away, pillowed her head on the sofa arm, and cried.

Betty felt each sob like a punch.

18

HELEN

Helen did her best to make her kitchen as cozy as possible for her play-reading guests, Catherine and Betty. She'd given up trying to heat the front parlor, when the fuel shortage was only growing; easier to make the kitchen the focus of her hospitality.

They sipped carrot tea at her table, nibbling on cake made with millet seed instead of flour and chatting about their daily lives. The other two women kept giving her confused glances. Helen knew they suspected they weren't there just for a play-reading, even though literature groups were one of the rare scheduled events allowed by the Germans.

At last Helen set down her tea and pulled a book of Shakespeare's plays toward her. "Which one shall we choose?"

"What's really going on here?" Betty demanded.

Helen just grinned. "Don't you just love the feeling of expectation?"

"Not if it's only about whether we choose a comedy or a tragedy," Catherine said dryly.

Helen lowered her voice. "I received another newsleaf."

Catherine matched her tone. "But I thought you still had a radio hidden?"

"I do, but the significance of this one is that I saw who delivered it."

Catherine gasped. "Who?"

"I can't tell you how many times I'd wait after each delivery, trying to discover his identity. But I'd eventually need to catch up on my sleep, and I'd miss him again. It was Mr. Garnier, the pharmacist's assistant at the chemist's in Saint Peter Port. I'm thinking of approaching him with an offer to help. I get the news—I have my father's typewriter, and I know how to use it. Surely they could use more typists or more people to deliver."

"That's so dangerous," Catherine said, although her voice sounded admiring.

Helen didn't want to be admired; it wasn't about that. "I just need to do something to help. That's why I called for this play-reading meeting—to find a way to resist the Germans."

Catherine bit her lip and looked away. Helen had known what her reaction would be, and although she understood Catherine's fears for her brother, Helen didn't think Richard would want his sister to wait passively for someone else to rescue them.

"What can we possibly do that would make a difference?" Betty asked. "Don't get me wrong—you know I'll help. I can deliver newsleafs, too. But what kind of resistance? The V is for Victory campaign made us all feel good for a while, but it didn't do anything to the Germans. We could flatten tires or damage buildings, but we'd probably just get caught, and again, what difference could we make?"

"I'm talking about something that might really matter," Helen said in a quiet voice, "like spying on the Germans."

Those words inspired a heavy silence, as Betty contemplated her with narrowed eyes.

"Helen, what are you saying?" Catherine asked in a tremulous voice. "Spy on what? For whom?"

"We can spy on anyone we have access to and gather information. I'm not sure who it would go to," she added falsely, submerging her guilt, "but perhaps we can find a way to get important information off the island. I *nurse* Germans. They want to talk to pass the time. Maybe I can befriend some of them until they let down their guard. Who knows what they might say?"

Catherine folded her arms across her chest and shivered. "I know what you're thinking. I have a German living right in my house. He says very little to us, just gets angrier and angrier every day. What am I supposed to do?"

"Search his bedroom?" Helen asked.

Catherine recoiled against her chair. "I can't do that! If he caught me, he could take his vengeance out on my whole family."

Helen sighed. "I do know that. I would never ask you to do something you don't want to. But you do speak German. Maybe you can listen in on conversations?"

"You mean wander the streets and hang around soldiers? That won't be suspicious at all."

"I can try to look through Franz's briefcase," Betty said.

Helen and Catherine both turned to stare at her.

"I know what you're thinking," Betty said, her lips a thin line. "It's what everyone is thinking, but I have not slept with him. I may have had no choice about dating him, but I can damn well use it for something good."

Catherine reached to cover Betty's hand with her own. "How did this happen?"

Betty allowed the comfort for a moment, and then pulled away. "He saw me in the restaurant and started asking for a date. Constantly. He wouldn't take no for an answer. He began to subtly mention my mother. I understood the threat."

Catherine said, "What an evil man."

"He's not truly evil," Betty said with irony, "or he could have forced himself on me. In his twisted mind, he seems to think we're not at war, that he's courting me. I guess I can be thankful for that," she added with a sigh. "But lately, he's getting impatient."

"He insisted on meeting your mother," Helen said. She tried to keep the anger and horror out of her voice, knowing Betty wouldn't want that.

"Frightened her half to death, as I knew he would." Betty lowered her gaze to her now-cold tea. "Oh, he was full of politeness, brought her chocolates and everything. But the way she cried afterward, the betrayed look she gave me, as if it was all my fault..."

"You didn't deserve that," Catherine whispered.

"Maybe I did," Betty said with tired bitterness. "Maybe I should have found a way to discourage him."

"Britain has been trying to discourage Germans for decades," Helen said. "They don't seem to get the hint."

Betty gave her a focused stare. "I'll help you resist. I'll see if I can examine his briefcase when we're together. I would be so relieved to have a purpose, to be able to look myself in the mirror again."

Helen's sorrow threatened to choke her. "I think you're one of the bravest people I know."

Betty gave her a skeptical look, but didn't reply.

"I'll talk to Mr. Garnier about the newsleaf," Helen said.

"And I'll keep my ears open," Catherine added. "I've been trying to ignore all the German spoken around me—as if I could somehow make it disappear. But not anymore. I promise."

Helen looked at her two friends with satisfaction. "We're going to do something to make a difference. But be safe—no information is worth risking your life."

They sat silently for a moment, and Helen knew they were each thinking about the men off fighting Hitler's army, definitely risking their lives.

Catherine reached for the collection of Shakespeare's plays. "Let's read. We don't want to give anyone a reason to think we're lying about this. I'm not the best liar," she admitted, blushing.

"I think you're underestimating yourself," Helen said. "You'll do what you need to do to keep your family safe."

They spent another hour dividing up the parts for Shakespeare's *As You Like It* and laughing as they created different voices. They promised to meet again the following week, with the unspoken understanding that they'd report on their progress.

Helen closed the door against the December chill and watched as her friends mounted their bicycles and started pedaling back to town. She turned around and let out a startled gasp as a man loomed silently in the hall.

"Jack!" she cried, hand to her chest as she sagged back against the door. "Why did you scare me like that?"

"Scare you? You don't think you've scared the devil out of me?" he demanded, towering over her.

She pushed at his chest, but he didn't move. "I don't know what you're talking about."

He held her upper arms and gave her a little shake. "I heard what you said to your friends."

"So now you're eavesdropping?"

"You're involving them in some crazy scheme to spy on the Germans and get information for me."

She lifted her chin. "I'm doing my patriotic duty."

He groaned. "It is not your duty to put your friends at risk. Did you hear how frightened Catherine sounded?"

Helen felt a pang of remorse. "I know. And therefore I didn't ask her to do anything risky."

"You don't think she'll worry she's not doing enough and find a way to do something more than eavesdrop?"

"She won't. I know her."

"I think you're a fool—you're all fools." He let her go and turned away, running his hands through his hair as he stood with his back to her.

"You know how I feel, Jack. We want to do our part, too."

He spun back toward her, his face a mask of frustration. "I can't even get off this island. You'll be risking yourselves for nothing."

"I don't believe that," she said fiercely. "If we discover something truly important, you'll find a way to get the information off the island. I trust you."

"You trust me? Why would you do that? I'm not any kind of man you should trust."

She took the last step toward him until they were so close she could feel the heat of him through his clothes. She laid a hand on his chest, above his heart. "I know what kind of a man you are. You're a hero, a man who risks his life every day for Britain. I admire you tremendously."

And then he leaned down and kissed her, shocking her, exciting her. She wrapped her arms around his neck as he pulled her against him. The kiss grew desperate, until at last Jack broke away.

"I'm not a hero," he said roughly. "A hero wouldn't take advantage of you like this."

"I don't feel taken advantage of." She reached for him again but he stepped back.

"I was always drawn to you, Helen," he said.

She blinked at him in surprise.

"It's true," he continued. "But you were formidable, so intelligent and aware of what you wanted. I knew I couldn't be the steady husband you deserved."

"Jack, you obviously thought you could make decisions for me back then—and you're still doing it. But you're not in charge here, and you can't keep me from doing what needs to be done."

"Then maybe I'll steal a boat and leave now, so you and your friends won't be tempted to do something crazy."

She put her hands on her hips. "And what information do you have right now that could truly affect the war? Where the guns are placed?"

His jaw tightened. "I cannot tell you."

"Because you don't have enough yet. We're going to help you."

"Helen—"

She put a hand up and walked back into the kitchen to start the dishes. He didn't follow her, and she was glad. She was still reeling from the kiss, the emotions he inspired, and the revelation that he'd actually noticed her all those years ago.

But she wasn't going to let him think he could change her mind.

19

CHELSEA

I stared at Grandma, who looked out the hospital window and blushed beneath the bruise on her cheek from her fall. I had so many questions about Jack, but she sidetracked me with a piercing look.

"Did you bring it?" she asked.

I looked over my shoulder. The faint ding of elevator doors sounded in the hall, but no one came in. We were alone.

I opened my purse, and the handgun gleamed dully at me. "Should I just...hand it to you? Where did you get it?"

"It's a German Luger. I kept it after the war."

I imagined what a German had done with that gun—how she had gotten it. I was full of questions. I trusted that she wouldn't recklessly use it—but she *had* been threatened.

I handed her the little sewn bag of bullets first—it had made me laugh when I saw it, but the reality of a weapon for killing had stifled my laughter. Glancing once more at the empty doorway, I lifted the gun and handed it to her. With a smooth motion, she put it in the bedtable drawer, sliding a bible in front of it.

I stared as she closed the drawer. "You don't think one of the nurses will find it?"

"They haven't looked in there yet," Grandma said with a smile.

I cocked my head. "You seem remarkably cheerful even though someone is threatening you."

"Perhaps near the end of one's life, fear of death isn't quite the same as in youth."

"You didn't seem very afraid of going against the Germans."

"Oh, believe me, dear, I was very frightened. Defeat was close, especially before the Americans arrived." She joined her hands in her lap and regarded me steadily. "Did you find out anything about Catherine's death?"

I nodded. "At first, I only found the same details as the obituary, with no cause of death listed. But, finally, I reached her granddaughter, Delilah, who recognized your name. She lives on Guernsey. In fact, all of Catherine's children and grandchildren still live there."

"Yes, she was very lucky to have all her family around her."

I couldn't help but stiffen a little.

Grandma noticed, of course. "You know I am not complaining. You call regularly. I know you're busy with your job and with auditioning. You're taking classes to improve your acting. So smart!"

Touched by her praise, I felt my face heating.

"Now go ahead and tell me about your conversation with Delilah."

"She said her grandmother had certainly died of natural causes," I began, "that she'd had a heart condition the last few decades of her life. I didn't tell her we were concerned she was murdered, just that you wanted to know that your old friend hadn't suffered. She died peacefully in her sleep with her children all around her."

Grandma released a sigh and turned her gaze to the window, blinking rapidly. I could imagine her relief, knowing that one of her oldest friends had not suffered—or been murdered.

My throat constricted, making it hard to swallow. I felt like I knew Catherine and could empathize with how frightened she'd been. I needed to know the rest. "Whoever wrote you that note about killing Catherine obviously wanted to frighten you," I said. "And you did get pushed down the stairs. You're concerned enough that you wanted"—I briefly lowered my voice—"a gun. Although I can't imagine what you'd do with it in a hospital."

Grandma shrugged. "Hopefully nothing. But there is a true scandal that's been brewing which might correlate with my problem."

Problem? A mild word for attempted murder, but then she was never one to over-dramatize things. "Go on, what's the scandal?"

"A journalist named Karen came to see me a few weeks ago. She was researching something about the war. I had forgotten all about it, what with my concern for Catherine. But now that my fears about my dear friend have been put to rest, I'm thinking of other possibilities." Her entire face wrinkled around the word. "I need to contact Karen. I tried to before my accident, and I haven't heard back."

"Let me do that for you, Grandma. You already told me overseas calls are difficult in the hospital. And I want to help."

She hesitated. I held my breath, then let it out in relief as she reached for her purse and pulled out a card. Her trust meant so much to me.

I took it and stared at it, but the name meant nothing. "There's no newspaper listed."

"She's an investigative reporter who sells her story after she's researched and written it. But she sells most of her stories to the *International Chronicle*. Start there."

"If this is about the war, what happened that she'd want to research?"

"I've been telling you what happened," Grandma said with a little exasperation. "Be patient, Chelsea."

Patient? When someone was trying to hurt her? "You don't want to tell me what you talked about?"

"Not yet. Just find her and see why she didn't call me back. See if she's...well."

Well? That sounded ominous.

I'd never been good at being patient, but I was way too good at being impulsive. I now had a connection on Guernsey Island, too, and I could do more research, as well as find her mysterious reporter. I wasn't going to let this go. I wanted my grandma to know she could trust me.

20

CATHERINE

That Christmas, there were no new toys to be had, so Dad worked a secret project to convert a neighbor's electric train set into a wind-up one for Timmy, after trading away Timmy's old three-wheeled scooter. Catherine sewed together old clothing fabric into new scarves for her family and made Timmy a jigsaw puzzle by gluing a page from a colored picture book onto thin wood. Mum knitted up a storm, finding more yarn by ripping apart old worn projects.

Food was scarce, but they made the best of it. Helen brought a sweet potato dish made with carragean moss that she'd scavenged from the beach, along with gifts of crocheted mittens for everyone. Betty had finally talked her mother into the leaving the flat for Christmas. Pale and perspiring from the several-block walk, Mrs. Markham huddled in a corner at first, as if the stimulation from people and noise after months of solitude was almost overwhelming.

Gradually, Mum won her over, and they were all sitting down to dinner, about to enjoy a special bottle of wine Dad had saved, when the front door slammed open and closed.

Lieutenant Schafer marched into the dining room and stared at their cozy celebration.

Catherine saw a myriad of expressions cross his face—sadness, longing, then frustration and rage. Suddenly Mrs. Markham screamed and fainted dead away.

In the commotion of reviving her and trying to stop Timmy from giving Lieutenant Schafer dirty looks—he would never forgive him for killing Sam the rabbit—the lieutenant picked up the small beef platter, heaped on some stewed potatoes, and retreated to his room.

Betty rallied her mother, and they tried to continue the holiday meal, but it was an awkward affair. The lieutenant's presence lingered over them like a storm cloud. Mrs. Markham couldn't leave soon enough.

At their next play-reading meeting just after the New Year, Catherine tried to apologize for frightening Mrs. Markham.

Betty snorted. "Don't worry about it. Sometimes Mum tries to forget that *everyone* is dealing with Germans, while she hides in our flat and pretends. It was good for her to see how the rest of the island is living."

Helen cheerfully distracted them. "Shall we bring our play-reading meeting to order?"

"Did you pick out a new play?" Betty asked dryly.

"Let's deal with more important business," Helen said. "I'll give my report first, because I don't have much. I've been trying to talk more to my patients, but it's harder than I thought to find English-speaking ones. Or they speak it so limitedly, that I can't really carry on a conversation. I wish I had your skill, Catherine."

Catherine blushed.

"And then there's Mr. Garnier, the druggist's assistant," Helen continued. "I haven't talked to him yet, but I managed to follow him for a bit, to see the few other houses he delivered the newsleaf to, but short of confronting him—and I don't know if that's wise yet—it was hard to get close but remain unseen." She heaved a dramatic sigh worthy of a play-reading meeting. "Not an auspicious start, I'm afraid."

"I haven't had much luck either," Betty said, slumping back into her chair. "Franz doesn't carry his briefcase every time we're together. And the few times he's had it, I was never alone with it. But I'm not discouraged," she added. "I'm sure every resistance takes time."

"Listen to you, Miss Optimistic," Helen said, smiling.

Betty nodded. "It does not come naturally to me."

And then they both turned to Catherine, who tried a smile, knowing it came out lame. "You know I've started teaching a German class, since the *Feldkommandantur* insisted children learn it. Well, an *oberst*—a colonel—came to school and asked if I'd be willing to take on some translating work."

"That's marvelous!" Helen said. "Who knows what they'll give you access to."

Catherine shrugged. "I asked what it was about, and basically, I'd spend several hours every week with officers new to the island who don't speak English and translate for them. I would also have to teach them some English."

Betty watched her carefully. "Do you want to do this?"

"Of course not!" Catherine let some of her frustration show. "I don't want to help them in any way. I worry I'll be seen as someone supporting our enemies." She glanced at Betty. "I don't know how you put up with it. You deal with judgmental people every day, and I admire you tremendously. But I'm afraid to be seen the same way."

"It wouldn't be the same," Betty said. "Most islanders are forced to work side by side with Germans, like your father, or their families will starve. They don't see me that way, even my own mother."

Catherine put her hand on Betty's.

Betty let out a deep breath. "I explained the truth to her, that I'm very unwilling, but she can't seem to understand the difference, although she pretends to. Sometimes I think her years of living in fear have altered how she thinks."

"I tell myself to pity her," Helen said coldly. "But I hate how she's making you feel, especially since *she's* the reason you remained on the island, and *you're* the reason she has food on her table."

Betty gave Catherine's hand a quick squeeze before moving it away. "I've given up trying to change Mum. I tell myself I'll be able to start over again, somewhere far away from here, when the war is over."

"You'll leave Guernsey?" Catherine asked in surprise. It had never occurred to her to want to live anywhere else. Her dream of the island after the Germans were gone seemed like a paradise she was afraid to want too much.

"I'll never be able to have a normal life here," Betty said. "People's opinions won't change, even when they hear that I had no choice in dating Franz. They'll think I *did* have a choice, that I should have done *something*. I understand people," she added bitterly. "They'll begin to see themselves as having silently resisted the Germans the entire time, a glowing revision of history, even though they huddled in their houses or just continued their jobs. Whereas I committed the sin of consorting with the enemy rather than letting myself be martyred."

The harsh statement brought a profound silence. Catherine was trying hard not to cry, and she saw Helen's jaw clench as she blinked rapidly. Betty hid her pain behind a wall of bitterness.

Catherine spoke before she could second guess herself. "I'm going to accept the translating position." She held up a hand when Betty started to speak. "This is my own decision. If I can find something that will help us get rid of the Germans, then I'll be proud of myself. Richard would be." Her voice trembled on her brother's name. "There's something else I've been meaning to talk to you about."

Helen and Betty exchanged a glance and leaned forward, as if what she had to say was so important. What was wrong with her that she was so quick to make light of her contributions?

"So, you know I've been trying to overhear German conversations around me," Catherine said. "Nothing has come of it, because they're just talking about whatever they happen to be doing—getting photographs developed, or buying something to send to a girl back home. I'll keep trying."

"Is Sergeant Doepgen leaving you alone?" Betty asked.

"A little. We've had far fewer conversations, although he continues to act as if we're friends—not that either of us has brought up the past. But at least he's not pushing for anything more. But I wanted to tell you about my neighbors, the ones who moved to the island the year before the war started. At first, we tried to talk to them in a friendly manner, but they made it clear from the start they were uninterested in being friendly. I know Mrs. Russell used to socialize with the wives of the Guernsey Controlling Committee, and they all considered themselves a step above the rest of us. I believe Mr. Russell is an engineer. Anyway, my point is, I see a car pick them up on an occasional evening. Much as the driver is always an islander, we all know who they're driving for."

"The Germans," Helen said coldly.

Catherine turned to Betty. "I've considered whether they could be in your situation, feeling like they have no choice. And that might be so. Except for the fact that my mother has never seen Mrs. Russell queue up *anywhere* in the village."

"That doesn't make sense," Betty said. "We all need to use our ration books for food. And wait—all the non-islanders were supposed to be deported last September."

Catherine shrugged. "Now can you see why I'm suspicious. Do you think they're collaborators?" She dropped her voice to a dramatic whisper, even though she knew no one could overhear. "And what should we do about it? They might be spying on fellow islanders, giving information about who still has a radio or which farmer keeps too much of his produce for himself."

"Good point," Helen said. "Can you keep an eye on them? I'm not sure yet what can be done even if we prove they're collaborators."

"We'll know who to be careful around," Betty said.

Catherine sat back, having said her piece, but wishing she felt more confident about it. Betty was risking her very life prying into Captain Lunenborg's briefcase. Helen was trying to become a part of an illegal underground newspaper and coerce German patients to confide in her, and what was Catherine doing? Hoping to translate something important? Not very helpful at all.

And then she heard a sound, something that hadn't been there before. "Did anyone else hear that?"

Helen tensed. "What do you think you heard?"

"I don't know," Catherine said with hesitation.

And then a mouse ran out from beneath the kitchen table.

Betty screamed and jumped up.

Catherine gaped at her friend's unexpected response.

But then a strange man rushed into the kitchen and, with a shriek, she fell back against the wall. Betty took a swing at the stranger, hitting him in the jaw.

The man barely noticed. "What's wrong?" he demanded.

Catherine realized he aimed that question at Helen, who sank back into her chair and wiped a hand down her face with exasperation.

"It was a mouse," Helen said. "Thanks for saving us, Jack."

"Jack?" Catherine echoed. "Jack Dupuis?" He looked very different from the skinny young man who'd left the island searching for adventure.

Betty was rubbing her knuckles, sending a reproving glare Helen's way. "You obviously knew about this."

Catherine stared at Helen in astonishment and with a growing undercurrent of hurt.

The tension went out of Jack's shoulders as he winced and gave Helen an apologetic look.

"You left the island," Catherine said in bewilderment. "How did you get back?"

"A submarine dropped him off," Helen said.

Betty arched a brow. "You're a spy."

He smiled, and the old Jack charm washed over Catherine. But she ignored it and turned to Helen. "You knew about this. Is he the reason you've wanted us to resist the Germans?"

"That was not my idea," Jack said. "And I don't agree with it."

"He was only part of the reason," Helen said, coming to her feet and pushing Jack aside to face them. "He gave me the best chance for our information to help the British."

"Other spies have been dropped off and missed their return trip," Betty said. "They turned themselves in when collaborators informed on them and the Germans threatened to kill the people who gave them aid."

"And did it work out for the spies?" Jack asked with faint sarcasm.

"It did not," Betty answered, then turned to Helen. "Tell us what happened."

Helen did. The entire time, Catherine watched Helen's face and the way she tried not to look at Jack too much. Jack listened with his arms crossed over his chest, stoic and impassive. Catherine felt a tension between them that was only partly about Jack's reluctance to accept Helen's assistance. Though he wasn't a close friend, Catherine remembered him. He was far more handsome as a grown man with a maturity he'd lacked in his youth. She was in awe of his daring mission on the island. But he, too, was trying to avoid looking at Helen.

"I can't believe you thought you couldn't confide in us," Catherine said quietly.

"I didn't want to drag you into something so dangerous." Helen's eyes were wide with earnestness.

"And I didn't want to drag Helen into this," added Jack. "But I remembered the cave, and I knew she lived alone. An offer of food and a change of clothes turned into..." His voice trailed off, and he gestured as if to include the whole house.

"Turned into what?" Catherine asked, a bit sharper than she intended.

Although Helen blushed, she met Catherine's gaze as she said, "I wasn't going to let him stay in the cave when I rarely have visitors. I have empty bedrooms, so he hides out here when he's not out doing reconnaissance."

Catherine relented. "I'm glad you're not alone out here. I've always worried."

"But what can you possibly do now?" Betty asked Jack. "Your submarine is not returning for you; the Germans keep laying more and more mines. You're trapped here. Any information you gather is useless."

"I refuse to believe that," Jack said. "I fully intend to find a way to get my report into British hands, even if I have to steal a boat."

"And I'd like to be able to include something in his report, something we've helped to gather," Helen said.

"But I don't want you to do this," Jack said, looking to Betty and Catherine. "I've explained this to Helen, but she's not listening. Perhaps you ladies can convince her."

"We support her," Betty said. "There is nothing worse than feeling useless."

"Yes, there is," Jack said coldly. "You could be discovered and sent to Germany."

Catherine hugged herself and glanced from Betty to Helen, but both looked clear-eyed and resolute. And Catherine didn't want to back down; having a purpose—a mission—had done something for her morale under this terrible occupation.

Jack shook his head. "You're all fools." He left the kitchen, and soon they heard the front door open and close.

"He just goes out during the day, when anyone could see him?" Catherine asked, aghast.

Helen shrugged. "No one lives within a quarter mile of me, and few people come down this lane unless they live here. He's careful. I've watched him as he looks out all the windows before he does anything. I was afraid all the time when he first arrived, but I couldn't stand to see him huddle in that awful wet cave for days on end."

Betty nodded, a faint smile on her lips. "I have to admit,

you continue to amaze me, Helen. I never thought you'd do something like this."

Helen blushed. "It just seemed the right thing to do, after all he's risking."

"But you didn't tell us," Catherine said, while inside, she thought, *You didn't tell me, your best friend*.

But her best friend could read her, and Helen turned a sober gaze on her.

"I'm sorry," Helen said softly.

Catherine knew she was being too sensitive, so she shrugged and forced a smile. "I understand. And it's good to know that if we find any valuable information, we might have a way to get it off the island." And how could she be angry with Helen, who thought she was protecting everyone? Catherine relaxed and gave her a real smile. "So the two of you keep each other company here every evening?"

Helen's blush deepened and she squirmed. "Sometimes. He's often gone. He doesn't want to put me at risk. But it's been...nice."

Catherine and Betty exchanged a look. "Nice," they both repeated, and laughed.

"I can see the wheels turning in your heads," Helen said. "Just stop."

"I don't know if I can," Catherine said primly. "Our boyfriends joined up before the war, leaving us lonely, and now an eligible man washes up on shore right at your cottage. I think I'm jealous."

"Don't be," Helen said, her smile fading. "He wants to be comrades in arms against the Germans, and that's all."

"Sounds like there's been a discussion about it," Betty said thoughtfully.

Helen threw her hands up. "Let's get back to the play."

21

HELEN

That evening, Helen sat alone in her kitchen, listening to the eeriness of the cold January wind off the channel whistling around her windowpanes. She huddled deeper into the blanket around her shoulders and sipped from a hot mug of dandelion coffee.

Jack hadn't returned. Restless, she'd placed a mousetrap in a dark corner and fixed a sparse dinner. She was reading by a single lamp, debating going to bed when she remembered her friends encountering Jack. Betty hitting him had been the high point, but Helen had felt...strange, watching Betty and Jack together. Betty had been the kind of woman Jack preferred before the war. There didn't seem to be a man who could resist the power of her presence, her beauty, her confidence.

And why should this even matter to Helen? What was it about Jack that twisted up her thoughts, her emotions? She couldn't stop thinking about their kiss, even though she knew that their resistance effort was so much more important.

There was a soft knock at the kitchen door, and Jack

stepped inside. Rain speckled the shoulders of his dark coat and dampened his hair. As he leaned back against the door and regarded her, she couldn't tell what he was thinking.

"I have to admit," Helen began, "I'm quite relieved that they know the truth about you. So many times, I would almost speak your name, and it complicated my every interaction with them."

"Did you plan my revelation?"

"I did not convince a mouse to startle my guests," she said wryly. "I was shocked at Betty's fright—Betty! It was hard not to laugh."

"I wasn't laughing."

She sighed. "I know. We had nowhere else private to meet but here. I gave you fair warning they were coming; you could have been gone, but instead you eavesdropped. Why?"

"Because I needed to know what dangers you were leading your friends into."

Helen regarded him coolly. "So I'm the reason a German lives in Catherine's house? I'm the reason Betty was forced to date a German?"

He let out his breath in a long sigh and took the chair opposite her. "No, of course not. But if something goes wrong—"

"We all understand the risks we're taking. We've spent months just existing under this occupation. That time is finished."

Jack studied her face for a long silent moment. "You have a passion for this work that makes your eyes sparkle, that makes you vibrant."

Her lips parted in astonishment before she could master herself. "Are you trying to say you want to kiss me again?"

"No." He sank back in his chair, giving her a wry smile. "It means I sometimes want to shake you in frustration."

"Because I'm passionate and vibrant." She felt bold as she said the words.

"Don't make light of this."

"I'm not. I feel proud that we're no longer so helpless, that we have a plan. We're sharing the experience, the danger, together. The girls and I are anyway." She lifted her chin, defiant.

Jack shook his head. "Good night."

"Don't you need to eat?"

"I already did."

She wanted to ask, "Where?" but he was a grown man and it wasn't her business to keep track of him. She watched him walk away, and all those defiant, strong feelings drained out of her.

~oOo~

The hospital was a place that had always made sense to Helen. While winter's chilly rain continued into March, each day the hospital's routine was both a comfort and a jarring reminder that life might have changed drastically under the occupation, but the art of healing the sick had its own rhythm that encompassed both islander and enemy.

Doctors were always men, always arrogant in their knowledge, convinced that only they could save patients, that what the nurses did was trivial. Of course, there were exceptions to this, and she had known a few, but the German doctors raised arrogance to a new level, even as they practically reduced island doctors to orderlies.

But the white corridors were clean, the equipment sterilized, the patients in clean bed clothes, with access to medicines. Helen and the other nurses were given what they needed to accomplish this, but she never assumed it would last forever. Now that the Americans had entered the war, how long could the Germans go on believing in their inevitable victory?

But her patients didn't care about that, not in their time of pain and need compounded by loneliness. Helen did what she could, using polite conversation or gentle hands when her patients couldn't understand her.

It was by keeping to her vow of healing that she stumbled on a German patient she hadn't met before. He had a private room, which implied he was an officer, but he was alone, his face turned toward the rainy window, his chest rising and falling swiftly as if he tried to master his emotions.

Helen walked in, and he turned his head toward her. It was then that she saw that half his face, including his eye, was covered in bandages.

She glanced at the chart to see his name. "Good morning, Lieutenant Beering. I am Helen, your nurse for today. Do you speak English?"

He nodded, watching her dully, still on a heavy dose of morphine. She felt a little spark of interest, but did not make the mistake of getting too excited. She'd been looking for a patient fluent in English, a way for her to test her persuasive skills, but the few soldiers who met her criteria were either too junior to help, in too much pain to communicate, or dismissive of her as merely an island prisoner.

"How are you feeling today?" she asked. "I see you're recovering from surgery."

He shrugged, then mumbled, "No one can tell me if I will lose my eye."

"Your surgery was recent. It takes time to recover."

"Everyone says that." He gave a deep, melancholy sigh.

"Would you like to talk about what happened? Sometimes that helps."

He shook his head, then winced in pain.

She repositioned his pillow. "Would you like something to drink?"

He nodded, and she helped him lift his head to sip his water through a straw. When he began to tremble, she eased him back.

He regarded her out of his bloodshot eye. "Why are you being so kind to me?"

"You are an injured patient. That is all a nurse should focus on." She frowned. "Has someone not treated you well?"

He sighed. "*Nein.* I've only been in the hospital since yesterday. It is only that most people on the island are distant. I have gotten used to that."

She gave him a professional smile. "There is a war going on, Lieutenant. You can't expect otherwise."

"It will not matter soon. With this injury, I will go home."

"That is probably true. I'm sure that will make you happy and help your recovery."

"I have a wife waiting for me—a new wife. We were only married a week when I had to leave."

"That must have been difficult to do, being a newlywed."

He shrugged. "We do what the Fatherland requires of us." He lowered his voice. "It would not have gone well with my family if I hadn't."

She seldom gave thought to the German soldiers themselves and didn't want to feel any pity for him. Who knew how many Allies this one had killed?

She couldn't believe how friendly he was, but she figured it must be the pain medication loosening his tongue.

As she began to change his bandages, and his body stiffened with the pain, she distracted him with questions.

"What did you do before the war?" she asked.

"I am a pharmacist," he answered between clenched teeth.

She paused unwinding his bandages in surprise. "A pharmacist? How did you become injured practicing such a profession?"

He hesitated, his expression stoic, his voice laced faintly with bitterness. "I was needed in other areas."

She assumed that meant he hadn't been permitted to practice his profession. "That must have been difficult," she murmured, continuing to loosen the bandages.

"I did what my country needed me to do."

"Of course."

When she at last saw the eye injury, a perforation, only her professionalism kept her from wincing. It would be lying to reassure him that his eye would recover, so instead she asked, "How did you get this?"

"An explosion. There was nowhere to run below ground."

"You're working in a cave?" she asked.

"No, just...below ground." He groaned as she gently dabbed ointment near his stitches.

Helen felt a jolt of excitement. Below ground? What were the Germans doing? She had a thousand questions, but she decided not to press for more answers. But she would.

After work that evening, she headed straight for the chemist's. The shelves were pretty bare, but behind the pharmacy counter, Mr. Garnier worked with the pharmacist, preparing the few medicines the Germans gave them access to, from creams to elixirs to capsules.

Helen's luck held, and she saw Mr. Garnier slip out the back door behind the counter, pulling a package of homemade cigarettes out of his pocket. Since she couldn't go behind the counter without attracting attention, she hurried outside and down a narrow alley. Dusk was already falling, and she knew she had to hurry or ride her bicycle home in the dark. Before the war, she would have stayed at Catherine's, but now Lieutenant Schafer was always there, looking at her too openly, filling her with unease.

Mr. Garnier was leaning against a low stone wall that separated the chemist's from a small car park filled with bicycles instead of cars. His hands were cupped around the match as he tried to light his cigarette. At last, he inhaled deeply, let it out, then squinted at her through the smoke that swirled around his balding head. He was a dark, wiry man, perhaps twenty years her senior.

He touched the brim of his hat. "Miss Abernathy, a good evenin' to you."

"And to you, sir." She took a deep breath, looked around to make certain they were alone, and leaned in to whisper, "I saw you delivering the newsleaf to my cottage. I wanted to thank you."

Wariness darkened his expression and his shoulders tensed. "I don't know what you're talking about."

She raised both hands. "I didn't mean to upset you, and of course you don't want to talk about it. It's just...I'm filled with admiration for what you and others are doing, and I want to help."

He took a few more puffs on his cigarette and then ground it out on a cobblestone. "You've got the wrong person, Miss Abernathy. But I found out recently—you're friends with that Betty Markham, aren't you?"

"I am. What's happened to her is not her fault."

"Uh huh," he said skeptically. "As if anyone could trust someone who's a friend of hers."

He slid past her and disappeared inside, while Helen stood still, hugging herself as if she might never be warm again.

Back at home, when she hopped off her bicycle, the last of the light was almost gone. She went to put her bicycle inside the garage, feeling the heaviness of grief weighing down her shoulders. She found the doors open, and Jack inside. He wore baggy old clothes, a cap pulled low over his brow, and his hands were covered in dirt.

"What are you doing?" she asked.

"I cannot sit in that house one more minute," he said over his shoulder. "I came out to help prepare your garden for spring planting. After all, I'm eating half of your food. But I got distracted—look what I found."

He stepped away from the tool bench to reveal a small crate. Frowning, she came closer and saw what seemed to be a bunch of feathers.

When she heard a faint chirp, she gasped. "Is that a bird?"

He snorted. "Of course, it is. It's wounded. I found it in your garden, unable to fly, limping itself into exhaustion to get away from me."

"And you're going to nurse a wild bird back to health." She wondered if he really was going a little stir-crazy.

"Not just any bird. It's a homing pigeon."

Her mouth briefly dropped open. "The Germans confiscated any homing pigeons when they arrived. This one can't be from the island. Is it being used for the war effort?"

He nodded, and she thought he was deliberately holding back his excitement.

"Look at the little tube attached to its leg."

She leaned in close, trying not to block the light of the single bulb. Jack was cradling the pigeon body with gentleness, but it weakly fought him. She saw a spattering of blood on its wings and body, but she forced herself to look past that to the tiny leg that he was showing her. There was a red tube attached by tiny leather straps. The top was open.

"The Allies airdrop pigeons to the French resistance fighters," Jack said, "so they can send messages to Britain. Perhaps this one was on its way home."

"Or it was simply lost." She gestured to the tube in disappointment. "It's empty."

He glanced at her, standing so close that his grin was powerful.

"No, it's not. I just unscrewed the top. Give me a moment."

He put the pigeon back in the crate, and then placed a makeshift cover of chicken wire over the top.

"You've been busy," she said, trying to hide her amusement.

"This is important." He held up what looked like a tiny round lid with a long matching spindle sticking out of it. "See how it's slotted?" he asked, holding it even closer to the light for her. "The end of the note was slid in there, and then the note was rolled around the spindle to make it small enough to fit in the tube."

"There was a note?" she asked with excitement.

He removed a tiny roll of paper from his shirt pocket. "It's made of very light paper." After he spread it open, he gestured for her to hold one end flat while he held the other. Shoulder to shoulder, they bent over it.

"It's just rows of random letters," she said, disappointed.

He nudged her shoulder with his own. "And why would they do that?"

"Oh, it's in code!" Her renewed excitement faded a bit. "Which means we can't read it."

"We can't. But it was important enough that the resistance fighters were trying to get it back to England. I think we could write our own note on the back."

He'd said "we," and that was almost as thrilling as the possibilities the pigeon represented.

"You could tell your commanders how to meet up with you," she said quietly.

"And we could tell them whatever important news we want to send. We'd just have to know by the time the bird is healthy, because I can't delay him any longer than that."

"Are you certain it's one of ours?" she asked.

"It's written on a printed note form with a typed place for the date, and even the bird's registration number. It could be a decoy, but I don't believe that."

In its cage, the pigeon gave another little pathetic chirp.

"Jack, will it live?" she asked, putting a hand on his arm.

He covered her hand with his. "I'll do everything in my power."

He looked down at her. Their hands were still touching. There was a long moment when she felt on the precipice of something she'd never experienced before, an intimacy born of shared history, and now the trauma of war.

But they both heard a distant drone of a plane—more than one plane. Not that it didn't happen regularly, but night flights often meant bombing runs, or so the BBC said.

He stepped away from her and cleared his throat. "One of her wings is broken. I had some experience with this as a boy. I'm going to do my best to fold it into place and then wrap a bandage around the body to hold it still. What I can recall is that it took a few weeks to a month before the bird could fly again. Until then, I'll feed and water it, and let it walk around for exercise."

"You've thought all this out."

He shrugged modestly. "Like I said, I only have the experience every young boy has. I hope it's enough. Do you have any old cotton fabric that I can cut into strips?"

She nodded. "And here I was about to tell you to take up a hobby like whittling, if you're bored. But you've found something more important to do."

He reached through the wire and gently petted the bird. "Getting him well enough to fly back to Britain might be a tall order. But it's a shot we're going to take."

22

CATHERINE

Catherine stood on High Street outside the grocer's, and told herself to go inside. The brisk March breeze carried a tang of the ocean, and her threadbare coat was doing little to protect her. She should complete her errand. But she was a coward, and nothing she did to resist the Germans changed her mind about herself.

She took a deep breath. Only her actions could prove she was a stronger person. Turning the door handle, she went inside.

The store used to have a fragrance of its own: spices, flowers, and oranges. Now, the empty shelves to the front of the room seemed to smell of dust and disuse. Near the back counter, shelves were sparsely stocked with the items one could use ration coupons for, everything from flour to candles. It must be hard to earn a living without access to items the islanders so desperately needed.

Mum's friend, Madame Caron, bent over a ledger. Her silver hair was drawn into a chignon at the back of her neck, and she squinted through glasses as Catherine approached. Her tense smile melted with relief.

"Ah, Catherine," she began, her voice threaded with a faint French accent, "it is good to see you. Your *maman* is not with you today?"

Catherine shook her head. "Not today, madame."

Madame Caron sighed. "I have little left for the ration books, so you might have come in vain. Unless you wish to buy other goods." Her voice had a tinge of hope.

Catherine gave her an apologetic smile. "No, madame, I came to talk to you." She glanced over her shoulder, but they were still alone. "Do you know Mrs. Russell?"

Madame Caron frowned her confusion. "Of course, I do. She used to come here regularly before the war."

"But now, not so much?"

The woman cocked her head. "No, not so much. I assume your *maman* told you that. Why does it matter?"

"Mum told me she does not queue anywhere."

"Anywhere? I assumed she was not choosing to patronize our store."

"Not anywhere, madame."

"Mmm." She frowned a moment, then looked back at her ledger.

Catherine was losing her, and she felt like a fool. She practically stammered as she said, "Do you know where she and her husband lived before moving to Guernsey?"

Madame Caron shrugged. "The south of France. I had the impression that when they were bored, they moved."

"I imagine they wish they wouldn't have come here."

"*Oui,*" Madame Caron absently said, not looking up from her ledger.

Catherine wished she had a coin to spare for gum or lipstick. She slunk out the door and headed for home, inwardly berating herself for not finding another way to ask questions.

"*Fraulein* Braun!"

She briefly closed her eyes as she recognized the voice. "Sergeant Doepgen," she said, when he caught up to her.

Though there were Germans everywhere, she still felt on display when talking to one, as if all the other pedestrians were judging her. Goodness, she judged herself.

He gave her a pleased smile. "It is a brisk day for a walk, *ja*?"

She nodded.

"Mind if I accompany you?"

"I'm in a hurry," she said stiffly. "My head has begun to ache."

And that was certainly true.

He gave a sympathetic nod. "Is it your students? They can certainly give one a headache by the end of the day, can't they? They were so good at testing me."

She shrugged, continuing to walk, but he strolled along with her.

"I remember one particularly challenging class," he continued. "For once, everyone was on task and working quietly at their desks. Then suddenly, one of the boys yelled out, 'I'm tired of this! Raise your hand if you want to go home!' And then everyone raised their hand."

Catherine had to bite her lip to keep from laughing. It all seemed so normal to share a story with a colleague. As the sergeant chuckled, she realized she'd almost forgotten what a man's laughter sounded like. She only worked with women now, since all the young men had gone off to war except for the headmaster, who was old enough to be her grandfather. She'd heard several teachers taking bets on whether he could make it up the stairs one more time. She almost told Lukas—

But she couldn't think of him as Lukas. He was Sergeant

Doepgen. Even though he wore a Nazi uniform, she felt a spark of attraction that hadn't gone away since their moonlit kiss.

She still didn't even know if he remembered her. She didn't want to ask, but it was as if he read her mind.

His smile fading into a look of intensity, he murmured, "We have not been alone since I arrived, but I wanted you to know that I have forgotten nothing about that night five years ago when we met."

They were hardly alone; a man jostled her going by on the narrow street, children chased a ball. But she barely noticed, so drawn inwardly to a more innocent time when she'd thought herself so grown up, her dreams of love and a family glimmering on the horizon of adulthood.

But she was a woman now, not a girl; she wouldn't let herself be deluded by romance. And she wouldn't ask why he'd never written back.

"I don't know what you're talking about," she answered coolly, then doubled her walking speed.

He didn't join her.

Soon, she opened the little gate to her yard, but before she could go inside, she saw movement out of the corner of her eye. It was Mrs. Russell outside in her garden. Without overthinking it, Catherine turned and went toward the half wall that separated their yards.

"Hello, Mrs. Russell," she called cheerfully.

Mrs. Russell held her hat against a gust of wind and squinted at Catherine. "Oh, hello...Catherine."

The woman had surprisingly remembered her name. Catherine saw an opening. "Oh, Mrs. Russell, your hat is divine." It was bright red, with a wide brim that shielded her face from the sun. It didn't droop; it wasn't faded. Catherine had only one good hat left, which she kept for church on

Sundays. She and most of the island's female population now wore scarves.

Mrs. Russell slid her fingers along the brim of her hat. "Thank you! I like this one so much I even wear it gardening."

"I have to say," Catherine continued, "I can't imagine how you must feel, knowing you moved here not a year before the war broke out. I bet you wish you'd stayed...I can't remember where you're from."

"London."

Her voice was noticeably cooler, but Catherine forged on. Madame Caron had said the south of France!

"Your move might have been poor luck, but you were very lucky last year. How did you escape being deported to Germany with all the other mainlanders?"

Mrs. Russell's smile was brief and forced. "I imagine my husband was smart enough not to list our recent immigration when we all had to register. It was good of the bailiff's office not to turn us in."

"It really was. But then again, we islanders have to help each other because certainly, the Germans don't care about us."

Mrs. Russell gave an uneasy look around. "Be careful what you say. You'd think you'd know better, with a German officer living with you. They have eyes everywhere."

With a last frown of warning, Mrs. Russell went indoors, leaving Catherine awash in frustration.

Not a week later, a detachment of soldiers arrived to search the Braun house. It was a Saturday morning and Catherine was home, helping to do laundry in the old tub. As she was putting the clothes through the wringer, the house suddenly shook with the pounding of booted feet on the front steps and banging on the door.

She rushed into the hall where all the family gathered in alarm. Timmy reached for her hand. Tears fell down Mum's cheeks, but she nodded to Dad who opened the door. Two soldiers rushed in with an officer right behind.

"What is the meaning of this?" Dad demanded.

The officer gave him a cold look. "We will search the premises for a radio."

"We gave up our radio months ago," Dad said in bewilderment. "One of your own officers lives with us—he knows what we have."

But they ignored him except to say, "It will go easier for you if you stay out of the way."

So they did. Catherine put her arm around her mother and they all flinched together as they could hear things break in room after room. Mum's tears tracked silently down her cheeks; Dad had his arms around Timmy, who buried his head in Dad's chest. The Germans could do anything they wanted and no one would stop them.

Her helplessness felt like a bottomless pit in which she kept falling. When the Germans left after having found nothing illegal, Catherine and her family went about the house picking up broken vases and tea pots, rehanging paintings on the wall, and trying to recover their sense of safety.

Catherine stood in the open doorway of Lieutenant Schafer's room and stared at the untouched interior. She sensed deep in her bones that this was their neighbors' fault. Catherine had questioned Mrs. Russell, and they'd gotten their revenge, though she could never prove it.

She was even more determined to discover if they were cozying up to their German oppressors.

23

BETTY

As usual, the restaurant was full of Germans. Betty stood near the servers' station feeling grim as she watched them chat and laugh, smoke rising about their heads in a way that reminded her of what hell must look like. The only thing missing were the flames.

Franz was in that crowd. He made sure she waited on his table so he could touch her waist or take her hand in front of his friends. And she had to keep smiling, always smiling, while inside she wanted to scream her outrage.

The only thing that kept her going sometimes was knowing that she had a goal now: discovering something Franz knew that Jack could use.

But she hadn't had any luck so far. He didn't usually bring his briefcase on their evenings out. At a dinner party with fellow officers and Guernsey women, Betty had even tried moving about the room, looking at the other men as if she could discover what they knew. She couldn't relax with the women either. They eyed each other uneasily, never knowing which of them was in this for fun, or who was being forced. One would have thought such a group of women might have some sympathy for each other, but how could Betty like or even understand women who wanted what the Germans could give them: exciting parties, good food, gifts like stockings or lipstick, the company of young men when all the young male islanders were gone.

She never saw Lucy, the young pregnant girl she'd met at her first German party. Apparently she and her baby were confined to the family farm. But her German lieutenant continued to visit her, Franz told Betty when she'd asked. Maybe Lucy had been right, and she'd be married by the end of the war.

When Franz did bring his briefcase on dates, he tended to leave it in the car with his driver. More than once, Betty considered kissing Franz while fumbling with one hand to move papers from his briefcase to her handbag. But she knew how low the odds were that she could make that work. She was just feeling so desperate to accomplish *something*, *anything* to make the torment of dating him worthwhile in the end.

Taking a deep breath, she returned to Franz's table. The sight of their laughing faces, square jaws, haircuts so precise, made her want to throw up. Franz was watching her, his eyes narrowed with speculation above his charming smile. He followed her from the table and spoke in a low voice.

"I feel like I haven't had a chance to be alone with you in ages, Betty."

She gave him a smile. "It does not seem that long to me."

He laughed. "After your shift tonight, come up to my room for a drink," he said.

"All right."

The words were out of her mouth before she could give

them much thought. Shock flickered briefly in his eyes, replaced by triumph.

Betty gritted her teeth and kept on smiling. He thought he'd won, thought he'd seduced her into acquiescence. She excused herself to go back to work. Her fellow employees certainly saw her in intimate conversation with the German. She was used to their sidelong disdainful glances, but even Margaret gave her a disappointed look before turning away.

Betty felt so alone.

At the end of her shift, she methodically finished the last of her duties preparing for the next day's service. No one spoke to her, so she focused on the evening to come. The hotel lobby was nearly deserted at this time of the night except for the clerk behind the desk. He was reading a newspaper, and Betty was able to sneak past him to the stairs. She knew where Franz's rooms were; more than once he'd managed to "forget something," forcing her to accompany him. She always remained near the open door, making it clear what she thought of his not-so-subtle tricks. And he never forced the issue.

Betty knocked on his door, and he opened it almost immediately. He surely thought her visit tonight was proof that his patience had paid off.

With a cool nod, she slipped past him and inside. The suite had three rooms: the sitting room, a bathroom, and the single bedroom beyond. The bed was not turned down, and she felt an absurd stab of gratitude. He had thrown his coat on the back of a chair, and a pair of shiny shoes rested neatly beside the door. To her dismay, she didn't see his briefcase anywhere.

She turned around as she heard the door close. Franz leaned back against it, hands in his trouser pockets, a lock of blond hair fallen over his forehead. It was the first time she'd seen him looking even a tiny bit disheveled.

As he studied her, he wore a half smile. "This is a pleasant surprise."

She shrugged her shoulders. "I've been here before."

"You barely waited in the doorframe, and would have been down the hall if you could have."

She arched an eyebrow, but didn't point out that she'd never had any choice from the beginning. Did he really like to pretend that they were a normal courting couple?

"Can I pour you a glass of wine?" he asked, moving toward the selection of alcohol he had set up on a small table.

"I'll take whisky."

He arched a brow in surprise, but didn't protest. "With ice?"

"Straight."

He brought her the glass of amber liquid which she finished quickly, eyes watering. She handed it back and lit a cigarette.

"Another whisky?" he asked, grinning.

She shook her head. She wanted to take the edge off, not end up drunk.

"We could sit down," he offered, gesturing to the little sofa.

She accepted with relief. There had to be a way to distract him and find the briefcase. But he sat very close to her, and without a drink to make it obvious she wanted to take her time, she would soon feel pressured to surrender to his advances. He'd kissed her plenty of times before, but always in his car—with Arthur studiously ignoring them up front—or once or twice in the shadowy corner at a party. There had been constraints on what they could do.

But not here. She inhaled smoke and released it.

He seemed to sense her inner turmoil, so he took her hand and rubbed it between his own. Perhaps he thought he was being reassuring.

"You're cold," he said.

Frightened half to death, she thought. She hated admitting it even to herself.

He lifted his gaze to hers, murmuring, "I could warm you."

The irony of his attempt at romance snapped her out of paralysis. "Another whisky might do the trick."

He chuckled. "Very well."

When he moved away from her, she took the opportunity to sweep her gaze around the room one more time, making sure there were no shadowy corners she might have missed. But nowhere could she see the briefcase. She glanced at the bedroom, and then away.

While he was pouring her drink, there was a sudden knock on the door, and she didn't know whether to be frustrated or relieved.

Franz frowned as he handed her the glass before crossing to the door. He opened it to find a subordinate officer standing there, twisting his hat in his hands.

Franz asked something in angry German, and the young officer, standing at rigid attention, answered. Franz responded, and the other man marched away from the door.

"I must take care of something, Betty. I won't be more than ten minutes. Please wait here." He shrugged into his uniform jacket and put on his cap before leaving the room.

She heard the door lock click and realized he'd locked her inside. But for once, she didn't care.

She vaulted to her feet and listened at the door, her heart beating wildly. She could hear their footsteps retreating down the hall, then the lift doors opening and closing. Racing into Franz's bedroom, she found it as neat as she'd imagined. A chest of drawers and a wardrobe stood sentinel on the wall across from the window, where a small desk and chair were stationed to catch the best daylight. Perched on the chair was Franz's briefcase.

Betty glanced through the door to the sitting room once more, then started unbuckling the briefcase. She thought about moving it to the bed, but every extra step she took would have to be undone before Franz returned.

Her fingers moved swiftly, and her mind was focused. Everything Franz had subjected her to, the shame and humiliation, the powerlessness, all of it would have had a purpose if she could find something to use against his evil government. He represented everything she hated about men as a group—their arrogance, their easy assumption of power, their ability to bully vulnerable women, their unshakeable belief in themselves—a belief that she'd once used against them as much as she was able. But she'd been helpless against Franz's onslaught, and the only thing in her favor was that he hadn't forced himself on her.

She flipped the leather flap of the briefcase back and found at least a dozen folders. She wanted to spread them over the bed, but knew she didn't have time. She grabbed the first and opened it.

It was in German.

But she'd been expecting that. She'd gradually been teaching herself the language with Catherine's help, though she never admitted it to Franz. She couldn't speak it well, but she was better at listening and reading.

She read the headline on the first page: "A survey of Guernsey roads," and decided that wouldn't be important enough. The next folder pertained to the railroad they built across the island—why would this matter to the Allies?

The third folder's headline read: "Munitions storage." Betty's heartbeat picked up.

And then she heard a key in the door.

Excitement exploded into fear as she dropped the folders back in the briefcase. She wasn't quite in the line of site of the door, and she couldn't risk looking as she tried to close the clasp. It wasn't working, so she had to abandon it. Picking up her drink, she sauntered slowly into the doorway. Her cigarette burned unattended in the ashtray, and she prayed he wouldn't notice. She casually leaned against the door frame, even as Franz paused when he saw her.

"Making yourself at home?" he asked, one eyebrow lifting as he closed the door to the hall.

The moment seemed to stretch on into a frozen tableau: her racing heart, his suspicion.

So she smiled.

He smiled back and came toward her, bracing both his hands above her on the door frame.

She was trapped. It seemed suddenly hard to breathe. She could smell his cologne.

"I was bored," she said languidly. "The rooms are smaller than I thought they'd be."

"I think you don't want to be bored anymore," he said quietly.

His lazy gaze moved down her body. Betty felt it as if a snake crawled on her, but she allowed no emotional reaction to show. This was the moment when everything could change; if she handled it one way, she could end up in a German prison camp, having accomplished nothing.

If she handled it another way, she could find something to help fight the Germans, or at least help liberate the island

—there'd still be a chance that she could make a difference in the war's outcome.

She put her hand on his chest, and he covered it with his own. When he moved toward her, she backed up, and he shut the bedroom door.

~oOo~

"You could move in with me."

Wearing just her slip, Betty came back into the bedroom, two glasses of whisky in her hands. "You know I can't do that."

Franz lay bare-chested, propped amid pillows against the headboard. He held out his hand when she offered him the second glass. "And why do I know that?"

"Because of my mother. She can't live alone, and I need to take care of her."

She could see he didn't have a solution to that. She took a drag on her cigarette. "Frankly, I wouldn't move in with any man without marriage."

"Especially a German," he added wryly.

"Especially a German." She felt daring—what did it matter what she said? He was getting what he wanted.

He chuckled. She wanted to smack his smug face.

After sipping his whisky, he looked at the glass as if in consideration. "I don't think I would have asked a woman to move in with me before the war."

You wouldn't have asked a German *woman because you respected them.* Betty gripped the glass so tightly, she was worried she'd break it.

"Why not?" she asked.

He patted the bed beside him, and she was forced to sit

down. Her slip rode up and he stared at her bare thigh a long moment before answering.

"Society's conventions, of course. And knowing that my mother would disapprove."

She wondered what his mother would think of his current behavior.

His smile faded. "But now each day is different, knowing it could be my last. War has made me rethink everything. I don't wait for what I want just because someone might disapprove."

"You waited a long time for me."

"That was different. Getting what I wanted—*how* I wanted it—was worth the wait."

Did he not see that such a relationship between captor and captive would always be unequal?

"I don't think of you as having a life before the war," Betty admitted, flicking her cigarette in the ashtray. "Were you in the military?"

"I had no plans to enlist after what my father experienced during the last war."

When he didn't elaborate, she didn't ask for details. She didn't care about Franz or his father, but keeping him talking and relaxed might help her future spying.

"What was your profession?" she asked.

He smiled at her like a man who knew he was handsome. "Can you guess?"

She didn't want to guess—this wasn't a game. But she made herself laugh. "A postman."

He rolled his eyes. "I'll give you a hint—I have a university degree."

She tried to think of the conversations they'd had, but she'd never asked questions about his past. Acting interested would have only made him think they had an intimate relationship.

"There are so many degrees, Franz. Architecture? Physics?"

"Business. I am good at keeping track of the *Fuhrer's* plans for the island."

Plans? Even more important to see inside his briefcase.

"How did you use your degree before the war?" she asked.

He placed his hand on her thigh. She'd given him the right to such intimacies, she thought bleakly.

"I worked in the business department of a factory. Nothing glamorous."

He must think the life of an officer in a triumphant army was far more glamorous and important. As often happened with men, the power had gone to his head. She should come up with more questions, but she was too annoyed by his fingers, which were now making little circles on her flesh. She beat back the feeling of despair about what the future held with Franz. Her mother had always let herself be trapped by overpowering men; Betty had sworn to never let that happen to her, so certain she knew men well enough to manipulate them.

She tried to tell herself that she *was* manipulating Franz, that eventually he would deliver useful information.

He leaned forward and pressed a kiss to her shoulder.

She briefly closed her eyes. "I have to go. My mother will be worried."

"Ah, I thought you might have evening plans with friends."

"This late?" she replied. "There is a curfew—or had you forgotten?"

He chuckled. "I had not forgotten. But not everyone

obeys the curfew. I believe your friend Helen lives alone, and that you girls occasionally spend the night. You read plays aloud, yes?"

Ice seemed to freeze her veins, but she kept her voice light. "How did you know that?"

"I heard you discussing it once. I think it is a smart way to keep your mind active."

"So we have your approval?" she asked dryly, even as she wondered how often Franz eavesdropped.

"You are saucy with your words now that we are lovers. I like that. I want you to feel free to talk to me however you'd like."

She stood up. "Then you'll understand that I have to leave."

"If you must. I'll have Arthur drive you home."

"You will not. It's late and he's off duty. I walk home at this time of night all the time."

"Then I'll walk you home."

"Franz—"

"No protesting."

They dressed, and he walked her down a back staircase to a rear door of the hotel—as if they had to keep their relationship a secret. Nothing was a secret on this island, except that they hadn't had sex before now. Everyone believed the worst of her, and now it was true.

Jerrybag.

24

HELEN

On a rainy, cold April day, Helen wasn't even certain that Betty and Catherine would attend their scheduled play-reading meeting, but they showed up on their bicycles wearing patched rain slickers.

Catherine was her usual talkative self, her hands weaving through the air, and it was always rare for Betty to get in a word. But Helen found herself glancing at Betty as they traipsed down the hall and into the kitchen where Jack waited. She seemed more subdued than normal.

"Hello, Jack," Catherine called.

Jack nodded to both women. "Ladies." He waited until they sat down before taking his own seat.

Helen poured them bramble tea, then looked at Jack expectantly. "Aren't you going to tell them?"

He raised both hands. "I don't want anyone's hopes getting too high, but I captured a wounded carrier pigeon that had been returning to Britain with a message in code. I'm nursing it back to health with the assistance of a nurse—"

Helen smiled.

"—and I hope to include a message about how to retrieve the information we've gathered."

"'Information'?" Catherine echoed, blinking in surprise. "That sounds so...official."

"If we *have* any information," Betty said darkly.

They all looked at her with concern.

"Never mind," she said. "Bad day."

Catherine leaned toward Jack. "What was wrong with the pigeon?"

"Broken wing. I saw it hopping away from a cat on the beach path. Now it's in a cage in Helen's garage."

Catherine opened her pocketbook and pulled out something wrapped in a wrinkled napkin. She spread it open on the table to reveal four squished cakes. "Mum has been experimenting with flour and ginger and syrup—there wasn't much ginger. Let me know what you think."

They all expressed appreciation by chewing and nodding. It was a little dry and tasteless, but they took their pleasure where they could.

"I've been very busy with Germans," Catherine continued, sitting back after a fortifying gulp of tea. "The new ones are so pathetically grateful to be stationed here instead of the Eastern Front. I could tell them it was a custom to walk naked into church, and I believe they would. As it is, I have to walk around town with them, helping to buy the things they need, introducing them to the frightened owners of homes where they're assigned to stay. But the worst is how some people stare at me, as if I'm the only person working with Germans."

Helen saw Catherine give Betty a wincing glance, as if she just realized how it might sound to a woman forced to date a German.

"You're not offending me," Betty said. "I know how I'm

seen. I'm still hoping it works out to our benefit. I had two minutes with Franz's briefcase folders. There was one about munitions, but he returned before I could read it."

"The German lessons have been working out?" Catherine asked brightly.

Betty gave a nod. "Thank you. I'll try his briefcase again."

Abrupt and to the point, Helen thought, her concern growing. Something was off about Betty, but she'd learned a while back not to offer too much concern or help. Betty was a private person who wanted to deal with her own problems. It seemed far too lonely a life.

"I heard an interesting clue," Helen said, trying to sound mysterious.

Catherine chuckled. "You're getting more and more dramatic. This play-reading group must be helping."

"Well, my German patient told me he'd been injured underground."

Helen saw the way everyone came to attention, their eyes sharp.

"Underground?" Jack frowned. "What did he mean?"

"He wouldn't say, and looked embarrassed at having revealed too much. I'll keep working on him. After that conversation, he talked mostly about his wife. It's been hard to steer him back without being too obvious. But he's a pharmacist, so we have medicine in common. We chat a little bit every day."

"Be careful," Jack said, but he spoke distractedly, his attention elsewhere.

"I spoke to Mr. Garnier, the druggist's assistant," Helen continued, "but he wouldn't confirm anything about the newsleaf." She kept his uglier words to herself.

"Good, one less way for you to get into trouble," Jack said.

She raised her chin. "I'm not giving up."

He sighed.

Catherine looked back and forth between them, barely hiding a smirk.

"You know that I've been getting only small acting parts in our local productions," Betty began slowly.

They all nodded.

"Suddenly, I'm the new lead. And I won't even be wearing make-up to hide my identity. Franz, of course, manipulating my life."

Where Betty usually sounded bitter, Helen mostly heard subtle traces of weariness and resignation.

"We're to give a special performance for the German officers," she continued. "And my fellow actors are not happy about it."

Helen bit her lip, feeling sympathy well up inside her and knowing her friend wouldn't appreciate it.

"Oh, Betty," Catherine murmured, reaching across the table to touch her hand.

Betty glanced at Jack and pulled away from Catherine, as if any emotion was unseemly before him.

"It used to be the place I could escape to," Betty said quietly. "But now that's gone. And I can't quit, if you're about to suggest that."

"I was," Catherine admitted. "Instead I'll pray that this damn war will be over soon."

Betty seemed to really look at Catherine, one side of her mouth turned up. "Did you just curse?"

Catherine spoke primly. "I curse."

Helen snorted a laugh. Catherine tried to hold onto her false defensiveness, but soon they were all laughing.

Not Jack. He stiffened, his head to one side, listening. "There's a car coming," he said.

They all came to their feet, humor forgotten. Helen hurried to the front hall and glanced out the window. "I see German flags flying."

She looked at Jack. They'd practiced what would happen in such a situation a dozen times—it was the only way he'd agree to stay.

She followed him to the cellar stairs, telling herself everything would be all right. Jack himself didn't seem to be flustered as he moved aside the crates covering the trap door.

He gave her a look. "Wait a long time before you open this again."

"I'll be careful," she said. "Don't you trust me?"

He held her eyes for a moment that seemed long. "I do. But that doesn't mean I won't worry."

She gave him a brisk nod of understanding. He went down into the cold cave without a coat, but they'd stocked the cave with anything he might need. She closed the door over him, pushed the crates back, and took the stairs two at a time.

As she closed the cellar door, she heard the front doorbell jingle. She touched her mother's brooch for luck. Catherine met her as she emerged into the front hall.

"Well, that's a good sign," Helen said as she headed to the door. "They usually pound when they want something."

Catherine stepped back to join Betty near the parlor. "Be careful."

Helen nodded, took a deep breath, and opened the door. Captain Lunenborg stood there, hat under his arm, smiling.

"Good afternoon, ladies," he said.

Helen closed her sagging mouth and glanced at Betty,

whose face was immobile until she permitted a small smile. It looked genuine—but Helen knew Betty's acting skills.

"Franz, what are you doing here?" Betty asked.

"I was so intrigued when I heard you had a play-reading group."

Helen knew Betty wouldn't have told him. Was he spying on them? She tried not to shiver as a chill of fear swept through her. If he knew about this group, what else might he know?

"Culture is important, is it not?" Helen asked.

"Of course, *fraulein*. And culture is something Germans and islanders both share a love of. May I join you? I even brought a contribution."

He held out a tin, and though she couldn't read the label, she knew it was food. To her chagrin, her stomach growled.

Captain Lunenborg pretended not to notice, but his smile deepened. He looked around. "A pleasant cottage you have out here. It is quite a distance from Saint Peter Port. Do you feel safe?"

Safe from Germans? she thought. Was that possible? "The island has always felt safe, Captain—until your soldiers came, of course."

Catherine gasped

Captain Lunenborg continued to smile as if they were all so amusing and harmless. "I trust you've seen that no one needs to fear us if they follow the rules."

Like their Jewish neighbors, who registered as they were told and ended up disappearing somewhere in Europe? Helen thought. Like the slaves the Organisation Todt brought to work under inhumane conditions? Her hatred and anger practically choked her, desperate to escape. Then she thought of Jack and how he needed her. "I follow the rules, Captain. And yes, I have felt safe here. It is my parents' home. I won't leave it. Now would you care for tea?"

Soon they were all seated in the parlor. She'd put the biscuits he'd brought on a platter, and it sat on a little table in the center of them, practically gleaming with sugar and fat, rare items indeed. She didn't want to take one, but Captain Lunenborg did, and when he glanced at Betty, she did as well. Catherine met Helen's gaze and they both reached for a biscuit. Helen managed not to moan as the sweet taste seemed to explode in her mouth.

"Thank you for the treat, Captain," Helen eventually said. She needed to fill the space, worried that in the silence, Jack might somehow be revealed.

"You are welcome." He took a sip of tea. "So tell me how your play-reading group started. I believe you all have known each other for years?"

"When you grow up on the island, Captain, you know almost everyone," Catherine said, her voice weak but gaining strength. "We wanted to keep things as normal as possible—hence, the play-reading group, for entertainment and distraction."

"Plays make sense, considering Betty's talents," Captain Lunenborg said.

Betty inhaled deeply, but said nothing before taking a drink of tea.

"And I imagine you gossip, as young ladies like to do," the captain continued.

"As do young men," Betty said.

He gave her a smile that was intimate enough to make Helen's uneasiness increase.

"You are correct, of course. My apologies," he said.

He was so polite, as if working hard to make them think of him as a guest before the war. But his uniform never let

Helen forget who and what he was, and what he represented.

"Don't let me keep you from your entertainment," he said. "What play are you reading today?"

Helen was grateful they'd always made sure to be prepared to continue their cover story, just in case. She lifted up her book and opened it to the dangling bookmark. "We are reading Romeo and Juliet."

"A tragedy," Captain Lunenborg said, shaking his head. "This seems rather depressing."

"A classic tragedy, yes," Betty said, "but the themes of the individual versus society are always an example we can learn from."

"Go against your family's expectations and die?" Captain Lunenborg answered wryly.

"No, follow individual expression regardless of society's disapproval and find fulfillment," Betty finished quietly.

Captain Lunenborg shrugged. "Not an easy path in these trying times."

"Life isn't always easy," she countered.

They were staring directly at each other, and Helen knew the captain was amused momentarily, but she worried Betty would push him too far.

"What parts have you all chosen?" Captain Lunenborg asked.

"I'm playing Juliet," Betty said, "and Helen is playing Romeo."

Helen shot a glance at the captain. He hesitated, as if debating what to say. To her surprise, she thought she saw emotions warring within his gaze. Betty watched him with a knowing expression, as if she knew exactly what he was going to say.

He turned courteously to Helen. "Might I play Romeo?"

Helen glanced at Betty, who gave a brief nod.

"I'll relinquish the part," Helen said, then added, "but we all have several parts. You'll also have to play the nurse."

Catherine covered her mouth with her hand, wide-eyed. Betty gave Helen a surprised look of respect.

Captain Lunenborg cleared his throat. "Very well, I'll give it my best shot."

It was a strange few hours in Captain Lunenborg's company. He played Romeo rather stiltedly, without an instinctive actor's flare. Betty's Juliet was subdued, but often she couldn't quite hide the youthful passion of the character, which slipped out.

Helen played several parts—Friar Lawrence, Lady Capulet, and a gentlewoman—but without much skill because she could never stop thinking about who hid beneath the cottage.

After they'd read half the play, Captain Lunenborg said he trusted them to do it justice without him during their next meeting. He insisted on putting Catherine's and Betty's bicycles in his car and driving them back to town because of the misty rain.

When Helen was alone, she briefly leaned back against the closed door, shoulders sagging, letting out a deep breath. She waited fifteen minutes before releasing Jack from his dungeon.

Catherine was horrified to be seen riding in a German car in Saint Peter Port. With one bicycle against her knees and the other in the boot, she tried to slouch as much as she could, tugging her head scarf down over her brow and cheeks. Betty sat in the front seat, cool and remote, as if she did this all the time.

Captain Lunenborg dropped Catherine off first, and she watched them drive away, worried about her friend. She tried to shrug off her unease, even as she hurriedly pushed her bicycle behind the house to the garage. She didn't think any neighbors had seen her, but looked around, and to her surprise, saw a car behind the Russells' house. Though no German flags flew from the bonnet, no one drove a car but Germans.

She saw Mr. Russell emerge from his back door, and when he looked around nervously, Catherine ducked behind the corner of the house. She peered out again to see Mr. Russell talking to the driver; then he opened the back door of the car to take a crate of items from the seat. Catherine thought she spied the brown paper of a small flour sack and several tins above the edge of the crate.

And then Mr. Russell's eyes locked on hers. He held her gaze until he said something to the driver, who drove away. Mr. Russell didn't look at her again, just went into his house.

Catherine slammed her door from the inside and leaned back against it, breathing hard. The Russells were receiving gifts from the Germans—what were they doing in return?

Unable to keep such an important secret, Catherine told her mother about their neighbors, then awaited her father's arrival home. They heard Timmy's voice first, shouting something to Dad before both came into the kitchen.

"Mum, you'll never guess!" Timmy began.

Dad's smile was already starting to fade as he saw the serious looks Mum and Catherine exchanged.

"We were down by the pier," Timmy continued, "looking at the boats, and *Monsieur* Naviaux said I could have a ride this afternoon. But only if Dad goes with me, because there'll be a German on board, too. Can I go?"

"What's wrong?" Dad asked.

The excitement in Timmy's eyes began to dim. Catherine felt an ache in her chest, knowing he would never again be carefree, that he'd grown accustomed to the feelings of wariness and danger.

And resignation. Catherine saw it at once, the knowledge that even a boat trip might be denied him.

"Go get dressed for a cold, wet ride on the boat," Dad said to Timmy, who grinned and ran off.

Dad sat down at the table across from Mum. "Tell me."

Mum looked at Catherine, who said, "I just saw a German car deliver food to the Russells."

No one spoke for a long minute.

"What should we do?" Mum whispered.

"There's nothing we can do." Dad's voice was stoic and tired. "But we need to be very careful and mind our own business. We'll do just fine."

Mind our own business? Catherine thought of the German soldiers she translated for, how she told every word to a spy hiding on the island. Fear stabbed her belly, but she fought it off. She'd been conquering her terror of the Germans and what they could do to her family; she wouldn't let her neighbors' treason make her sink back into despair.

Ten minutes later, Timmy came bouncing into the room, a rain slicker over his arm. A sudden knock on the front door made them all jump. Dad went to answer it, and when he returned, his face was gray and drawn. Mum closed her eyes, lips pressed together. Timmy trailed Dad uncertainly.

"What is it?" Catherine demanded.

"A telegram from the Red Cross," Dad said gravely. "Richard has been taken prisoner."

Mum cried out, and Catherine blindly reached across the table for her hand, her own emotions veering from shock to disbelief to terror. Dad pulled Mum to her feet, and she sobbed against his chest. Timmy wiped his eyes with his dirty hand, leaving a smear across his face.

Catherine looked at the people she loved in pain, knew that somewhere her brother was alone and frightened and under the control of the enemy.

And the Russells were taking food from the Germans, perhaps doing their bidding, betraying people, all for the sake of their own comforts.

A white heat of rage seemed to explode out of her chest. She was on her feet and running up the stairs before she even knew what she meant to do. Distantly, she heard her parents calling for her, but she ignored them, her anger focused on one place: Lieutenant Schafer's bedroom and everything he represented.

She burst inside. Any evidence of Richard, except for her memories, was long gone. She flung open the door of the wardrobe and stared at his uniforms, before pushing them aside as if looking for a monster hidden there.

"Catherine!" her mother cried, grabbing her by the waist and pulling. "What do you think you're doing?"

Catherine shook her off and opened drawers, wanting to fling all the clothes to the floor.

Her father caught her arm this time and didn't let go. His voice was quiet and compassionate as he said, "Come, Catherine, this isn't how to handle our sorrow. You'll only make things worse."

She hadn't even realized she was crying, that the tears were dropping onto her blouse, that she couldn't catch her breath.

"It's...his...fault," she cried between sobs.

Mum was crying, too, and just held onto her, pressing her hot face into Catherine's shoulder. As if in a daze, Catherine saw Timmy standing at the door, eyes red and frightened. She reached out to him and he ran to hug her. Dad's arms came around them all, and they stood in Richard's room and cried together at his fate.

At last Dad herded them toward the door, and Mum closed it behind them as they trudged in line down the stairs. In the kitchen, Mum boiled water, and they all drank the terrible acorn coffee; but it was hot and soothing and Catherine tried not to think about anything in the depressing silence.

"I'm sorry," she said at last, her voice husky. "That was... foolish of me. I could have gotten us in worse trouble. But Richard—" Her voice broke.

"All we can do is pray," Mum whispered, her hands clasped together.

"I've been praying for years," Catherine said bitterly. "What good has it done?"

Mum met her gaze earnestly. "You won't know what good it has done. You must have faith."

"I'm sure the mothers of all those dead soldiers would disagree with you."

"Catherine." Dad spoke her name quietly, a bit disapprovingly.

She looked at him, and they both turned to Timmy, who was biting his lip, eyes downcast. Richard was his brother, too, and she was just making things worse.

"I'm sorry," she said, forcing herself to sound more encouraging, more hopeful. "I will pray, but we can write to Richard, can't we? Perhaps someone will agree to send our letters through."

"That's a good idea," Mum said. "Surely the Red Cross can make the Germans see reason."

So that evening they wrote letters to Richard. It gave Timmy something to focus on; it helped distract Catherine, at least until Lieutenant Schafer returned. She didn't come out of her room, worried her hatred would be too obvious as she glared at him.

Not three days later, the Germans raided their home again. Catherine returned from school to find her mother shaken, their furniture toppled, dishes broken.

"Mum, are you okay?" She clasped her mother's upper arms, hoping to read in her eyes what Mum might not say in front of Timmy.

Mum nodded wearily. "I'm fine, although I can't say the same for the house. It's such a mess..."

"Did they say what they were looking for? What do we even have?"

Mum just shook her head, lips trembling. "They found nothing, but they ruined so many things." She looked around helplessly.

And then Catherine realized something. Only three days ago, she'd seen the Russells accept food from Germans, and Mr. Russell had seen her watching. Was this another retaliation? Or a warning?

But she said none of this to her family. Suspicion might only put them in more danger.

~oOo~

"I know it was him, but I don't know what to do about it," Catherine said in frustration.

She sat between Helen and Betty on the bluffs overlooking the channel near Helen's cottage. The spring wind was almost punishing, the way it whipped them, but Catherine's anger and helplessness were too big to be contained indoors.

Helen put her hand on Catherine's arm as if to comfort her.

Betty stared out to sea, frowning, and said in a low voice, "Mr. Russell needs to be punished. He's a traitor."

Catherine's gaze shot to her friend, who said the words aloud she'd been thinking for the two days since the raid had happened.

"We have no real proof," Helen said.

Betty eyed them both. "Don't we? They have more luxuries than anyone we know, they don't stand in line for food, and now we've seen them receive food from Germans. You don't receive secret rewards for no reason at all. And he works at the power station. Who knows what he could be doing for them?"

"But..." Catherine trailed off, then started again. "There's no one we can tell. And waiting until after the war—who knows when that will be?" And then she realized her brother would be a captive all that time, and she drew in her breath on a sob.

Helen put an arm around her. "Oh, Catherine, I'm so sorry. Richard will be all right, you'll see. He's so strong and brave."

Helen was a good friend, but her sympathy didn't help the pain that felt like it would live in her heart until the war was over.

"There's no reason we can't start telling people what we know," Helen said, "planting rumors about the favoritism the Germans are showing them."

Betty's smile was cold with triumph. "And make them wonder what he's up to at the power station."

Catherine's emotions veered between fear and hope. "I don't want to lie—then I would be no better than they are."

"We're not going to lie," Helen said. "All we have to do is tell some of the truth and let people come up with their own conclusions."

"We'll have to be careful," Betty said, her smile disappearing into seriousness. She gave Catherine a measured stare. "Helen and I can do this if you don't think you can."

Catherine felt immediate affront, opened her mouth... and then closed it. She gave Betty a rueful smile. "We might not have been close friends our entire lives, but you know me pretty well already."

"You've never had to lie," Betty said quietly, "never had to pretend to be something else. I envy you. And I don't want to change you."

"But this is all because of *me*," Catherine cried.

"This is happening to all of us," Helen insisted. "You have a German *living* with you and a collaborator next door. I think that's enough stress for anyone to deal with. Let Betty and me start some rumors."

"You are good friends to me," Catherine said, her voice husky. "I will try to help. And I'll keep an eye on what goes on next door."

26

BETTY

B etty worked her next shift at the restaurant, a Saturday, when the tables were dense with Germans. She realized immediately that any conversation with the few islanders in attendance would easily be overheard. She put aside her plans to spread rumors until the following Tuesday when islanders came between meals to avoid Germans.

Betty chatted with the regulars, who were not as judgmental as people on the street. She settled on Madame Edouard and her friend Mrs. Hewet, nosy old ladies who liked to talk to everyone, even Jerrybags, Betty thought. They preferred their gossip from every source, but were seldom cruelly intentioned, which was why Betty chose them. They wore hats that had seen better days, like most women on the island, and their gloves were well mended.

"Ladies, good afternoon," Betty said as she approached.

They smiled up at her with such good-natured cheer, Betty was almost taken aback. Was she growing so cynical, so used to people's reserve or outright disdain, that friendliness was unusual?

"Betty, how do you do today?" Madame Edouard asked, her faint accent more pronounced than most of the islanders.

"I am well, madame, thank you for asking." Betty turned to share her smile with Mrs. Hewet. "Might I bring you ladies some tea?"

A meal out was a rare treat, even for two widows once considered very well off. It was only later, when Betty brought them their spider crab soup, did she say quietly, "Such a shame what I heard about some of our neighbors." After the ladies shared an interested glance, Betty made a point of looking crestfallen. "I've spoken too freely. I should stop."

"Oh no, dear!" Mrs. Hewet quickly said. "We all should know what is happening on our island, the better to protect ourselves."

"That was my concern, too," Betty said meekly. Had she ever spoken meekly in her life? Did it even work for her? But the two ladies only seemed eager.

"Do tell us what is on your mind," Madame Edouard said, patting her hand.

Betty made a point of glancing around, even though she knew there were only two other occupied tables on the opposite side of the dining room. She tried to look sheepish. "Do you know the Russells? I've heard something... disturbing about their food situation."

Madame drew herself up. "I've never seen them queue for anything, ever."

"Really?" Betty said. "I just assumed I must have missed them."

"Their clothes are so fine," Mrs. Hewet said, "their manners so free. I have not thought kindly of them."

"Well, they're mainlanders, aren't they?" Madame said with a sniff.

Betty leaned closer and whispered, "But it turns out they didn't need to queue because the Germans are giving them food."

Mrs. Hewet gasped while Madame Edouard covered her mouth in shock.

"You saw them?" Mrs. Hewet whispered.

"My friend did."

Madame Edouard's brows drew together. "That is just unthinkable. It worries me what they're doing to receive such a benefit."

Betty nodded solemnly, but inside she felt satisfaction warm her to the tips of her toes. "You know where he works, don't you?"

Mrs. Hewet's eyes widened and she hissed, "The power station!"

Betty felt like a rag doll nodding her head so much. "I worry about what he might be doing there to benefit the Germans."

Madame Edouard grabbed Mrs. Hewet's hand. "To think, a neighbor could be an enemy!"

"But they're not our own, are they?" Mrs. Hewet countered. "They're not from the island. Who knows what plans they had when they moved here?"

When another customer signaled her, Betty excused herself, leaving the two widows with their heads together, whispering intently.

The rest of the day passed slowly. Her face hurt from smiling at German officers, her feet hurt, even her back hurt from when she'd jerked sideways to avoid a roving male hand. The Germans thought they could do anything they wanted, *with* anyone they wanted.

In a bitterly ironic moment, she realized that her relationship with Franz usually protected her from more men trying to make advances.

In the kitchen, she helped finish the last preparations for tomorrow's breakfast. She had a sort of truce with the rest of the staff. They knew who she was seeing, but her hard work had some of them treating her with politeness, and others grudgingly holding their tongues. Or maybe fear of Franz did that, but she hoped it was a sort of respect.

Was she fooling herself? Who knew, but it was easier to live inside her own head believing that.

The toughest part was that Margaret, the waitress who used to chat with her and offer lifts home when she had a car, was one of the staff who'd become coolly polite. Betty understood. Most people kept to themselves as much as possible, hoping the Germans would ignore them.

But Betty knew that without the friendship "foisted" on her by Helen and Catherine, she would have been far lonelier and depressed. She appreciated their thoughtful concern more and more each day.

When she left the hotel, it was dark outside, the warm spring air turned cool and windy. She tucked her sweater tighter around her, lit up a cigarette, and walked at the back of the group of employees heading toward High Street.

And then she saw the glow of another cigarette, and the outline of a man leaning against his car. He straightened when he saw her, and much as she would have rather put her head down and kept going, she couldn't. She came to a stop. Margaret looked back over her shoulder, then turned quickly away and kept going.

She could see Franz's lean face by the dim light of a bare bulb over the rear door.

He took his cigarette out of his mouth and blew smoke

to the side, where it faded into the shadows. "I haven't seen you in a while, Betty, love."

She wanted to flinch at the endearment. "We've both been busy."

One corner of his mouth turned up. "I think you've been avoiding me."

"Do you blame me?" she asked with frankness. "You eavesdropped on my conversation, and then you barged into my friend's home without an invitation."

"She didn't seem to mind," he said wryly, then took another puff of his cigarette.

She could have slapped him—instead she clenched her fists. "Do you really think that? Is it so easy to forget how things stand between everyone on this island?"

"I don't forget, no."

"So you just don't care," she said bitterly.

"I care about being with you, getting to know the person you are with your mother, with your friends."

Was she supposed to be flattered? Did he think he was falling in love with her? She wanted to give a bitter laugh, but could not.

Franz dropped his cigarette and ground it into the pavement before coming closer, until his body brushed up against hers. She heard his swift inhalation of excitement, while she controlled a shudder of revulsion.

He put a hand on her wrist, and slowly slid it up her arm. Her heart pounded hard with the need to escape, but there was no escape for her, not anymore.

He leaned down and kissed her, his lips firm and warm, a deception if there ever was one. She accepted it passively, participating only as much as she had to.

He lifted his head and looked down on her, a faint smile on his face, the gleam of a challenge in his eyes. That's what she was to him—a challenge, a bauble to dangle from his arm. He only wanted to know about her relationships with friends and family because it was one step closer to conquering her. She put her cigarette to her lips as if he didn't concern her.

Taking her hand, he led her back through the hotel entrance and up the servants' stairs. Once he pulled her into his room, he closed the door, put out her cigarette, and began removing her clothes, one item at a time.

When she was naked, she said coolly, "I'll take a whisky."

Smiling in triumph, he complied.

~oOo~

Later, when Franz closeted himself in the bathroom, and she heard the water running in his bath, Betty jumped naked from the bed and went swiftly through his briefcase. She found similar papers on munitions, spelling out how many were ordered and where they'd be sent. She took the summary paper and tucked it into her handbag.

Her heart began to slow as she picked up her clothes. She was fully dressed by the time Franz emerged in a robe.

Frowning, he said, "Aren't you spending the night?"

"You know I can't. My mother will be terribly worried."

"I'll take you home."

"No, that'll take too long," she said. "Good night."

And before he could protest, she was out in the corridor, running for the stairs.

27

HELEN

Helen found Jack in the garage, his shoulders hunched as he stood over the work table. It was dusk, and she'd known he was somewhere about when she got home, but not being able to find him felt a little terrifying. Since when had she come to depend on him so very much?

He must have heard her arrive, but he didn't turn and face her, which only brought back her worry.

"Jack?"

"The bird died."

She gave a little gasp of shock, putting a hand on his arm. The little bird lay on its side in the cage, unbound from its bandages days ago, but somehow never able to adjust.

"Probably killed himself," he said, half amused, half bitter.

She gave his arm a squeeze. "He did not. He was a good little bird."

She'd watched Jack tenderly feed the bird with an eyedropper when it was too frail to stand up and peck on its own. Eventually, she'd caught him petting the little bird, who would lean into Jack's finger and chirp softly. For a man who guarded his emotions, who'd seen too much violence, he'd grown surprisingly attached to his little pet. It had shown Helen a side of him she'd never imagined. He'd once represented excitement and danger, but now he proved to be a man with a tender heart he kept submerged.

Jack sighed. "He probably never would have made it back to England. Too long a journey for a wounded bird."

"You did your best."

He picked up a shovel. "Do you have a burial ground for pets anywhere?"

She came up short, eyes wide in surprise at the sudden memories his words evoked. "We do. It's my favorite place to sit and watch the channel. Follow me."

She waited while Jack wrapped the bird in an old towel. Outside, she moved through the trees near the house, and then across a meadow, tall with wavy grass in the mild breeze off the channel.

They rounded a curve in the cliff where the house was no longer in view, and it was just the land, sky, and water. She'd spent her childhood there, beneath the little copse of trees, sitting on a rock, imagining the world beyond the horizon.

Just past the roots of one of the trees, several rocks jutted up. "Those rocks mark the graves of my two dogs, Dab-Dab and Jip." She caught his smile out of the corner of her eye. "I know, I know, I was a Dr. Doolittle fan, just like every other child. Hardly original."

"I think you're original."

She willed herself not to blush. He could mean anything.

While Jack dug a new hole beside the others, Helen searched for a suitable rock to mark the grave. When she returned, he laid the pigeon inside. Once the grave was filled in again, she placed the rock atop it, and they stood side by side in the silence, staring down at it.

Saying a prayer seemed ridiculous, but Helen found herself saying aloud, "Please, Lord, let this war end before anyone else—man or bird—has to die."

A foolish wish, but she thought she saw Jack's lips form "Amen."

Then, as if they read each other's minds, they turned to face the channel and sat down in the grass. Helen inhaled the salty smell of the sea and tried to recapture the peace this little cliff always gave her, but it proved elusive.

"Why is this your favorite place?" Jack asked.

"Partially because I felt closer to my pets here, of course. When I was a child, I'd squint across the water and imagine I saw France. It represented the wider world, only miles away from me. It meant—freedom and adventure."

"That way no longer lies freedom," he said quietly.

They sat in thoughtful, sad silence. Without taking her eyes from the horizon, she reached over and found his hand, giving it a squeeze. He linked his fingers with hers. It felt as if they were alone in the world, lovers who had nothing but time between them.

But the future felt as doomed as the little bird.

They weren't lovers, and they certainly weren't alone in the world. Beyond the cliff, her beloved beach was strewn with mines. On the next jutting cliff, the Germans had built an artillery battery that rose up like a concrete idol of the god of war.

Helen said, "Those batteries the Germans are building to rim the island with guns remind me of the square-headed statues of Easter Island, but without the personality."

He made a choked sound, and when she glanced at him, he was struggling to keep a straight face.

"I'm not sure it's appropriate to laugh," he finally said.

"What else can we do but laugh whenever given the opportunity?"

He shrugged. "You're right. And this is your favorite place, so it's up to you to decide which emotions are appropriate."

She rolled her eyes. "You sound like a counselor."

"Now you're *really* trying to make me laugh. As if I could ever counsel anyone on their emotions."

"Why not?"

He let go of her hand and leaned back to prop himself on his elbows. The breeze ruffled his hair, which had long ago ceased being militarily short.

"It seemed such a waste to overly think about how I felt about—anything." he said, forehead wrinkled in a thoughtful frown. "I spent my childhood running and jumping and playing, not *feeling*. Or at least that's what I told myself. My school years were consumed with a desperation to leave, to see the world instead of being trapped on this little island."

"Seeing the world brought you right back here," she said wryly, "trapped on this little island."

"At least I'm with you."

Their gazes met.

He looked away. "I shouldn't have said that."

"Why not? Are those words you'll have to forget, just like you've forgotten about our kiss?"

"Oh, I haven't forgotten. But I'm adult enough to realize that some things are more important right now, and leading you on isn't helping anything and only confusing you."

And how could she answer that without sounding like

the war was less important than her need for another of Jack's kisses? It made her feel selfish to want any more of him than he was willing to give her.

"Have I hurt your feelings?" he asked softly.

She forced herself to smile. "It's a waste to think how I'm feeling, right?"

"Helen," he said, his blue eyes soulful, "you know I don't want you to regret anything. But if we do more than share the occasional feeling, you'll regret I ever came back into your life."

Never, she thought vehemently, but couldn't say the word aloud.

"Helen!" A woman's voice seemed blown in on the wind.

Helen turned and saw Catherine waving to her, racing up the path from the house, Betty following behind. Helen and Jack rose to their feet.

"What is it?" Helen called. "Is everything all right?"

Catherine's breathing was fast as she stumbled to a halt. But she wore a triumphant smile, gesturing to Betty. "Look!"

Betty pulled several sheets of paper from her handbag and thrust it toward Jack. "Munitions order."

Frowning, he took the sheets, but kept his gaze on her face. "This is the original copy?"

She nodded.

"What if he misses it?"

She shrugged. "I had little choice what to take. He was about to return."

"Next time, make a copy," Jack said, "and if you can't, don't take the paper. It's not worth your life."

Betty's face remained impassive, but there was an edge to her voice as she said, "I need to help."

"I understand that," he said with exasperation, "but we don't want you arrested."

"When the bird's ready—" Betty began.

"The bird died," he interrupted. "We just buried it."

Catherine flinched, her expression almost comically shocked.

A muscle in Betty's cheek jumped as if she'd clenched her teeth. "I refuse to believe I did this for nothing."

"You did not," Helen insisted. "We will get our information out when we can."

"Tell them the rest," Catherine said.

Betty rolled her eyes. "It wasn't much. I told the Widows Edouard and Hewet a few rumors about the Russells."

Helen clapped her hands together. "Oh, jolly good for you!"

"What?" Jack said sharply.

Helen sighed, feeling disgruntled with him. "This is none of your business, Jack."

Betty and Catherine turned their heads toward her in wide-eyed unison.

Jack frowned. "What is this about?"

"It's about doing something to protect our neighbors from snakes within our midst," Helen said coolly.

He rounded on Catherine. "What is she talking about?"

Catherine's shoulders came up. "I—I—"

"Stop trying to scare her," Helen insisted.

"I'm not trying to scare anybody." But Jack's voice had grown milder. "I'm sorry, Catherine."

"It—it's all right," she said, clearing her throat and putting her shoulders back a bit. "I'm not scared—not of you, Jack. But my neighbor made certain my house was raided—I know it—because I saw him receive a German food shipment."

"Why didn't you tell me?" Jack demanded.

"*This* is why," Helen answered crossly. "Our friends and

family need to know the Russells can't be trusted, so Betty gave some hints to her customers, and I talked to fellow nurses. It's not much, but we have to do something so people don't trust collaborators."

He held up both hands. "I think you ladies need to stop right now. This is too dangerous. The type of man who conspires with the enemy in the midst of an occupation will resort to anything."

No one spoke for a long minute. Hands on her hips, Helen looked out at the white-topped waves and felt a moment of self-pity, wishing desperately that her island gave her the peace it used to.

28

CHELSEA

When I entered the hospital room, Grandma's eyes were closed. She looked serene, not like a woman who'd been carrying secrets her whole life. I hesitated—maybe she needed her rest.

Grandma opened one eye. "I'm not deaf. I know you're here."

I smiled and leaned down to kiss her. "Hi, Grandma."

"Punch up my pillow a bit, please."

After I did so, she looked me over, one eyebrow arched. "Well?"

I sat down on the edge of the bed. "Like you, I couldn't reach your journalist friend, Karen."

"Oh, dear. I was hoping my telephone calls were just missing her."

"I called the newspaper you thought she might be selling the story to, but they haven't heard from her either. The secretary did accidentally tell me Karen was researching a story about Guernsey during World War II."

"We know that," Grandma said patiently.

I rolled my eyes. "Apparently the secretary's not

supposed to discuss their stories. She stopped abruptly, and then someone else got on the phone, demanding to know who I was. I hung up."

"Good girl."

"Then I called Delilah. I thought if you were contacted about what happened on the island, perhaps Catherine had been, too." I paused to heighten the suspense.

It was Grandma's turn to roll her eyes.

"Apparently Karen visited not long before Catherine's death. Karen told her she was researching the suicide of a key Churchill aide."

Grandma's forehead began to wrinkle in a growing frown. "I know all about Mr. Riley."

"Of course you do," I said dryly.

"You don't forget someone who committed treason."

I caught my breath. "Treason?"

"I've been telling you his story for days now."

I blinked at her in surprise. "Well, I didn't know. His name hasn't come up."

"It won't for a while yet. Do go on about Catherine."

"Apparently she was getting forgetful near the end."

"I did receive a repetitive letter or two," Grandma murmured, her mouth turned down with sadness.

"All Catherine told her daughter was that a journalist was looking for proof of a collaborator who'd been working with the Germans on Guernsey during the war. Delilah didn't take it very seriously—what could possibly happen over fifty years later?" I asked with irony, gesturing to Grandma's broken leg.

"We spoke too freely about the Russells after the war, trying to clear up—so many things. Someone cared enough to write our accusations down in a local newspaper article no one paid any attention to at the time. Decades later, Karen stumbled across it."

"She was determined to dig for more," I said. "Catherine wrote down another appointment to meet with Karen, had Delilah make her best scones, but Karen never showed up. This was only about ten days ago."

Grandma pursed her lips. "This is not good."

"It's not, so I asked if Delilah knew where Karen had been staying. It was a little Bed and Breakfast in Saint Peter Port. I called, and they said she left but never checked out."

"Left?"

"Disappeared. She left behind some clothes, too."

"And they didn't think that suspicious?"

"Apparently, they were too annoyed to make that connection at the height of tourist season and with a room they could have filled. I told Delilah what I'd learned and suggested she call the police."

Grandma leaned toward me. "I don't have a good feeling about this."

I shook my head soberly. "They'd found a body they couldn't identify floating beneath a dock."

She covered her mouth, eyes wide with shock.

"It was Karen," I confirmed. "The police believe it's a tragic accident. Do you, Grandma?"

She shook her head, wet her lips, and spoke softly. "Not a bit. They believe I had an accident, too. Apparently, the secret that the government had concealed for so long is not a secret anymore."

"What secret?" I demanded. "You've told me about the collaborator you discovered. With a journalist investigating and losing her life over it, I can't believe this is just about a man who accepted German payment to tell stories on his neighbors."

"It's not. And I have proof."

I gaped.

"I didn't give it to Karen, of course," Grandma continued. "It's locked away in a safe deposit box. But I did allow her to have a copy, and whoever killed her must have it now."

"A copy of what?"

"German orders regarding a most unusual request. And now, someone knows I have the original."

29

CATHERINE

Two weeks later, Catherine walked slowly home from school, letting Timmy skip ahead of her. She kept her head down, lost in sad thoughts, barely noticing the last blooms of daffodils in flower boxes that hadn't been given over to vegetables.

Every day when she had to walk past the Russells' house, she was confronted again by the failure of their plan to hurt Mr. Russell's reputation. He sauntered through the town like a Victorian dandy as he went to the power station, twirling a walking stick and whistling. He didn't care that some people gave him wide berth and others scowled. He hadn't lived on the island long enough to cultivate a social circle whose ostracization might have hurt him. The power station remained vital, and certainly its board of directors did not want to offend the Germans by either censuring or firing Mr. Russell.

Catherine felt so helpless and frustrated that patriotism was rewarded with hunger and deprivation, while collaborating with the enemy only brought full bellies and a secure position. All she could hope for was that someone would be saved from being spied on with knowledge that the Russells were collaborators.

She kept her face deliberately turned away from the Russells' house as she passed by, so she was startled when she heard the man himself calling her name.

"Miss Braun! Miss Braun, do slow down a moment."

Timmy, unaware, ran up the stairs to their home and disappeared inside.

Stomach clenching, Catherine took a deep breath and turned to face Mr. Russell, who gave her a satisfied smile that could only be termed "oily."

"Miss Braun, I've been waiting to see you."

She swallowed but managed a faint smile. "Can I help you with something, Mr. Russell?"

"Like so many of us, Miss Braun, I've been assigned a German officer to reside in my home. I was told you would be assigned some translation duties. Rather than wait until tomorrow, could you meet him now? We feel quite at a loss with no way to communicate."

"Oh...of course." Catherine's stomach almost rebelled at the thought of going into that house, but she couldn't think of a reason to say no and avoid German punishment. Every step closer made the front door loom larger and larger, and curtains ruffled as if she was being watched.

Before she knew it, she was inside. The Russells' son was playing with a set of blocks in the parlor, flying a toy airplane off the top of it. He glanced up at Catherine then away without interest, which was strange for a child not yet of school age. Her teacher's mind started wondering if he was being given enough attention—or were his parents more focused on earning rewards from their German masters?

The house itself smelled of warm spices, as if a delicious Christmas goose was cooking. In the dining room, a German officer jumped to his feet when he saw Catherine. A part of her was relieved, worried she'd been lured inside for a more sinister reason.

The officer removed his hat and briefly bowed his head.

Mr. Russell gestured to Catherine and said, "*Fraulein* Braun."

"How do you do?" Catherine asked in German.

The young man beamed happily. "Ah, someone who speaks my language. I am Corporal Pollock, *Fraulein* Braun. It is good to meet you."

She gave an awkward nod. "Mr. Russell says you'll be living here now?"

Corporal Pollock thrust a paper at her. "Is this the right place? I believe so. So many twisting roads on this island."

"Many of the roads were planned when there were only horses to deal with." She heard herself sounding like a teacher, a professional, and that made her relax just a bit.

After all, what could happen when Mr. Russell's son and probably his wife were in residence?

Catherine scanned the piece of paper with the Russells' address printed. "You're definitely at the right place, Corporal."

He gave another bright smile. "Good, good." He bobbed his head at Mr. Russell.

Catherine felt a moment's discombobulation. It was as if she was meeting a foreign visitor to Guernsey Island, something which used to happen quite regularly. He was just so obviously happy to be there.

Besides being unhealthily thin, he had the pink line of a newly healed scar along his jaw. She wondered if he'd recently seen worse action, as so many of the Germans had before being assigned to what must seem like a tropical holiday.

In English, Catherine said, "Mr. Russell, what would you like to do next?"

"We'll show him to his room—it's right upstairs. Follow me, Miss Braun."

Catherine opened her mouth to protest, but Corporal Pollock was looking confused again. In German, she said, "Come with us to your new room."

He nodded with eagerness, picked up his suitcase, and followed her to the stairs. Catherine saw Mrs. Russell standing in the doorway to what must be the kitchen. Her face was expressionless when she met Catherine's gaze before turning away. She wore rouge and lipstick, a beautiful blue silk dress, and a white apron. Her auburn hair was pinned into upswept rolls that brushed her shoulders and circled her head. She looked perfectly put together and untouched by hardship. Catherine's bitterness was a knot in her stomach that made her feel somehow ashamed.

Mr. Russell was waiting at the top of the stairs, and they marched in a line behind him to the end of the hall.

"In here," he said, gesturing.

Catherine repeated the words in German, her hands fluttering nervously as she spoke, and the corporal stepped past them.

"Tell him when he's unpacked, to return downstairs for dinner," Mr. Russell said.

Catherine repeated it, then said in English, "If you don't need me..." She started toward the stairs.

Mr. Russell stepped in front of her. "Not so fast, young lady."

His face wore a smile, and his tone was pleasant,

perhaps in case their German visitor overheard him. But the words that emerged were far from pleasant.

"I know you're the reason there are rumors about me."

She stiffened and could not look away from his face. "Rumors?" she repeated stupidly.

His smile widened, which made his lips thin beneath his mustache. "No one else knew about the food delivery."

"I don't know what you're talking about."

"Oh, I know it's not just you—it's also that Jerrybag friend of yours, and the nurse."

"Did you call my friend a Jerrybag?" Catherine asked coldly. "*You*?"

"So it was you, then."

"I did not—"

"Quiet."

The pleasant tone was almost comical, but she heard the menace. And then he took an angled step, forcing her to back up against the wall.

"I'll scream," she said with a calmness she wasn't feeling.

"Don't be silly. I'm not going to hurt you in my own house. I'm not going to hurt you at all—not physically. But I know all the right people now, Miss Braun. There are plenty of soldiers looking for girlfriends, and you are available. I'll let them know."

She frowned her confusion. "But—"

"And then there's your family. I do believe you all count on your father's position at the airport?"

The terror chilled its way through her, though the house was warm with baking. She wanted to protest, but didn't have a clue what to say.

"I suggest you stop the rumors and hope I don't make you suffer too much." He looked past her shoulder and his smile became placid, as if the soldier watched. "I'll escort you downstairs, Miss Braun. This way."

He turned his back and walked down the hall toward the front stairs. Catherine's legs didn't want to move at first, but then she followed him and went past him right out the door. She didn't take a breath until she was in her own yard, and it came out as a gasp.

She came to a stop when she saw Sergeant Doepgen sitting on her front steps.

"Is Lieutenant Schafer not here?" she asked in dismay, without even greeting him.

He twisted his cap. "I am here to see you, *fraulein*."

And it was suddenly too much. A wellspring of courage rose up inside her, taking her by surprise. "Stop paying so much attention to me. You are a German officer and I am your captive. I'm not going to date you!"

His brown eyes went wide, and he raised both hands as if to placate her. "I would never ask such a thing of you in the middle of war, Catherine."

She flinched at his personal use of her first name. "Then what do you want of me?"

He looked over his shoulder and at her house, as if worried they'd be seen. Were her parents watching? What would they think? When he came toward her, she took a giant step back.

"No, you misunderstand," he insisted, his voice so soft she had to strain to hear it. "I need your help."

She hugged herself as if in protection. "*My* help? How can I help *you*? And why would I want to? You are my enemy!"

It was his turn to take a step back as if she'd struck him, and she found herself angry at his deliberate ignorance. She wanted to shout about the innocents his people had killed —that her brother was a prisoner, suffering in ways she couldn't imagine.

"I don't want to be your enemy," he said hoarsely. "I want to stay here, to...to defect. Will you help me to hide?"

30

BETTY

Betty regarded herself in a mirror as she dressed. The navy blue silk dress hugged her hips and showed off her slim waist. Her neck looked particularly bare, and she draped her simple string of pearls around her neck. They weren't real, of course, but her mother had given them to her on her eighteenth birthday, and they were sentimental favorites even though she wasn't a very sentimental person.

"You're wearing those?"

Betty turned around to see Mum standing in the bedroom doorway. She wore a housecoat and slippers, her face getting thinner, her hair uncombed, a cigarette trembling in her fingers. It was hard to see her mother deteriorating in front of her, but then so many people were getting thin. Betty had to tighten the belt on her dress to make sure it didn't gap at her waist.

"You gave the pearls to me," Betty said. "They mean something."

"So you'll wear them—for him."

The bitterness in her mother's voice struck a pang in Betty's heart. Mum had been in denial about Franz, had been ignoring the reasons Betty stayed late after the restaurant was closed. They never talked about it, which was why Betty was so surprised now.

Arching a brow, Betty said, "I'm wearing them because it makes me remember a time before the war, and reminds me that this war will be over eventually."

"Stay home then."

Betty let out a long sigh. "And what do you think would happen? He would come here looking for me." She turned and faced her mother fully. "Do you think I *like* this, Mum?"

"I don't know any more." Her mother's chin trembled as she looked away.

"Then I guess you don't know me after all."

"Don't say that!"

"What choice do I have? All of my choices were taken away when the Germans invaded. If I protest, bad things will happen. I could lose my position. I could be forced to date other men. Do you want that?"

Mum put her hands over her ears like a child and squeezed her eyes shut. "Stop it! You're just saying these things to hurt me!"

Betty blinked at her in silent disbelief. When the phone rang, she was grateful. She moved past her mother into the parlor.

"Hello?" she said into the receiver.

"Betty, it's Catherine."

Betty frowned. "I can barely hear you."

"I'm whispering because my family is nearby. I just wanted you to know that Mr. Russell knows what we did, and he's threatened me."

"Oh no." Betty briefly closed her eyes. "What happened?"

"He said he'd tell soldiers we were looking for boyfriends, and he said my father could lose his job."

"We'll stop spreading rumors, of course," Betty murmured.

"I don't know if he cares. I just wanted you to know, so you could protect yourself."

"I have a protector," Betty said bitterly.

Catherine hesitated. "I'm sorry. I—I have to go and call Helen now. Good night."

Betty hung up the receiver. She'd known Mr. Russell might find out about the rumors, and didn't much care. He couldn't do anything more to her. But Catherine and Helen —her friends might suffer in this. What could she do to help? Perhaps convince Franz to do something without telling him the whole truth? But that meant asking him a favor.

Like she hadn't done him so many favors, she thought, bitterness a tightness in her chest that seemed to only grow day by day.

The doorbell rang. Her mother gave a theatrical gasp, as if Franz hadn't come to their flat before, then hurried into her bedroom and slammed the door.

Betty quickly applied the lipstick Franz had purchased for her on one of his many trips to France, took a deep breath, and opened the front door. Franz stood there with fresh flowers. When he cleared his throat, she realized she was just staring blankly at the flowers.

She gave him a faint smile and reached for them. "Thank you. I'll find a vase."

He stepped in without waiting for an invitation and then followed her into the kitchen. She knew he was looking around at the sad old furnishings and ancient range, but she didn't much care. Maybe it reminded him why it was so easy to get her to do what he wanted, how desperate she was to afford even the little that she had.

But she didn't think he was that aware of others, only of himself. She was proven right when, after she had the flowers in a vase, she turned around and found him smiling at her—

Like he wasn't forcing himself on her.

Like she was perfectly willing to live in his dream world where he was courting her as if she wasn't his prisoner.

She *was* living in his dream world, she thought, mentally sighing.

"Might I have a cup of coffee?" he asked.

"I'd rather get to the party."

And not put her mother through any more of this.

And find a way to return the munitions list she'd stolen.

"It *will* be fun," he admitted. "Very well, let's go."

His car had the streets practically to itself on a Friday night that had once been filled with people enjoying the beginning of the weekend. There was plenty of open parking in front of the dance hall, and Franz insisted on opening her door with a gallant flourish.

He was so ridiculous—how did he not see that?

Because he was so enamored with himself. And he was getting away with his behavior, after all. The Germans had their own little kingdom on the Channel Islands, only seventy miles from Britain, but it felt like half a world away, especially when Britain did little to help them.

But the military had sent Jack, and other spies as well. Maybe some hadn't been discovered, and were even now doing their work unseen. Betty couldn't let herself think of the worst, that they'd been abandoned by Britain.

Inside, the room was warm and loud and full of the smell of smoke and sausage. The Germans loved their sausage. Laughing women wore lipstick and nylons, things they couldn't get on the island. Not that there were all that many young island men.

And that was part of the problem. Too many of these women were bored and desperate for the attention they thought themselves entitled to as young single women.

To her surprise, she saw Sergeant Doepgen, the man who'd been bothering Catherine. He looked pale and solemn, not a man enjoying a party. When he caught her staring at him, he gave a brief bow, then turned away.

After downing a quick drink, Franz pulled her onto the dance floor for a foxtrot, and then brought her close for a waltz. Later, he took her into a group of men and women, where the men conversed in German. Betty pretended to be as clueless and bored as the other women, though she was avidly listening. But the conversation was about nothing more than reassuring each other that Germany was going to win the war.

Franz was watching her a little too closely, so she excused herself for the bathroom, where several women were chatting in the sitting room as they reapplied makeup in the big lit mirrors. One very young woman whose name she didn't know was silently crying, dabbing at her eyes with a handkerchief as if desperate to protect her makeup.

Betty paused beside her. "Are you all right, miss?"

The girl shook her head and blew her nose. "What does it matter?" she asked with a faint thread of bitterness. "There's nothing anyone can do until the war is over, and even then—" Her voice broke and tears spilled once more down her cheeks.

Betty understood all too well.

Two of the women eyed the girl with open derision and whispered something to each other before laughing.

"That's enough," Betty said sharply. "We all have our reasons to be here—mind your own business."

One woman looked as if she'd respond, but the other pulled on her arm to turn her away.

Betty lingered as long as she could, fussing with her hair, smoking a cigarette, while the crying girl tried to repair her makeup. They returned to the party at the same time, and the girl gave her a grateful, sad glance before reuniting with a German officer old enough to be her father.

Betty didn't spot Franz at first, but she did see someone she knew—Lucy, the young girl who fancied herself in love with Lieutenant Hamachers. She was obviously no longer pregnant, although her apple cheeks had thinned out with hunger, just like everyone else on the island. Her blond hair was tucked into a neat coronet of braids, and she held hands with Lieutenant Hamachers, who still looked at her like the sun rose and set in her eyes.

Lucy's eyes went wide when she spotted Betty, and after saying something to her lieutenant, she practically skipped across the room.

"Hello, Betty!" Lucy cried, leaning forward to kiss her cheek.

Surprised, Betty accepted the intimacy that didn't seem deserved—although they did belong to a very small sisterhood. "Hello, Lucy. How are you—and how is the baby?"

Lucy glowed like so many new mothers. "Wonderful! Tobias comes to visit us often and is the perfect father."

"That's good to hear. I was concerned that he might not...*take* to fatherhood."

Lucy chirped a laugh and waved a hand as if negating any doubts. "Everyone thought that, including my parents, but I knew better. We are planning our wedding. It won't be permitted until after the war, of course, but he will move here with us. My father has even offered him a position on the farm!"

Betty blinked in disbelief. She could not imagine a German—the enemy—being permitted to live on the island after the war. "If anyone can make it happen, you can."

Lucy blushed. "I am very determined. You don't give up on love when it's so rarely found." She hesitated. "Do you love the captain?"

Betty didn't bother hesitating. "No."

Lucy's smile faded. "I'm sorry to hear that. Being with a man must be very sad when there is no love."

Betty didn't let herself think about what life would have been like if she'd found a man to love before the war. She spotted Franz. "I have to go."

Lucy squeezed Betty's arm gently. "Good luck."

Betty turned away, then frowned as she examined Franz's conversation partner who seemed so familiar. He wasn't wearing a uniform and was in his thirties, with a mustache and hair polished with pomade. He and Franz were talking with their heads close together, their expressions serious. Franz made a gesture with his hand, his cigarette flaring.

And then Betty had a moment of clarity. The man was Mr. Russell, Catherine's neighbor—the collaborator.

Betty moved back along the wall, as if heading toward the refreshment table, all the while keeping Franz and Mr. Russell under surveillance. Mr. Russell's eyes were narrowed in a frown—could he be discussing the rumors about him? But why would he do that with Franz, who worked in munitions rather than with the locals? She was thinking she should wait for Mr. Russell to leave, but after she had some punch and sipped it slowly, she saw Franz looking around the room with some distraction.

He must be searching for her. Resigned, she let herself be spotted and lifted the glass to him, silently asking if he wanted something to drink.

He shook his head and gestured with his chin for her to approach. Walking toward them at an unhurried pace, she felt the stares she always received, some admiring, some envious. But in this room, at least no one was disdainful, she thought with irony.

She saw when recognition dawned on Mr. Russell's face, before he quickly hid his surprise behind a cool smile. Would he tell Franz what Betty and her friends had done to him? Would Franz even care?

This was becoming a tangled knot she had no idea how to untangle.

"Betty," Franz began, "have you met Mr. Charles Russell?"

"I haven't had the pleasure," Mr. Russell said.

Betty let him take her hand. "Mr. Russell."

"But I know who you are, of course." He squeezed her hand meaningfully and let go.

She arched a brow and waited, not the sort of person who dwelled and worried on what might happen. Best to deal with reality rather than waste energy on what might never be.

But she wasn't alone in this dangerous situation now— Catherine and Helen would be affected. She'd never had people who counted on her, people to worry about except her mother. And now this man was a threat to all of them.

"You know me?" Betty asked.

"I do. You're a friend of my neighbors, the Brauns."

"It's a small island," Franz added.

She held her breath, wondering what Mr. Russell would say next. He paused in a very deliberate fashion, until even Franz looked from one to the other in confusion.

"How do the two of you know each other?" Mr. Russell asked.

Betty met Franz's gaze, and his slow smile might well have been a declaration of the things they did in bed together. It took everything in her not to blush, but to simply regard him coolly.

"Ah," Mr. Russell said with a nod.

"We have a special friendship." Franz took her hand.

Showing her off, Betty thought. Just another Jerrybag in a room full of them.

Mr. Russell bowed. "It was good to see you again, Captain."

"We can talk another time," Franz said lightly.

A little too lightly, Betty thought.

And then Mr. Russell slipped away into the crowd, and Franz swept Betty into the center of the dance floor.

~oOo~

Later that night, Betty lay in bed until Franz fell asleep. She waited a long time, used the bathroom to dress, and then waited even longer, until the moon dimmed behind clouds. By touch, she found Franz's briefcase and slid the stolen munitions paper back into a random folder, as if it had just been misplaced. She took another folder, hid it beneath her blouse, and went back to the bathroom, where she thumbed through it far too slowly, her German skills still woefully weak.

And then she saw the word, "invasion."

31

HELEN

Helen looked in on her special patient, the German officer with the eye injury. Lieutenant Beering was wearing a patch now, the eye long taken, a festering infection in the socket lingering painfully. He would be leaving soon, shipped back to Germany to recover. Perhaps the war had ended for him. He couldn't seem to decide how to feel about that, as if his manhood could only be proven by remaining a soldier.

He was much more guarded with her now about his current assignment, and she blamed herself for prying too hard. It was definitely an art to persuade people to talk, and she didn't have the skills. She tried leading with inquiries about his wife since he received regular letters from her—lucky him, she often thought bitterly. What she wouldn't give for a letter from a distant cousin or old school friend. Mentioning his wife always seemed to work; he was happy to talk about his life before the war, the endearing way he'd courted his wife, the pharmacy he hoped to own someday.

She gave a bright and cheerful smile as she changed his sheets while he sat near the window. It was a little too easy to chat with him, but it was necessary, she told herself. "I bet the sun on your face feels good," she said.

He shrugged listlessly, something unusual for him.

She put on a fresh pillowcase, fluffing it before putting it back on the bed. "Your wife will be happy to see you."

"I don't think so."

She put her hands on her hips as she faced him. "You sound like she would prefer you die rather than come home missing one eye."

He sighed. "Hearing you say it makes it sound foolish. But my brain doesn't seem to understand."

"Be patient with yourself," she said. Inwardly, she winced at how easy it was to be kind to a patient who was also her enemy. "You've been through a trauma that your brain is still dealing with. And you know that your wife will be thrilled to have you home. Otherwise, you're saying she doesn't love you."

Lieutenant Beering looked startled. "We love each other very much."

"See?" she teased.

His lips turned up at the corners, and she decided to press the advantage. "Will you tell her how it happened?"

He looked back out the window. "I don't know."

"So you haven't written to her about it."

"No."

"Then you can tell her in person," Helen said matter-of-factly. "She loves you and will want to be there for you. It could help if you practice telling her." She pulled a metal chair over near his and sat down. "Go ahead, tell me. It will help."

He smiled at her, and she found herself smiling back. He had an endearing way about him, as if he were a puppy. He reached for her hand and, surprised, she let him take it. "Greta," he began.

She felt a thrill of satisfaction. He'd never told her his wife's name before.

But then he paused, studying her hand before looking at her with his one good eye. He suddenly released her hand. "You're not my wife, and I don't feel comfortable pretending you are. Why are you so interested in helping me?"

She tensed, but her nurse's outward calm steadied her. "Because a good nurse is always interested in helping her patient. You're in distress. Talking about it and making plans for how to deal with it will help."

"I can't talk about it," he said firmly.

She'd lost him, and she had to accept her failure. Lieutenant Beering wasn't going to be the one to help her —directly.

She stood up. "Then I'll stop bothering you. But my advice is to be honest with your wife. You'll both feel better in the end."

She left the room, determined not to feel defeated. The lieutenant was hiding something, and there were other ways to find out. She'd seen him in long friendly discussions with another patient of hers, Sergeant Menz. Maybe the sergeant knew about whatever underground work was going on.

She found the sergeant outside, enjoying the sun. She took a deep breath, grateful for the scents of cut grass and salty sea air, rather than the constant antiseptic used in the hospital. He wore a robe over his hospital gown, and someone had helped prop his broken leg on a stool. A weather-beaten man in his late thirties, he was frowning at his leg as if it offended him.

Helen set a glass of water on the little table at his side.

"Hello, Sergeant," she said.

He nodded at her. "Nurse Abernathy, good day," he said, his accent thick but understandable.

They spent a few minutes chatting about the weather under the guise of him practicing his English.

When there was a moment of silence, she gave a sigh and spoke regretfully. "I just came from Lieutenant Beering's room. Do you know him?"

Sergeant Menz nodded. "He has been here a long time. Everyone knows him."

"So sad what happened to his eye."

The sergeant lowered his voice. "He knew he was going over his bounds."

"Going over...overstepping his bounds?" Helen said.

Sergeant Menz's face lit with a smile. "*Ja*. The prisoners were ordered to be working at the new hospital. He should not have been among them, trying to help. The accident wouldn't have affected him at all, yet he pushed a worker aside and bore the brunt of it."

She didn't even know where to start with so much information and still sound like she knew what he was talking about.

"He tries to be a good person," she murmured, then threw caution to the wind. "I did not realize it was a new hospital they were working on underground."

He shot her a wide-eyed look, then turned away, whispering fiercely, "Do not tell anyone I spoke to you of this. It is not to be discussed with islanders."

"I already knew," she said, hoping to placate him. "It's not your fault that I know."

"Lieutenant Beering told you?" he asked, aghast.

Oh, this was all going so wrong. "I—he was sedated. He didn't mean..." She trailed off before she could make things worse.

"I cannot speak of this anymore," Sergeant Menz said. "Please leave before someone is suspicious. I'll talk to Lieutenant Beering."

Panic shot through her like a zap of static electricity. "Sergeant—"

"Just go."

Pressing her lips together in frustration, she turned back toward the hospital—and saw Lieutenant Beering standing at his window, palms against the glass, staring down at them. Guiltily, she glanced at Sergeant Menz, who gazed up without expression before limping away on his crutches. Helen felt trapped by the lieutenant's focus, the stiff way he held his body, even though she couldn't quite make out his expression. She'd made a muddle of everything.

Feeling panicked, breathless, she hurried back inside. After a consult with a doctor about another patient, she found herself outside the lieutenant's door, as if she might apologize to him. She could hear voices inside and knew Sergeant Menz had beaten her there. She couldn't make out their conversation, just the tone of desperation from Lieutenant Beering and sternness from Menz. She didn't think the sergeant would turn his friend in, for it would implicate himself as well. He'd talked to her, too.

Helen backed away from the door. There was nothing to be gained by pressing these two men further. They were her enemy, and even though she'd tried to erase that truth for her own purposes, they would never forget.

She spent the next hour going from task to task, patient to patient, trying to squash her frustration in hard work. But she couldn't stop thinking about the lieutenant, the way he'd stared at her through the window, the desperation in his voice. Uneasiness made her show up at his closed door again. She listened a moment, but when she heard no sound, she went inside.

Lieutenant Beering sat on the side of the bed, pills scattered all over the blanket as he poured a handful into his mouth.

Her stomach spasming with horror, Helen was at his side in two strides, striking the remaining pills from his hand. His eye was wet with anguish as he stared up at her. She stuck her fingers into his mouth and swept side to side, like one would a choking infant. Pills scattered from his mouth like the spew of blood from an artery.

"Did you swallow any?" she demanded urgently.

When he shook his head, she couldn't believe him. She shoved her finger down his throat until he gagged. Mercilessly, she did it again until his lunch of soup and mushed vegetables came up to splatter all over his hospital gown and the floor. No pills.

Her heart was pounding so hard it almost made her light-headed. The lieutenant quietly cried, face buried in his hands, while she gathered up every pill, then searched every drawer, every curtain fall, every clothes pocket in the wardrobe. When she was confident that she had them all, she put them in her own pocket. Gently, she helped him change his clothes, then guided him to sit beside the sunny window while she cleaned his bed and the floor. At last, she sank down in the chair opposite him, straightened her cap, and waited.

He said nothing, just looked out the window, the lines of his face etched with bleakness as if he'd become an old man in just hours.

"I guess you know enough about pills, being a pharmacist," she said tiredly. "You've been planning this for a long time."

A tense minute passed before he said in a hoarse voice, "Not planning it, no. I just wanted to be...prepared. It was easy enough to claim the pain was worse than it was, the last week or so."

"I thought you couldn't wait to return to your wife. Surely your experiences haven't been worth killing yourself over."

He turned and looked at her, eye narrowed. "I told you something I shouldn't have. And you told someone else. I *saw* you."

She felt the blood leave her face at the realization that he'd tried to kill himself because of her prodding for information. But she couldn't let herself think about that now or she'd be overwhelmed. He was still her patient.

She leaned toward him. "I only spoke to Sergeant Menz because he's your friend, nothing more. I just wanted to find a way to help you."

"That's not what he thinks."

He spoke without anger, just a despair that kept her fear for him like a knot tied in her throat.

"Then he's mistaken. Lieutenant, ask yourself—what could I possibly do with the knowledge that you injured yourself *saving* people. And as for the underground building, hundreds of people know about it—think of all the people building it! Even if I told someone, the knowledge isn't leaving the island." She was so shocked by her own ability to lie that it scared her.

He didn't say anything, just bit his lip. But at last, he looked at her. She kept her expression as calm and kind as she could, honed by several years of nursing dying patients who needed to believe they could fight and live.

Then he started to shake. She guessed that he felt overwhelmed by how near death he'd come—at his own hand.

"Promise me you won't do this again," she said, leaning forward to put a hand on his arm. "It isn't worth it. You're going *home*. The war is over for you."

His head drooped forward as he nodded a few times.

"And Greta is waiting," she whispered.

He lifted his head and gave her the ghost of a smile.

The door suddenly opened, and her friend Bridgette ducked her head through. "Helen, can I speak to you in the hall?"

Helen blinked in confusion as she came back to the world outside this room where tragedy had almost struck.

A tragedy she'd almost caused.

She cleared her throat. "I'll be right with you, Bridgette."

When Bridgette retreated, Helen looked back at the lieutenant. The color had come back into his face, and his breathing had slowed. She couldn't stay here and watch him for the rest of the day.

She went to his bed table and handed him the photo of his wife. "Remember your bride, Lieutenant. Family is truly what we live for."

He nodded, and his smile seemed a bit less tortured.

"I'll check in on your tomorrow."

He caught her hand as she turned away. "Don't tell anyone how foolish I was," he said, low and urgent. "They'll never leave me alone."

She studied him with narrowed eyes. "Very well. But I'm trusting you."

He slumped back with a deep sigh. "Thank you."

He had trusted her, and she'd betrayed him.

This was *war*, she told herself.

But it was like two parts of her were fighting over her soul.

When Helen reached the hall, Bridgette was tapping her foot obviously anxious to start her next task.

"Helen, there's a man to see you. He's waiting at the front steps, and said he doesn't have time to come in."

"Do you know who it is?" Helen asked, untying her apron and laying it over a nearby chair.

"I think he works at the chemist's?"

Helen inhaled swiftly, even as she gave a casual nod as she moved past Bridgette. At the front steps she found Mr. Garnier, his cap in his hand as he regarded her with penetrating eyes.

"Mr. Garnier," she said coolly. It was hard to forget that he'd said he wouldn't trust someone who associated with a "Jerrybag."

"Can you walk with me a spell?" he asked. When she hesitated, he added, "Please."

She nodded and moved with him onto the lawn, away from the hospital. "What can I do for you, Mr. Garnier?"

"I need a favor."

She arched a brow.

He said, "I heard that you and your friends tried to reveal a collaborator. It was bravely done."

It was not an apology, but almost as good.

"Our attempt proved fruitless," she said with faint bitterness.

"None of us know the long-term results."

She shrugged and rubbed her arms against the cool breeze blowing off the channel. "What kind of favor are you asking?" she repeated.

He looked over his shoulder, as if judging the distance back to the hospital. "I need you to deliver the newsleaf tonight—just tonight."

She caught her breath even as she glanced at him in surprise. "Me?"

He winced. "I'm not one to risk a lady if I don't have to, but people depend on us, and my regular who delivers out your way is...detained."

He didn't volunteer any more information, and she knew better than to ask.

"It's just tonight," he repeated.

"You know I'll help whenever you need me to."

He grimaced. "War is no business for ladies."

"I work in a hospital," she said sharply. "I see more of war than you ever will."

He eyed her narrowly, but finally gave a reluctant nod. "I keep underestimating you."

"Hopefully you'll think twice before doing that with all the ladies in your life."

Mr. Garnier harrumphed. Helen thought he might be married, or if not, he was at least someone's son.

"Come to the chemist's at dusk," he said. "I'll give you the packet and tell you your stops. I don't want to do it here. Too many Germans."

Helen nodded. "I'll be there soon."

After her hospital shift, she met Mr. Garnier behind the chemist's, as if they were spies. Maybe not spies, exactly, but she was doing something illegal, something that could get her arrested and sent to Germany. She tried not to think about that.

He gave her a large envelope which she placed in her bicycle basket.

He looked at it dubiously. "People will see it."

"And what will they think? I'm wearing a nurse's uniform riding home at dusk. They see me do this every day. And it's my risk to take. Is the list of homes in there?"

He nodded, and she unclasped the envelope to look.

He pushed it down in the basket. "Not here!"

"We're in the alley."

"Wait until you're away from town."

She glanced up at the sky. "I don't have much daylight left."

"Then go quickly." He started to leave.

"Mr. Garnier, thank you," she said quietly.

Turning back to her, he frowned. "You're thanking me for asking you to do something that could get you arrested?"

"I'm thanking you for giving me a purpose. I've spent too much time trying to do something for the war effort and feeling like nothing ever works out." She thought of Lieutenant Beering and suppressed it immediately. She couldn't consider her culpability now.

"You've revealed a collaborator, and now you'll help people get news of the outside world. You've done your part. Stop trying to do more."

She watched as he went back inside and shut the door firmly. Then, looking at her basket with determination, she started pedaling. Outside town, she stopped on the side of the road and opened the envelope, shooting a guilty look over her shoulder. No cars were coming—the only people with cars were Germans, after all, and why come out into the countryside in the evening? There were ten houses on her list, and she knew almost every single occupant. But she didn't want them to know what she was doing—the less people who knew, the less who could talk. She would have gone home to wait for nightfall, but Jack was there, and he would question why she was going out after dark. Better to explain later.

Where the road traveled along the cliff, she found a perch to admire the view for an hour, until dusk melted into a dark grayness, when she headed off on her bicycle again.

At the first house, she left her bicycle in the grass near the road and crept silently across the lawn. A dog barked in the distance, and she stiffened, but nothing happened. She stepped onto the porch, hoping that a board wouldn't creek. After sliding the newsleaf under the door, she ran away.

Feeling a little giddy, she hopped on her bicycle, her stomach full of butterflies, her limbs bursting with energy. She'd succeeded! Now she only had to do it nine more times.

The next two houses were even simpler; the front lights were off, and there were no animals to alert them to her presence.

She had a scare at the fourth house—she could actually hear the doorknob turn. Jumping off the porch, she crouched behind the shrubbery and held her breath. These people wanted the newsleaf—what would it hurt if they accidentally found out who delivered it?

No, there was a reason all the spy movies made clear you only revealed what you had to.

After another house, she turned onto her own road, which ran another half a mile toward her cottage on the cliff. Every home was familiar to her; it made creeping up the lawn easier, but she still didn't want her neighbors to know her identity, in case some were looking for a person to turn into the Germans.

She had to stop being so paranoid. Not everyone was a collaborator like the Russells. She refused to believe the worst about neighbors she'd known her whole life.

She was so focused on her disdain for the Russells that she was far too reckless going up the next drive. Wilbur, the Fentons' herding dog, rushed at her out of the darkness, and she gasped loudly in surprise. He only jumped up on her chest to lick her face, but he interspersed that with joyful barks.

"Shh, shh, down boy!" she whispered, pushing him away.

It was all part of the game to him.

The back veranda light was on, but not the front. If she could just get up on the porch and—

The light came on, and the door opened. Helen was frozen in place, Wilbur darting excitedly up and down the steps between her and his master.

She stiffened when she saw that it wasn't his master, but a stranger with short gray hair and a scruffy beard.

"Who are you?" he asked gruffly.

She opened her mouth, but just then Wilbur pounced, driving her back a couple steps.

"Wilbur, down!" she and the stranger said together.

To Helen's relief, Mrs. Fenton came to stand beside the stranger. She was a widow in her sixties whose daughter Helen used to play with before the girl grew up and moved to the mainland. Helen had called on Mrs. Fenton every so often, checking up on her, but the woman was taking the occupation in stride. She'd lost her husband during the Great War and had always had a strength about her.

"Helen, is that you?" she asked curiously, eyes narrowed as she tried to see beyond the porch light into the darkness.

Helen was glad the newsleaf was tucked into her sweater pocket. "Hello, Mrs. Fenton. I found Wilbur on the road and wanted to bring him back." She was surprised at how friendly and normal she sounded—and how easily the lie had tumbled out of her mouth.

Mrs. Fenton stepped out onto the porch. "Helen, dear, how very kind of you. You know how Wilbur loves to roam. I should be careful—there are so few dogs left on the island. I know some people sent theirs to roam free on Sark because they couldn't take care of them, but I could never do that to Wilbur."

The man grumbled something under his breath, frowning at the dog.

"Ignore my brother." Mrs. Fenton smiled as she elbowed the man. "He's a curmudgeon. I can't believe he came to visit me from the other side of the island."

Spoken as if that was hundreds of miles away instead of nine, at the most.

"That's kind of him," Helen said. "I won't keep you from your dinner."

"You could come in," she said hopefully. "We're long done with dinner."

Helen ended up having carrot tea in the tiny kitchen, Wilbur's soft head on her knee, listening to Mrs. Fenton and her brother chat about the weather, the growing season—anything but the Germans.

By the time Helen could escape, it was truly dark, but she wasn't far from home. She walked her bicycle slowly down the road, unable to see holes in the packed dirt. There'd been no one to fix the roads since the occupation began, especially this far away from town. She ran across a lawn, glad she knew it so well, and slipped another newsleaf beneath a door. Only one more left.

The final lawn was long and dark leading to the house. But the front porch light was on, and she was just trying to decide the best approach angle when someone grabbed her from behind.

The shock of being dragged up against a tall man's body with an arm around her waist almost caused Helen to scream, but a hand covered her mouth before she could. Fear shot through her, and she started to struggle.

"Helen, it's me," whispered an urgent voice in her ear.

Jack.

She went totally still.

"Don't say anything."

He released her mouth, and she turned toward him. His face was shadowed, but his narrowed eyes gleamed down at her. She opened her mouth to whisper, but he shook his head, pointing toward the patch of woods off the side of the road and gesturing for her to follow him.

She didn't know what was going on, but she trailed behind him, leading her bicycle. After laying it on the ground in the brush, she slid between two trees and found Jack crouching down in a very small space. There wasn't much room but she hunkered down, their shoulders brushing.

"What's going on?" she whispered.

"Besides you not coming home? I come looking for you and find you creeping onto people's lawns." Then he held a finger to his lips and peered out between the trees toward the road.

"Jack—"

He put his lips against her ear, causing a shiver, and said very softly. "I'm following someone, and he's getting closer. We can't get caught."

She nodded, but her excitement, already heightened, surged even higher. She waited a few minutes, staring at the road just as Jack was, but nothing seemed to be happening.

"Who is this person?" she whispered.

She couldn't see the expression on his face, but she imagined he was irritated by her questions. But he answered, "A German soldier. I was trying to stay ahead of him and see where he went, so I was crossing lawns and staying near trees. He should be coming around the bend soon."

As if Jack's words conjured him, Helen saw the outline of a man gradually appear in the near darkness. He carried an electric torch, but of course, why would a German soldier fear being seen?

Helen held her breath as he walked by. He moved with purpose, as if he knew exactly where he was going.

When the soldier was past them, Jack whispered, "I'll take you home and keep following him."

"And risk losing him? No, I'm coming. I know how to be quiet."

He hesitated, and she thought he might be about to protest, but she heard him sigh. "Stay close and stay on lawns to avoid stepping on twigs."

The moon was only half full, riding low in the sky, as they crept from lawn to lawn, ducking beside half walls or sliding behind trees. She didn't try to see the soldier, knowing Jack wouldn't lose him.

At least a hundred yards down the road, Jack halted. From between the trees, Helen could see the German as he turned up a drive and switched off his torch.

"Do you know these people?" Jack whispered.

"Not well. They didn't have children, which meant I didn't play at their house."

There was a faint light in the front window, and the German soldier stood near it, head cocked. Was he listening to a conversation? Or listening for an illegal radio? Helen prayed her neighbor wasn't about to get in trouble.

The German suddenly vaulted onto the porch and pounded on the door. Helen gasped, and Jack put a hand on her arm.

"Do something!" she hissed, even as she realized he couldn't, not without revealing himself.

The front door opened, and the soldier barged in.

"Wait here," Jack ordered, then sprinted up the lawn.

She saw him slide into the shadows beneath the window even as she crouched in the shrubbery. The German came out a few minutes later and marched down the road with something in his arms.

Helen held her breath while he went past, feeling like his evil nature wafted over her. He had no problem terrorizing defenseless people.

Jack reappeared beside her.

"Are we going to follow him?" she asked softly.

"No. Let's go home."

He sounded stern, and she imagined he was going to have something to say to her, but she didn't care. He'd called her cottage "home."

She forced herself to stay focused as she said, "But I have to finish—"

"Delivering the newsleaf?" he interrupted sarcastically.

"You know?"

"I *saw*. Anyone could have seen you."

"But only you did," she said smugly.

"Helen—"

"I have one more left to do. And my bicycle is there."

"Helen!" he hissed her name, but she ignored him.

She kept expecting him to stop her as she hurried back the way they'd come, keeping off the road. Her eyes were used to the dark, and it only took her a few minutes to see the gleam of her bicycle lying on its side in high grass, but she went past it. The front windows of the final house on her list were now dark, so she slipped the newsleaf easily under the door.

Back near the road, she found Jack with her bicycle. When he saw her coming, he turned and headed for her cottage. She didn't bother to keep up, letting him have his moment of pique. After he put her bicycle in the garage, they met up again at the back door, but he didn't speak.

Inside, she closed the door and leaned against it as he turned on a light. "Are you going to be quiet all night?" she asked.

He paused, head bent near the lamp. She could see the tension in his shoulders, the spasm in his cheek muscles as he gritted his teeth. She should feel uneasy, contrite, when instead she felt—alive.

At last he turned around and folded his arms across his chest. "How did you come to play a part in this?"

"They needed me," she began, and then the whole story spilled out.

He gestured toward her. "Look how you're dressed. I could see you from a distance."

She glanced down at her light blue dress and dark stockings, then chuckled. "It's not as if I have my white apron on. And these people *want* the newsleaf."

"You're taking this too lightly."

Her smile faded as she approached him. "I am not. I know the risks. And it's exhilarating."

He arched a brow. "War is not exhilarating."

She stopped right in front of Jack and looked up into his eyes. "But doing my own small part for the war effort is. Why do you keep resisting my need to help?"

"I don't want you hurt," he said gruffly.

She realized he was looking at her mouth. It was suddenly difficult to breathe.

He added, "And I'm not resisting you much at all."

She put her arms around his neck. "Then why do it?"

He leaned down and kissed her, pulling her body against his. She moaned into the kiss, and for a long moment, she didn't think of anything but how wonderful she felt in his arms, and how incredible it was to be falling in love with him. She wanted him to love her back.

But when she put her hands on his chest, her fingertips touching the bare skin at his throat, he lifted his head, breathing heavily, staring down into her eyes. For a long moment they looked at each other, and she didn't hide her longing, her love.

He stepped back. "Helen, we have to stop."

It was a blow she hadn't been expecting. She turned away, putting up a hand to ward him off. He only wanted her when he could not control his emotions—and he needed that control.

She blinked away tears and turned to face him, hoping

her face was as impassive as his. "What did that German say to my neighbor?"

"He made him give up a box of food and some money in exchange for the German not turning him in for an illegal radio."

Helen blinked. "The German had to have known—he went deliberately to his house."

Jack shrugged. "I don't know how they first met up. Perhaps the German searched people's houses and left radios alone until he needed something. The perfect petty blackmail."

"Is there anything we can do?"

"You know I can't risk my position over something like this."

"I know. I'm perfectly aware of all the things you cannot risk."

"Helen—"

"Good night, Jack." She went up the stairs with slow deliberation, as if she wasn't affected. But tears rolled down her face.

Alone in her room, her sadness swamped her, as if she floated in choppy seas with no land in sight. Lieutenant Beering appeared in her mind, and how he'd looked at her in despair, pills in his mouth because of her. Maybe she should have told Jack what had happened; maybe he could have assured that her things happen in war that you can't predict, that you can only do your best.

Or maybe it would have been proof of her ineptitude, another reason for him to condemn her efforts.

It was a long time before she could sleep.

33

CATHERINE

Catherine stood alongside hundreds of islanders outside the cemetery, carrying their wreaths decorated in red, white, and blue. The bodies of two RAF pilots had recently washed ashore. Though German orders stated that the funeral be private, she and her family weren't alone in wanting to show their respect. Mourners lined the streets leading to the cemetery, all of them defying their occupiers to honor men who'd given the ultimate sacrifice.

Catherine's defiance of the Germans continued. She was determined not to enter the Russells' home ever again. The Germans might insist she work for them, but as long as Corporal Pollock had no cause to complain, she should be in the clear. So rather than seeking him out, she waited until he knocked on her door with a request for help, even though his appearance startled her mother. Mum held up a hand to stop him from entering and turned to Catherine.

"What does he want?" Mum whispered.

Catherine patted her arm. "He's one of the Germans I've been assigned to help. He seems harmless enough."

"None of them are harmless," Mum said sharply.

"I know, but I'll be all right in public."

Frowning, Mum let her go, and Catherine went out onto the front porch. Corporal Pollock was waiting at the bottom of the stairs, their gazes leveled, and he gave her his puppy-dog grin. Catherine wasn't fooled for a minute. He was the enemy.

"Can I help you, Corporal?" she asked in German.

"I have papers, *fraulein*," he said, holding out a stack. "The Russells are not at home, and I knocked papers off the dining table—I am so clumsy. These are in English. Are some of them mine? Do some belong together? I need help sorting."

The stack was at least an inch thick. He was feeling guilty for disturbing an *islander's* papers? If anything marked him as a newcomer, this was it.

He looked at her expectantly, and since she wasn't about to enter the Russell home ever again, she invited him inside. Her mother was waiting in the hall, nervous but composed as she twisted her hands together.

"Mum, this is Corporal Pollock," she said in German. "Corporal Pollock, this is my mother, *Frau* Braun."

Mum said in formal tones, "Pleased to meet you."

"You speak my language," he said in delight. His big smile faded when she didn't return it.

"My grandparents taught my parents, who taught me," Mum said.

"And you taught your daughter. Thank you. She has helped me tremendously."

Mum nodded and gave Catherine a narrow-eyed look.

"We need the table to sort papers," Catherine said. "It shouldn't take long."

Catherine led the way into the dining room and set

Corporal Pollock's messy stack on the table. "Let's spread them out and turn them right side up, at least."

He knew enough to be able to help that small bit. Soon, Catherine was gathering together household lists about cleaning and cooking and taking care of their son, and even one with places to travel. My, how ambitious the Russells were, she thought with bitterness. There were many letters addressed to people in Europe, as if the Russells were able to get their mail off the island. She glanced through each one of them, conscious of Corporal Pollock standing with his hat in his hand.

"Do sit down," she said.

He did so, and continued to watch her with interest and relief. Would he tell Mr. Russell that Catherine had read every single paper—even though she really hadn't? She hoped the corporal would want to hide his clumsiness as much as possible and say nothing. She couldn't let herself take too long, but she felt...eager, curious, aware that she was seeing into the private life of a man who was a traitor.

And then the contents of one paper rewarded her for her thoroughness, and her breath left her lungs in a gasp that she quickly covered with a cough. Corporal Pollock looked around as if for water, but she waved his concern away.

"It's nothing," she insisted. "I'm almost done."

She read through the paper a second time, while her heart pounded, and her fingers trembled. She controlled herself by straightening all the piles of paper and telling Corporal Pollock how to keep everything separated. She found a bill addressed to him from a tailor.

He blushed. "I bought trousers for my father. Such fine quality, and back home..."

He trailed off, and while he looked away with embarrassment, Catherine quickly slipped the Russell note into her skirt pocket.

After the German had gone, she stood frozen in the dining room, her hand on her pocket, her mind racing.

Timmy came in with a deck of cards. "Are you done? Mum and I are going to play. Do you want to join us?"

Catherine didn't even know how to answer. Her mother arrived next, searching her face worriedly, then putting on a smile for Timmy.

"Catherine, say you'll join us," he pleaded.

Mum glanced at her again, and Catherine realized everything that was at stake—she should destroy the letter, pretend she never saw it. It would keep her family safe.

And then Catherine thought of everything Betty had risked to find information for Jack. How could she do less?

She couldn't. Taking a deep breath, she forced a brisk smile. "I need to make a telephone call, and then I'll be right back to play with you."

By the time she was done calling Betty and Helen, Catherine wandered into the parlor looking for her family, but it was empty. She searched the ground floor, then went outside, believing she heard voices. To her surprise, she found Timmy at the rabbit cages with the Russells' little boy, who was alone. He couldn't be even five years old, and he was watching the rabbits with rapt attention as Timmy fed them.

"Hello," Catherine said brightly, but cast a curious glance at her brother.

Timmy shrugged. "I found him here. He didn't want to go home, and I didn't think I should leave him to fetch his mum."

"Willy!" came a frantic shout as if on cue.

Willy didn't stir. Catherine walked around the side of the

house until the Russell home came into view. She saw Mrs. Russell emerging from their gazebo, her face full of fear.

"Mrs. Russell, Willy decided to come see our rabbits," Catherine called. "He's fine."

She saw the woman's shoulders sag, as if she'd begun to fear the worst. Then she marched to the gate separating their properties and came through.

Catherine smiled politely as she approached, but the woman just swept past her with determination. Bemused, Catherine followed her to the rabbit cages in the garden.

"Willy!" Mrs. Russell said firmly.

He didn't look up from where he was petting the rabbit Timmy held.

Mrs. Russell turned back to Catherine. "How dare you bring him here without telling me."

Catherine stiffened. "You're mistaken. Willy arrived alone. You're lucky Timmy found him before he wandered somewhere else."

Mrs. Russell pressed her lips in a narrow line, then turned back to her son. "Willy, it's time to leave."

"He's teaching me about bunnies," Willy said, a whine in his voice.

"This is Timmy," Catherine said to the boy. "And I'm Miss Braun, a teacher at school. Perhaps you'll be in my grade someday."

"Willy—" Mrs. Russell began.

"Mum, no!" Willy cried, stepping closer to the cages.

"I don't mind showing him the rabbits," Timmy said.

"Only for a minute," Mrs. Russell said with a heavy sigh.

She didn't meet Catherine's eyes, but Catherine wasn't about to leave the woman alone with her brother. She didn't know what Mrs. Russell knew about her husband's collaboration, but she wasn't a very pleasant person.

~oOo~

Helen and Betty arrived after dinner, exchanged pleasantries with Catherine's family, and then the three young women retreated to the garden. Catherine chatted about school, while Helen and Betty frowned at her and barely kept up their part of the conversation. Betty smoked.

"What is going on?" Helen finally whispered, still smiling.

Betty folded her arms across her chest. "I can't believe you needed us so quickly to talk about school."

"No, I didn't, but I wanted to make sure no one followed us out here." Catherine took a deep breath, and then explained what had happened with Corporal Pollock, and how she'd found the note.

"What did the note say?" Helen asked eagerly.

Catherine looked at Betty. "It's about a German weapon. Captain Lunenborg wrote it."

Helen frowned. "Mr. Russell knows the captain?"

"I saw them speaking together at a party," Betty said slowly.

Catherine stared at her. "Why didn't you tell us?"

"I didn't think much of it, except that it was more proof to me that Mr. Russell is a traitor."

"I don't know what good it is to have proof," Helen said bitterly.

"It depends on the proof," Catherine said. "Apparently, Mr. Russell is altering weapon schematics for Captain Lunenborg."

"He's helping Germans with weapon research—from Guernsey Island?" Helen asked with confusion. "Why wouldn't they take him to Germany? Unless they have some kind of laboratory in the underground rooms they're creating."

"Maybe because it's not meant for the Germans?" Betty asked. She took the note and examined it. "The Germans are smuggling it to someone in the British government."

Catherine frowned. "Mr. Russell altered a German weapon and they're deliberately giving it to their enemy?" Then she gasped. "Oh!"

Betty nodded grimly. "It sounds like the military is supposed to believe they're stolen plans for a new German weapon."

"They'll work to develop it quickly for our side," Helen said, wide-eyed, "but it won't work correctly."

"And men will die," Catherine whispered, the cruelty and horror almost too much for her mind to contemplate.

"Someone in the British government is allowing this to happen," Betty pointed out, flicking cigarette ash to the side. "He's an accomplice, not someone who thinks he's helping Britain win the war."

There was a long moment of shocked silence.

Catherine felt her chest squeeze. "I can't believe we're right about this."

"Why not?" Betty asked. "The Germans are doing everything they can to win. And if they don't do something big, now that the Americans have joined the effort, it could be too late."

Catherine held out the paper. "Jack needs to see this."

"He does." Helen took the paper, folded it, and put it into the pocket of her trousers.

They all looked at each other, and in that sober moment, a spark of triumph moved between them with just a glance. Catherine had never felt such a communion of purpose, of understanding, outside of her family. The three of them had set out to find some way to help the British cause—and perhaps succeeded.

"Jack has to get this news off the island," Betty said.

And Catherine's excitement faded at the reality of the situation. "Soldiers could die if he can't get away."

"*If* we're reading this correctly," Helen pointed out. "But regardless, yes, he needs to leave. And he'll forget about being angry with me."

Betty eyed her curiously. "Why is he angry?"

"He's upset with me because I delivered the newsleaf last night."

"What?" Catherine said.

Just then, Lieutenant Schafer stepped through the door to light a cigarette. Though Sergeant Doepgen joined him, the lieutenant made no pretense of ignoring them. He watched them and smoked, as if they were as interesting as a radio program or newspaper while he enjoyed his cigarette. Sergeant Doepgen kept up a conversation they couldn't make out, and the lieutenant answered occasionally.

"Just keep talking," Catherine said. "Since we can't hear them, they can't hear us." This was the first she'd seen the sergeant since his crazy request for help, and she felt even more flustered than normal.

"Look at you," Betty said, "unafraid of the Germans."

Catherine blushed. "Oh, that's not true. I'm trembling inside. But Helen, why did you deliver the newsleaf?"

As Helen told them the story, including the scary part where Jack grabbed her from behind, Catherine couldn't help noticing that Lieutenant Schafer was watching Helen. Though she kept her voice down, Helen spoke with a liveliness that she didn't often display, especially not in front of a German officer.

"I was glad to accomplish something for the war effort,

because my hospital spying has failed miserably," Helen continued.

Catherine watched Helen's demeanor change before their eyes, her gaze dropping, her fingers twisting together as if they were restless spiders. Something had happened.

Helen continued, "All I found out was that my first patient was injured as they constructed an underground hospital."

"That's all you found out?" Catherine asked, leaning toward her. "Why don't I believe you?"

And to her surprise, Helen quietly began to cry.

Catherine wanted to enfold her in a comforting embrace, but didn't want to alert the German officers. "What's wrong? Please tell us."

"Lieutenant Beering saw me discussing him with another German patient. Then he—he tried to kill himself b-because of me!"

Betty slipped her a handkerchief, and Helen accepted it, trying to hide that she was dabbing her eyes.

"Surely not because of you," Catherine said gently. "Hasn't he been worried about his injury?"

"No, I mean yes, but no, it was definitely because of me. He admitted it. He was saving up pills in case the pain got too bad. I reassured him I was only trying to help him recover by talking to his friend about him—what a lie," she added, her voice harsh with bitterness.

"This is war," Betty said impassively.

"I know that!" Helen glanced at the German officers and lowered her voice. "I keep telling myself I'm doing what I have to—he and his fellow soldiers are trying to kill our men, after all. And he accepted my excuse. But...but I'm surprised how sad and guilty I feel. It's been hard to let it go."

"You're a good person," Catherine said. "Of course you feel bad. But he didn't die. And is he feeling better about it? Did he believe your reasons?"

"I think so."

"Then let it go," Betty said. "You can't change it now and you just have to live with the knowledge that you did what you had to."

Catherine studied Betty's emotionless face and knew she wasn't only talking about Helen.

Helen took a deep breath and let it out. "Back to the reason I interrogated the lieutenant. Why would they need an underground hospital?"

"The island would be a logical place to bring wounded soldiers if they're planning to invade Britain," Betty said.

Catherine studied her. "But the Blitz didn't succeed. The news reports say they've changed their mind about an invasion strategy."

"They haven't." Betty pulled another paper from her pocket. "I found this in Franz's things. My German skills are too rudimentary, but I know the word 'invasion.' Am I right, Catherine?"

Catherine held the paper with trembling hands. "There's not much detail, other than munitions orders necessary for the coming invasion."

They were all silent, imagining an invasion and the people who'd be killed.

"This story is probably not news to the army," Betty said. "It's been Hitler's goal to invade."

"But everyone thought he'd changed his plans," Helen said.

"I'm sure they've been preparing, regardless," Betty continued. "Catherine's news is much more important."

"*All* that we've uncovered is important," Catherine insisted.

"It'll have to be, because I probably can't get more." Helen sighed. "My German patients now turn their heads away when I walk in. Word has gotten around that I ask too many questions."

Catherine touched her arm. "I'm sorry, Helen. Do try to be careful."

"I saw *him* there, too, Lieutenant Schafer." Helen glanced at him. "He was visiting Lieutenant Beering, my patient who tried to—to—" She gave a heavy sigh.

The German soldier puffed his cigarette and continued to watch them.

"Why won't they go inside?" Betty asked, her voice laced with frustration.

Helen took a deep breath. "Maybe Lieutenant Beering said something to him about me."

"Let's not assume the worst," Betty said. "He tried to kill himself because he thought you might reveal something he said. Why would he risk that himself? I think it's time for us to go home. We've done all we could. It's up to Jack now."

"Take your invasion document back to Captain Lunenborg," Helen said. "He'll miss it, and there's nothing in it the British absolutely need."

Betty hesitated.

"Take it," Catherine said, holding out the paper. "You're already in too much danger."

Betty took it with reluctance, then eyed Catherine. "You seem skittish."

Catherine sighed, and sank back on the bench, crossing her arms over her chest as if she felt cold. "You know how Sergeant Doepgen has been visiting here a lot?"

Helen put a hand to her mouth, eyes wide as if anticipating the worst.

Catherine shook her head. "It's not what you think. I finally got up the nerve to tell him I wouldn't date him, and he said that wasn't what he wanted. He—he wants to defect and wants me to help hide him."

Both women gaped at her, and Catherine shot a guilty glance at the two German soldiers, but they were talking and smoking, for once ignoring them.

"What did you tell him?" Betty asked.

"I was too flustered to tell him anything!"

"Good," Betty said flatly. "You cannot risk yourself or your family for the enemy."

"We could ask Jack's opinion..." Helen began.

Catherine stiffened. "No. He has enough to deal with. I've been giving this much thought, and I agree with Betty. I can't risk my family."

"Do you think he'll hurt you?" Helen asked.

"No." She believed that without reservation. They had so much in common that in another place and time, they might have...but she stopped her thoughts from wandering in a dangerous direction. Regardless of how sympathetic he might seem, he was her enemy.

After Helen and Betty left and the Germans went inside, Catherine stayed on the bench as dusk settled like a blanket around her. Her mind was racing, full of too many worries, and she needed the peace of her garden to calm her.

And as if she'd known what would happen, Sergeant Doepgen approached her as he was leaving. Catherine started to rise, but he put up both hands.

"I don't wish to disturb you, *Fraulein* Braun, but I wanted to know—"

In a rush, she interrupted. "I can't help you. I cannot risk my family, and that's what would happen if I was discovered."

His shoulders sagged a bit, but he didn't look angry. "I'm almost relieved. I had begun to worry about the same thing. How could I live with myself if I caused you harm?"

Catherine didn't know what to say as a strange tension hummed between them.

He twisted his cap in his hands. "I think...I wanted to stay because when I look at you, I see a future I haven't let myself imagine since this blasted war started. At night I dream there is no war and I meet you again."

She was hot with embarrassment tinged with guilt. "Don't speak of such things."

He looked off into the dark distance. "I won't, ever again."

"What—what will you do?"

"I will go where I'm assigned, and be thankful that I'm a medic, where killing people is not required." Bitterness tinged his voice.

"You could give yourself up once you're off the island. The Allies will take you in."

He nodded, but she didn't think he was listening.

"Good night, *fraulein*."

He turned and started walking away before she even answered.

"Good night," she whispered.

34

HELEN

At dusk, when Helen hopped off her bicycle and headed for the garage, a low fog was creeping up over the cliffs, its tendrils curling around trees as it approached the house. There were no lights on in the windows—no surprise, since Jack was good at pretending he wasn't there.

She hurried inside, tossed her sweater onto a chair, and turned on a lamp. "Jack?"

He appeared from the shadows of the hallway, and she jumped with fright.

Frowning, he said, "What is it? What's wrong?"

"Nothing's wrong. In fact, everything is finally right. Betty found a letter in Captain Lunenborg's briefcase about the munitions for an invasion. Everything makes sense now—no wonder they're building an underground hospital."

"Wait, slow down."

Helen couldn't. "We didn't let Betty keep the paper, like you told us, but there really wasn't anything on it more important than the fact that an invasion might still happen. And there's more! Something so important that we have to get it off the island."

Jack watched her warily. "You sound so shaky that I'm concerned. Sit down, have some tea."

"No, you have to listen." But she did sit down after pulling the paper out of her pocket. She spread it on the table, smoothing the wrinkles out. "Read this, and tell me if we're crazy thinking that the Germans are using Mr. Russell to alter the schematics for a new weapon."

He bent his head to read. She watched his face, unable to hide her fascination with the furrowed lines of his brow, the way his hair swooped over it, the intelligence lighting his eyes.

She was giving something that would make him leave the island, make him leave *her*. As the implications of that dawned on her, he looked up and met her gaze, and they stared at each other for a long time.

"You have to go," she whispered.

He nodded. "I stole a boat a while back and have been slowly siphoning enough gas for the trip."

Her mouth dropped open. "You didn't tell me?"

"I didn't want to get your hopes up. But now you've gotten *my* hopes up. This is the final information I needed, and you and your friends helped me get it."

Her lips trembled, so she pressed them together. He reached across the table for her hand.

And then they heard an engine coming down the road.

Helen tried to ignore it and focus on this connection with Jack, who'd soon be gone.

But his focus was no longer on her.

She suddenly remembered that none of her neighbors had cars anymore.

The engine stopped near her house.

They both rose, and when she would have shut off the

lamp, Jack held her arm and spoke into her ear. "That would be suspicious."

She shivered. "Take the radio and go hide."

"I'm not hiding."

"Jack!"

Someone knocked on the kitchen door. The Germans always came to the front, hoping neighbors would see and be intimidated.

"I'll be nearby if you need me," Jack said. "Just say my name."

"I won't."

"Do it if you need to."

As the door rattled under a louder knock, Jack disappeared back into the hallway shadows.

Helen made sure to stomp hard as she approached the door, as if she'd come from a different part of the house. Swallowing, she called, "Yes? Who is it?"

"Please open the door," said a man's German-accented voice. "I've broken down on the road and need to use your telephone."

Could it be as easy as that?

But his voice was familiar, and fear crept higher up the back of her throat.

The knob turned and the door swung open. She'd been so anxious to get to Jack that she hadn't locked it. Not that that would have stopped—

Lieutenant Schafer.

He stepped up into her doorway and smiled at her. "*Fraulein* Abernathy, aren't you going to invite me in?"

He did not need to use the phone; he'd come here deliberately, and he slurred his words as if drunk.

She tried to shut the door on him, but he held it open.

Don't come out, Jack, she thought. *If he sees you, it will ruin our plans.*

"Lieutenant Schafer, this is not a good time."

He grinned, a sight she'd never seen and hoped never to see again. He took a step into her kitchen, and she was forced to back up or be too close to him. She skirted a chair and put it between them.

"I just wanted to pay you a compliment, *fraulein*. We have a mutual friend."

"I don't know who you could mean."

"Lieutenant Beering, of course. Your patient."

"I didn't know you knew each other," she lied.

"We do." Schafer leaned against the back of another chair, gripping the backrest.

His knuckles were broad and scarred. How had she never noticed that?

"Beering says you treated him kindly," Lieutenant Schafer continued.

That surprised Helen, but it was a fleeting thought. "A nurse is always kind to patients. It's our duty."

"Other nurses were cold to him."

"Perhaps they're frightened."

"You weren't frightened."

She was frightened now, and it was growing worse the longer he lingered, drunkenly talking nonsense, avoiding his true purpose. She was afraid for herself, but mostly afraid for Jack.

"I envy Beering," Schafer said, stepping closer to the chair between them. "He has a wife waiting for him at home who writes him long letters, who brightens his day. I have no one."

His gaze traveled down her blouse.

She crossed her arms over her chest. "Soon this war will be over. You'll meet a nice girl and get married."

He cocked his head, his smile almost boyish with drunken silliness. "But that doesn't help me now. I need a kiss, and then I'll be happy."

"You don't need a kiss," she said, her voice shaky as she tried to sound brisk.

He grabbed the chair between them and tossed it aside. Helen didn't scream, only flung herself toward the kitchen cupboard, looking for something to hit him with, if necessary.

Schafer laughed as he chased her. "You're such a tease."

She brandished a wooden spoon at him. "Lieutenant Schafer, I insist you leave. I will not be kissing you."

He took the spoon out of her hand. "Then we can skip the kissing."

Fear consumed her, mixed with hatred at what he and his people had done. Now he thought he could rape her without consequence? Was this how Betty felt, day after day, angry and helpless, fending off a German officer?

He leaned his body against her, pressing her hard against the cupboard. She reached blindly behind her, grasping at anything. Kissing her neck, he breathed alcohol fumes on her. She felt light-headed, appalled, so afraid—

And then she grasped a handle, brought it around, and slammed the hammer into the side of his skull.

He dropped hard to the floor and didn't move.

The sudden silence was unnerving as she gaped at him.

Jack burst into the room, stared wide-eyed at Schafer, then back up at her. "He looks dead."

Her legs suddenly weak, she sank into the chair she'd just used as a shield and dropped the hammer on the floor.

"Oh, my God. He's not dead, just unconscious. He'll wake up, and I'll be arrested."

"You're not going to pass out, are you?"

She shot him a look. "I just defended myself against a German. I don't faint."

He bent over Schafer, turning his head to see where she'd struck, and then feeling for a pulse at his neck. "No, he's dead. He has a deep indent in his temple. Good aim."

It was as if she'd been struck herself, so shocked she burst into tears.

Jack pulled her out of the chair and held her.

"What have I done?" she whispered shakily against his chest. "Someone might know he came here. They'll come searching, they'll find you—"

"I'm not going to be found out, and neither are you," he said with easy confidence. "I'll take Schafer out of here. No one will know."

"It's a body, not so easily gotten rid of. We don't even have a car."

"We have *his* car."

"We'll have to dig a grave—people will notice fresh earth."

"We won't dig a grave. We have the sea."

Helen lifted her wet face from his shoulder and stared up at him. He was Jack the soldier, Jack the spy, so full of confidence and ready plans. She wanted to believe him.

"If they find him at the base of my cliff—"

"We'll take him closer to town and leave his car near the shore. It's near full dark now; we have all night to accomplish this." He took her shoulders in his hands and gazed into her eyes. "We'll do this, Helen, and no one will find out. You were so brave. I need you to be brave a little longer."

She frowned. "I'm not falling apart." She pushed against him, and he let her go.

And then she saw the body again and froze. She'd killed someone, though she'd sworn only to heal.

But he'd been her enemy, a German, an invader who meant to rape her. She wasn't going to feel guilty.

Then why was guilt one of the emotions that seemed to be tearing her apart? Her chest ached, her throat felt tight, her eyes hurt from suppressing more tears.

"Do you have an old blanket to wrap him up in?" Jack asked.

Helen flinched, but whispered, "I'll get it."

Together they wrapped him up, dragged him to his car, and bent him to fit in the boot. She felt ill touching him, remembering his hands on her and what he intended to do.

Jack closed the boot. "We can't leave yet. We have to wait until well after midnight. My knowledge of the timing of the patrols is finally paying off. And here I thought it was useless information." He chuckled.

Helen stared at him, her eyes wide.

Jack's smile faded. "You get used to this, you know," he said quietly. "You tell yourself you won't, that you don't want to be a killer, but in war, you have to think of them as the enemy, not just another bloke you might have had a beer with when you visited Europe."

She shuddered and hugged herself, staring at the car. "We thought he was shy and awkward when he first moved into the Brauns', almost...nice. But this war changed him."

"He thought of you all as his enemy, and not as people anymore. He thought of you as the spoils. It infects some men worse than others."

Jack drove the car to the side of the house, out of sight of headlights that might come down the road, while she carefully washed the hammer and put it with her father's tools in the basement. To think, she'd only brought it up to pound a loose nail.

Then they sat in the kitchen. She twisted her hands together, staring into the distance.

"Maybe you should read a book," Jack suggested.

She shot him a look in disbelief.

He shrugged. "Shall we turn on the radio?"

They listened to the BBC through the last news program at midnight, then sat in the dark for long minutes.

"You still need to leave the island," she said firmly. "I'll be fine."

Though she couldn't see him well in the shadowy darkness, she could practically feel his uncertainty.

"Jack, this is war. Your information is needed. I have my friends—I'll be fine."

"My brain knows that, but..." He trailed off.

What had he meant to say?

A tense hour later, Jack tried to make her stay behind, but she refused. She would see this through to the end.

She didn't even understand her own dazed emotions as she sat in the car next to Jack. There was a body in the boot, like something out of the mystery novels she loved. Could she ever read a mystery novel again? she thought, feeling a little hysterical.

"There are mines on the beaches," she said quietly.

"I know. We won't go to a beach."

The fog had retreated. They drove to a low cliff just outside of town. Why hadn't she thought of that? But her brain kept flitting wildly from thought to thought, and overrunning it all was a terrible fear that they'd be caught, jeopardizing Jack's chance of leaving the island with news of the altered German weapon.

"We have to hurry," he said, as he shut off the engine and left the key in the ignition. "They sometimes patrol the island by boat."

They met at the boot, and he opened it up. She tried to help with the body, but only he had the strength to reach inside and lift.

"Dead weight," he grunted, pulling the blanket from under Schafer's body and handing it to her.

"That's not funny!"

"But it's true. Do you have the torch?"

She turned it on and aimed its weak beam out in front of them. The moon was a sliver in the sky, and the waves crashed below them, as if determined to take bites out of the rocky coast.

Jack trudged slowly to the edge of the cliff, where grassy rock gave way.

"Don't get too close," she whispered, her fear rising again. "The edge could crumble."

"You think"—he huffed—"I haven't been here before?"

He gave a sudden heave, and the body hit the edge of the cliff, rolled once, and was gone.

Helen felt frozen staring out to the dark channel, where the moon touched the tips of waves, and the wind seemed determined to push her back.

Jack caught her arm, and she flinched.

"Let's go," he said. "We have a couple mile walk in the dark."

For a while they tried to stay off the road, in case someone drove past. They were breaking curfew. But the farther they got from Saint Peter Port, the more they risked the easier path of the road, which they could see beneath the star-filled sky without needing to waste the torch batteries.

When they turned down her own lane, the tension eased a bit in her chest. She began to think they might truly get away with murder.

Murder.

She was so focused on the awfulness of that word that she didn't hear Jack's whisper, didn't know anything was wrong until he grabbed her arm and pulled her off the road and straight through shrubbery which tore at her clothing and scratched her arms.

Her breathing came fast, making her light-headed with fear. They were going to be caught. Jack's mission would be a failure, and she'd lose everything.

Then she heard whistling, and realized someone was strolling unconcerned down the road toward them. Helen soon recognized him, that blackmailing Nazi who demanded things from their neighbor to keep silent about an illegal radio.

She sank down and put her hand over her mouth to keep from laughing hysterically. She knew Jack was staring at her, but she couldn't stop. Her stomach heaved with silent laughter; tears streamed down her face.

Minutes later, when she'd almost gotten herself under control, Jack irritably demanded in a low voice, "What is it?"

And she was snickering again. "He...he's blackmailing my neighbors over a radio, when...when...he could be blackmailing me for m—murder."

Jack didn't laugh, and she knew it wasn't funny, but something inside her felt wild with emotion, so unlike herself.

"Can you walk?" he finally asked.

She gulped and nodded, letting him lead her back to her little cottage. They went in the back door, and she bolted it and leaned heavily against it. It seemed as if no one had followed them.

She turned away from the door and found Jack watching her in the shadows.

"Will you be all right?" he asked quietly. "We could talk, if you'd like."

"You already told me I'll get used to murdering people." She tried for lightheartedness, but wasn't managing it.

He winced. "You know I didn't mean *you*. I meant soldiers in wartime who have to kill over and over again."

"I don't want to do that," she whispered, then fiercely met his gaze. "But I will if I have to."

"I know. I thought I was coming to rescue you tonight, and when I saw him on the floor and you wielding that hammer..." He trailed off, shaking his head.

"You didn't think I had it in me," she said.

"That's not true. I knew you were more than capable." He took her face in his hands. "My brave Helen."

When he leaned down to kiss her gently, she gave a long sigh and leaned into his chest. He made her feel so safe, but it was over now. He was leaving her.

He broke the kiss, only to put his lips against her forehead as he murmured, "I was going to leave a note without saying good-bye."

"You still can."

He chuckled. "I was worried I wouldn't be able to leave you."

"I want you to go. I want everything my friends and I have done to be worth something."

He nodded and stepped away, and it was as if her heart went, too.

He stooped to pick something off the floor. "You dropped

this," he said, holding up his hand where her flower brooch gleamed in the low light.

She reached for it and held it tightly in her fist, closing her eyes in relief.

"You always wear it," Jack said.

She nodded. "It was my mother's. It helps me remember them during these dark times. To think I almost misplaced it because of...that man."

He wrapped his hands around hers. "You know you'll always have your memories, regardless of what happens to this brooch."

She tried to smile. "How like a man to say that. I know you're trying to make me feel better. And I promise I'll get there." She took a deep breath. "When will you leave?"

He let her go. "Right now. I have to change."

He went upstairs, and she looked around at her cottage that she'd once thought of as cozy and private. And then Jack had returned, bringing with him the war, and danger, and the chance to be of use. That was going away along with him. Who knew if she'd ever see him again?

She marched up the stairs without even making a conscious decision. Opening the door to his room, she found him wearing only trousers, barefoot. He stared at her in surprise, and then his eyes widened even more as she began to unbutton her blouse.

"Helen." He spoke her name hoarsely.

"I don't want my last memories of you to be of *him*." She gestured with her chin toward the window.

When he didn't say anything, just watched her with hooded eyes, she let her blouse drop to the floor. She didn't stop until she was as naked above the waist as he was. And then she put her arms around his neck and kissed him.

~oOo~

Later, Helen came awake from a doze and found Jack sitting on the edge of the bed, the faint moon coming through the window to bathe the silhouette of his face, set and determined.

"Now?" she whispered, coming up on one elbow to kiss his back.

"Now." He sounded impassive but tired.

She put her arms around him from behind, but could think of nothing to say that would make either of them feel better.

"I'll do my best to return our information to Britain."

"I know you will. You've spent your life around boats—a little one won't defeat you."

He gave a soft snort and looked over his shoulder at her. "I want you and Catherine and Betty to know that every sacrifice you've all made will have been worth it."

She leaned her cheek against his shoulder blade, closing her eyes, inhaling the scent of him.

"This war will go on a long time," he said, "and I don't know what will happen. I won't make any promises to you that I cannot keep."

She opened her eyes. "If I don't hear from you, I'll know."

"I don't want you to wait for me, to give up any sort of life on a chance that might never happen."

"I won't." She heard herself sounding distant, certain, and thought that even Betty would be impressed with her acting ability.

He briefly leaned his head back against hers, then rose to his feet. She watched him pull on his clothes.

At last he stood beside the bed. "Good-bye, Helen.

Promise me you'll take no more chances. What good would it do without me here to pass on whatever you uncover?"

She sat up against the headboard, pulling the sheet up beneath her arms. "You know I can't promise that. I don't know what will happen."

"Promise to stop trying to find out more German secrets?"

"I'll try, and *that* I can promise."

In the shadows, she saw his mouth quirk in a half smile. He leaned down, kissed her lips swiftly, and was gone.

I love you, she thought.

35

CATHERINE

E arly in the morning, Catherine was out in the yard, feeding the rabbits. Her mind was distracted, unsettled, darting in a thousand directions at once. It was hard to believe that something so crucial to the war could be happening on Guernsey. What was Jack doing with the information? Would he even tell them his plan?

And then there was Lieutenant Schafer. He hadn't returned last night, which was rare for him. He hadn't even shown up for duty, according to a fellow officer who'd come looking for him.

She was so focused on her thoughts she didn't hear the approaching footsteps.

"Miss Braun, I'm glad to find you alone."

She jumped, dropping seeds all over the ground. Mr. Russell simply smiled.

"What are you doing here?" she demanded as quietly as she could, trying to project displeasure instead of fear.

"I was here last night, waiting for you to be alone."

Her mouth suddenly went dry. "You didn't approach me."

"That's because I happened to overhear some distressing news while I waited. Apparently, you and your friends have been keeping the whereabouts of a spy hidden from the authorities." He smiled at her, obviously pleased with himself.

Catherine felt the blood drain from her face, but she wasn't going to give him the satisfaction of swooning.

"It seems I don't have to threaten your father's employment," he continued, "I simply have to threaten *you*."

"I don't know what you're talking about." She sounded weak even to her own ears.

His mustache was like a hairy umbrella over his smile. "Anyone who harbors a spy will be arrested."

"If you wanted to have me arrested, you would have done so already. What do you want?"

His smile vanished as he spoke coldly. "My letter. You stole it from me, and I want it back. If you don't give it to me, I'll tell the authorities what I know."

Once he had the letter, he'd turn her in regardless—she knew that. But she didn't know what to do, or how much he'd actually heard.

"I don't have the letter," she said between gritted teeth.

He frowned. "You're lying."

"I'm not." So he hadn't heard the entire conversation. "Why would I keep it here, risking my family, especially since you're right next door?"

He stepped toward her menacingly. "If you don't give it to me, I'll have you and the spy arrested—maybe even your whole family sent away."

Fear seemed to freeze her into immobility, but she managed to keep talking, keep thinking. "Then you'll never have the letter, will you? The extent of your collaboration will be exposed."

He clenched his jaw.

"Why are you helping them?" she demanded.

"The same reason you are—to survive!"

She felt like she'd been slapped. "I am not helping them!"

"You teach German in their schools, you translate for them, your father works at their airport."

"Those are *our* schools, *our* airport, and we need our work to feed our families. But I certainly didn't *volunteer* to help by hurting fellow islanders!" She looked back over her shoulder at the house as she realized her voice was rising. No one came out.

"I'm protecting my family, too," he insisted.

Did he think there wasn't a difference, or did he just not want to see it? British soldiers—maybe even her brother, if he'd been freed—could die because of what Mr. Russell was doing. But she didn't want Mr. Russell to know they might have figured out his part in this treason. It could make him even more desperate and dangerous.

She didn't know what Jack's plan was, but somehow, she had to stall this man.

"When will you have the note?" he demanded, as if it was a foregone conclusion she'd submit.

She pretended it was. "I don't know exactly where it is."

"Find out," he ordered. "I want it back by tonight, or I'll reveal what I know about the spy."

"And if you do that, I'll reveal what I know about your plans."

"And then your families—yours and your friends'—will be arrested. Mine won't."

"Not right now, anyway."

But he was right. No matter what she did, her family was going to suffer. Unless Jack could help them find a way to defeat this man. "We can keep threatening each other, or you can go away and let me try to get the letter back."

"Be at the gazebo behind my house tonight at midnight. You'd better have that letter or your family will suffer the consequences."

Catherine watched him stride away with a confident swagger, while her mind was awash in confusion and fear. She went back inside, and everything seemed so normal for a Saturday morning—her father reading the newspaper, her mother cooking at the oven.

"Where's Timmy?" Catherine asked, afraid for any of her family to be out of her sight.

"He's down the street at John's," her mother said, not looking up.

"I'm going to run to Betty's," Catherine said.

"Will you be back by lunch?"

"I don't know. Don't save anything for me. I'll be fine."

There was so little food to go around that her mother didn't protest. Catherine found her handbag in the front hall, grabbed a sweater, and opened the door in time to see a car pull up out front, disgorging three German officers. Fear stabbed through her. As they marched up the walkway toward her, she took several steps back, knowing it was useless to shut the door.

Had Mr. Russell already turned her in? But it had barely been five minutes since they'd spoken, and he knew if he revealed Jack, she and her friends would reveal his treason.

Unless they were all being rounded up before they could say anything. She hadn't thought her fear could ratchet any higher, but she'd been wrong.

"*Fraulein* Braun?" The man swept his hat off his blond head.

"Y-yes? What do you want?"

"We are here to question your family about Lieutenant Schafer."

That's why this German seemed so familiar; he'd visited the lieutenant before. And then his words truly penetrated.

"Lieutenant Schafer isn't here," she said slowly. "He didn't return last night."

"That's because he was found dead this morning at the foot of a cliff outside town."

She drew in a breath with a gasp.

"Who is here?" he asked.

"My parents," she said weakly. Did she sound guilty? She felt very guilty and nervous all the time, just not for this! She cleared her throat and straightened her shoulders. "Please be seated in the parlor. I'll bring them to you."

"We'll accompany you."

Did he think she and her parents would run out of the back door to escape? Or did they think her family had something to do with Lieutenant Schafer's death?

She turned to lead the way, but her parents were already coming through the kitchen doorway, her father's expression stern, her mother's worried.

"I'm Mr. Braun. What is going on?"

The German gave a brief nod. "I'm Captain Müller. Please be seated in your parlor. I have questions for you."

When Dad gave Catherine a worried look, she said, "They've found Lieutenant Schafer dead at the base of a cliff."

Mum clutched Dad's arm and, grim-faced, he led her to a chair in the parlor, while Catherine sat beside her father on the sofa. Two German soldiers stationed themselves near the hall, staring straight ahead.

Captain Müller loomed over her family, hands linked

behind his back, and spoke sternly. "When did you last see Lieutenant Schafer?"

"Yesterday evening after dinner," Dad said. "He drove away with his friend, Sergeant Doepgen."

Had something happened to Sergeant Doepgen, too? Surely a second body would have been mentioned. She didn't want to care, but she did. Perhaps it was just the longing for a memory of a time when life had seemed full to bursting with promise.

"Did they say where they were going?" Captain Müller asked.

"No, he never does," Dad said.

The captain turned to face Mum. "Did Lieutenant Schafer seem upset?"

Her eyes were stark with tears. "I—I don't know. He doesn't talk to us unless he's angry."

"Then why are you acting nervous?"

A tear slipped down her mother's cheek, and Catherine gripped the sides of her skirt in anger.

"Why shouldn't she be nervous?" Dad demanded. "You are questioning us about a death, and we don't know why. What happened?"

"I will ask the questions," the captain snapped.

The front door suddenly slammed open. "Hey, Mum—"

Timmy ran into the hall and then froze as two German soldiers whirled toward him, raising their guns.

Mum gasped out a cry, half-rising from her chair.

"It's just the boy," Captain Müller said.

The two soldiers lowered their weapons. Timmy still hadn't moved.

"Come in here, boy," Captain Müller said. "Your name?"

Timmy came into the room, and Dad pulled him onto the sofa next to Catherine.

"Timmy," her brother said.

He sounded calm enough, and Catherine realized with a pang that living under German rule would shape his childhood, his behaviors, and his memories forever.

"Did you see Lieutenant Schafer leave last night?"

Timmy glanced with confusion from Mum to Dad. "Sure."

"What time was it?"

"I don't have a watch, but it was just before dark. I only saw him because I was coming back from my friend's. I have to be home before dark."

The captain turned back to Catherine. "What was Schafer doing before he left?"

She tried to speak calmly. "He took a plate of food to his room to eat, and then both men came outside to smoke."

"'Came outside.' You do not say 'went outside.' You were already there?"

She swallowed and nodded. "My friends were visiting, and we sat in the garden to talk."

"Did you talk to Lieutenant Schafer?"

"No."

"Did your friends?"

"None of us did."

"I will need their names."

Catherine hesitated, wishing there was a way to keep them out of this. But everyone was staring at her. "Helen Abernathy and Betty Markham. But they left before Lieutenant Schafer did." She was asked to explain where they lived and worked, and her mind spun frantically as she prayed that she could warn them, and that their families would be left alone.

Dad cleared his throat. "The lieutenant drove away, and you only found him dead this morning."

"Dead!" Timmy said loudly.

Catherine gave him a quick shake of her head.

"Did he drive off the cliff?" Dad asked.

Captain Müller hesitated, as if he wouldn't answer, then said, "His car was left on the cliff."

Dad nodded. "So he fell or jumped."

"Or was pushed," the captain countered angrily.

"Or was pushed," Dad echoed. "Captain, I assume you're going to question Sergeant Doepgen, the last person with him. You can ask any of our neighbors who might have seen him drive away."

Oh God, Catherine thought, what would Mr. Russell say if questioned? She could only hope that fear of the letter falling into the wrong hands would keep him silent.

At last the captain left, his expression grim and unsatisfied, and his men followed after retrieving the lieutenant's suitcase and all of his things. The Brauns stared at each other for a frozen moment, then Mum covered her face, her shoulders shaking. Dad leaned toward her and put a hand on her back.

"Dead," Timmy echoed in wonder. "We won't miss him. I wonder what happened?" he asked Catherine. "Maybe his friend was drunk and pushed him off the cliff."

"He wouldn't do that," Catherine said too quickly.

Both her parents stared at her.

She jumped to her feet. "I have to warn Helen and Betty."

She raced for the telephone in the hallway, but when she dialed, Helen didn't answer. Betty was at home but on her way to the restaurant.

"Might I come over afterward?" Catherine asked, then lowered her voice. "Can you make sure your mother isn't there?"

Betty agreed without even asking why.

36

BETTY

Betty opened the door to her stairway and found Catherine on the top step, handbag clutched in both hands, her face white with strain.

"Is your mother gone?" Catherine asked, before Betty could even greet her.

"She's visiting our neighbor. She never stays more than an hour, though."

"I hope I won't need that much time." Catherine stepped inside and began to pace.

Betty folded her arms across her chest, bemused. "What's wrong?"

Catherine shot her a look. "As if *everything* isn't wrong?" Her expression twisted. "I'm sorry—that was so unnecessary. Lieutenant Schafer is dead, and the Germans might interview you, since we're some of the last people to see him alive." Catherine collapsed into a chair and put her face in her hands.

Betty sank slowly onto the sofa and reached for her cigarette. "This is unexpected. Does Helen know?"

"I couldn't reach her at home, and I didn't want to try at

the hospital. There's too much to say and no privacy." Words spilled out of her about everything that had happened with the Germans that morning.

"Sounds like he was either too close to the edge—"

"Maybe drunk," Catherine interrupted.

"—or he killed himself."

"You don't think someone killed him? The Germans hinted as much—as if we'd risk everything to kill him for no reason! And then there's Sergeant Doepgen, who drove off with him."

"Do you think your old beau is a murderer?"

"He's not my old beau, but...no."

Betty shrugged. "I guess I don't really care either way. And if the Germans interview me, I'll tell the truth about what I saw. Helen will, too. There's no reason to worry."

"Yes, there is," Catherine said bitterly. "Mr. Russell was eavesdropping on us last night. He heard almost everything."

Betty stiffened. "So he knows we have the letter."

"And he's going to turn in Jack—and us!—if I don't give it back to him at midnight tonight."

"You're full of news today," Betty said dryly. "Shall we go tell Helen and figure out what to do?"

Catherine sighed heavily. "You know how she feels about Jack. And he'll want to protect all of us by doing something foolish."

"That's his mission, after all."

They rode their bicycles to Helen's house and arrived before she did. While Catherine rested on a garden bench, Betty walked around to the back of the house, curious. It seemed very quiet, too quiet. Jack would see it was just them —why wasn't he coming out?

"Hello!"

Betty heard Catherine's voice and walked back around the house to see Helen riding down the lane, her blue nurse's skirt flapping behind her. She hopped off her bicycle and let it drop.

"What is it?" Helen asked, looking from Catherine to Betty.

Betty was wondering if Catherine would want her to explain, but Catherine took a deep breath and said, "Mr. Russell overheard us last night. He knows about Jack. He's demanding we give him the note back at midnight tonight, or he's telling the Germans we've been harboring a spy."

Helen briefly closed her eyes, her expression pained. Betty found herself tensing, though she didn't know why.

Helen sank down on the front stairs, looking out toward the channel glistening in the summer sunlight. "Both Jack and the letter are gone, somewhere out there." She gestured tiredly toward the blue waters of the channel.

"Gone?" Catherine echoed, her voice breaking.

Betty sat down beside Helen. "He didn't waste any time."

"He'd stolen a boat weeks ago and had been slowly accumulating enough gas. He knew how important the letter is."

"But—" Catherine began. She backed up a step, staring wide-eyed at the other two women. "What will we do? What will *Mr. Russell* do to us? To our families?"

"There's no one we can go to for help," Helen said weakly. "We'll just have to appeal to him somehow."

"No, we're not doing that," Betty said. "It's his word against ours. We're going to meet him tonight and deny it all —the note, Jack, everything."

Both women stared at her.

"We don't have a choice," Betty insisted. "Jack is gone, and his important work is going on. I feel such a sense of pride that we helped the war effort. Don't you?"

They both nodded. Catherine's eyes were damp with tears, but Helen was looking at the ground. Betty understood what Jack's absence meant to her, but Helen bravely wasn't mentioning it. Some things were more important.

Then Helen straightened, her expression resolute. "If Russell goes to the Germans, his own guilt will be evident, too. He lost the note, after all. Maybe he won't risk it. Maybe he'll just keep quiet and let the Germans think they're still safe. We know he cares about money and himself more than either country."

"Good point," Betty said, feeling the first stirrings of relief. "And the longer we can delay the Germans knowing anything about Jack, the more chance he has to make it to the mainland. It's only 70 miles."

They each looked at Catherine, who was trembling.

"You don't have to go tonight," Helen said quietly. "We'll meet him."

Catherine gave her a quick frown. "Not without me, you won't!"

Betty patted her shoulder, so impressed by how Catherine had conquered a fear that had once almost immobilized her. The fears weren't gone, but she was in control. "Let's not forget our other news about Schafer."

Betty couldn't miss the expression that came over Helen's face—terror. She paled so quickly that Betty thought Helen would actually faint.

Catherine took Helen's hand in hers and patted it. "What's wrong, dear? You don't look well."

"W-what about Schafer?" Helen whispered.

"The Germans came to my house this morning," Catherine began, "and said they found Schafer's body at the base of a cliff, his car at the top. They're talking to all of us who saw him last night. You were with us, so all you have to say is the truth..." Her voice trailed off.

Helen pulled her hand from Catherine's and briefly covered her face before taking a deep breath. Her face was blanched white, her eyes glistening. She pressed her lips in a firm line as if to stop them from trembling.

"Just tell us," Betty said quietly.

"He came here last night, drunk, and tried to attack me. I killed him." The last words were bleak and hopeless.

Catherine gasped. "Oh, Helen, oh no! You poor dear. Tell us what happened."

The story spilled out of Helen, hesitant at first, until her outrage overcame her fear. She finally finished with the tale of Jack leaving her for good, and the three of them sat on the steps, watching the sun slowly sink in the west. Betty thought there might be a bit more to Jack's final hours with Helen, but it wasn't any of her business.

"So I've broken my oath to heal." Helen spoke with tired resignation.

"You know it was self-defense," Betty said. "This is war."

"I know. But I still don't feel any better about it."

"You're safe and unharmed," Catherine murmured. "That is more important than any of it."

"But you said they're going to question us?" Helen asked.

Catherine shrugged. "All we need to do is tell the truth about him watching us in my garden."

"Do you think you'll be able to remain unemotional?" Betty asked.

Helen gave a faint smile. "So as not to make them suspicious? I hope so. Do you have any acting tips for me?"

"Only to believe in the truth of what you're telling them, and don't think about what happened later."

"You mean create a character who's innocent?" she asked with sarcasm.

"You aren't a murderer, Helen," Betty said. "You *are* innocent."

No one said anything for long moments.

"Should we just wait here until we have to meet Mr. Russell?" Catherine asked. "I don't think I could face my family. And someone might see me try to leave at such a late hour."

"Let's go to my flat," Betty said. "We should ride while there's still daylight. I'll get my gun and then it's an easy walk to your house."

37

HELEN

Helen felt incredibly awkward at Betty's flat. Mrs. Markham kept bringing tea as they played cards, and would have tried to feed them from her bare kitchen, except they kept insisting they were full. Helen couldn't stop staring at Betty, who had no real explanation for how she'd gotten a gun, and wouldn't be dissuaded from bringing it to protect them.

Captain Müller tracked them down and questioned them about Lieutenant Schafer's death, but Helen and Betty told the truth. He didn't seem happy to see them with Catherine, as if they'd all memorized one story, but he left them alone at last, his eyes narrowed with suspicion.

Just before midnight, long after Mrs. Markham had gone to bed, they started walking to Catherine's, only a few streets away. In the distance they heard the pop of an occasional weapon, but they'd grown used to that, as drunken soldiers sometimes shot into the air at this time of night.

The lights were still on in the Brauns' front parlor as they kept to the shadows and went into the garden.

Helen's mouth was dry. Every step across the dark

garden was a step closer to the man who held their future in his hands. Could he be reasoned with? There was no way of knowing.

She hadn't realized how much she'd relied on Jack until he was no longer there to help or protect them. She kept asking herself what he might have done in their place, but her mind was too frazzled to think of anything other than their impending confrontation—and Betty's gun.

Catherine led them across the back of the lawn and over the half-wall into the Russells' garden. The white wooden gazebo seemed to glow in the shadowy moonlight. Helen glanced at the house with apprehension, but there were no lights on in the back.

"Should we wait inside?" Betty whispered. "I feel pretty exposed, even in the dark. And we can't use a torch."

Suddenly they heard a low moan coming from inside the gazebo.

Betty leaned near the arched doorway. "I think there's someone lying on the floor."

Helen peeked over Betty's shoulder at what seemed like a pile of rags—until it moved. Catherine gasped. Betty stepped inside.

"Don't get too close," Helen urged. "It could be a trap."

The moan echoed again, and then a weak voice said, "Betty?"

It wasn't Mr. Russell. When Helen heard Betty fumble in her pockets, she tensed, but when she only clicked on her torch, they all stared in shock at Captain Lunenborg lying on the ground, his torso stained with blood.

Helen glanced swiftly at Betty's face which only showed shock. The light clicked off, and Helen could see nothing until her eyes adjusted to the gloom.

She heard Betty drop to her knees and say, "Franz, what happened?"

Captain Lunenborg cradled his stomach, and the darker shadow on his fingers was obviously blood. "Russell told me...you were involved," he wheezed between pained gasps. "I didn't...mean that to happen. He...bungled his assignment...lost the orders...I told him he was done, that I'd... report him. He wouldn't be paid. He...had a gun. I tried to get mine...he shot me."

Russell wasn't just a collaborator, Helen realized—he was a killer.

"Where is he?" Helen glanced in fear at the house, but didn't see any movement. He could be anywhere.

"Franz, do you know where he is?" Betty demanded.

"The house...talking to his wife...consults her...about everything." His breathing seemed to rattle in his chest. "Go now, Betty. Save...yourself."

His pleading eyes glistened in the faint moonlight. Helen couldn't help wondering if he loved Betty in some twisted way.

"Too late," Russell said from the doorway.

Shocked, Helen crouched. The blaze of a shot from Captain Lunenborg made Russell grunt and jerk back, but not before he got off a shot of his own. Captain Lunenborg sagged with a harsh gasp of pain. Catherine screamed, and Betty lunged toward the captain's body.

When Helen realized Betty was going for the gun to defend them all, she shouted, "No!"

But it was too late—Russell shot again, Betty fell back, and it was the captain who whispered, "No!" into the sudden quiet.

As Catherine wept, Helen thought that nothing could

possibly be real in this nighttime realm of shadows thick with the smell of blood.

And then she remembered how to move again. After a quick look outside where it seemed like Mr. Russell had disappeared, she fell on her hands and knees beside Betty. She didn't know where the torch was, couldn't see where Betty was hurt.

"Betty? Betty!" she cried. "Where are you shot?"

She could hear Betty breathing harshly with pain, and that was some relief. Catherine was still crying, but she'd come down beside Helen and tried to quiet herself.

"I don't want to die," Betty whispered.

"You're not going to die! Where are you shot?" Helen cried with desperation. "Catherine, find the torch!"

Catherine rummaged on her hands and knees as she tried to stifle her sobs.

Helen began to run her hands over Betty's torso and felt the blood. There was so much of it already, from her chest to her stomach, as if an artery had been ruptured. The realization of what that meant made everything inside her seem to grow still, calm; she'd experienced this too many times before.

"Betty," Helen said quietly, "we'll make sure everyone knows how brave you are, how you sacrificed everything for your country, for your friends."

The moonlight gleamed briefly on Betty's face as her grimace eased, and her expression turned peaceful.

"My final curtain call," Betty whispered, her smile crooked. "Tell my mother I love her..."

Helen watched the life fade from her friend's eyes. The wrenching loss finally penetrated her nurse's calm, and she gave a moan of grief.

"I found the torch!" Catherine cried.

She turned it on to reveal the stark scene of Betty and Captain Lunenborg dead beside each other, blood a dark stain across them both. Catherine dropped the torch and gagged.

Helen sagged back onto her heels, her arms and her head too heavy to lift.

"We have to call an ambulance," Catherine whispered.

"It's too late."

"Oh, no," Catherine said, tears in her voice as she reached out to touch Betty. "She can't be—not Betty—oh, Helen, no!"

The danger of their situation was beginning to penetrate the fog in her brain, and Helen realized that Russell could be back any moment.

"We have to go," she said dully, then with more force, "We have to go!"

"We can't leave her!" Catherine said, her voice aghast.

"How will we explain this if we stay?" Helen grabbed her arm and pulled them both to their feet. "She won't want us to get caught. And we have to be free to tell her story!"

They both knew how this tragic scene would look—a lover's quarrel gone wrong.

"We're in the middle of a war, Catherine, and Betty would understand. I want to live long enough to tell people what she tried to do."

Catherine was still crying, but she didn't protest. "The gun," she said. "Should we take it? In case Mr. Russell..."

"We can't take the captain's gun—it has to look like he used it. But Betty's gun—I don't know if she was going for it or for Franz's gun when she..." She couldn't go on speaking, even as she felt in Betty's trouser pocket and found the weapon. Betty was so still, as if she was only sleeping.

"What are you doing?" Catherine hissed.

"I'm keeping this for our protection."

With a last look at the shadows of Betty and the captain, Helen pulled Catherine out of the gazebo.

And they stumbled over Russell, who was lying just outside in the shadowy darkness, unmoving. Helen felt for his pulse.

"He's dead," she whispered. "We have to go before his wife comes out."

~oOo~

At dawn, Helen and Catherine were still huddled together on the sofa at Catherine's house after a night of crying. They'd heard the police and the German authorities arrive at the Russells' home almost an hour after they left. Mr. Braun had woken up with the commotion and gone outside, only to return white-faced.

One of the hardest things Helen had ever had to do was listen to Mr. Braun tell them their friend had been murdered, and pretend she knew nothing.

But their tears were real.

When the telephone rang just as the sun was coming up, Catherine answered, her voice dull. Helen watched her eyes widen and fill with new tears.

"Of course, we'll go," Catherine said at last. "I'm so sorry, Mrs. Markham." She hung up the phone.

Helen winced. "I never thought about how Betty's mother would hear the news. I wish we could have told her."

Catherine drew in a shuddering breath. "She sounds terrible. At least it was the police who notified her, rather than the Germans. She wants us to go to the hospital because she can't. We need to see if the hospital will release Betty to the undertaker, and bring home her things."

Biting her lip, Helen nodded. "Let's go."

At the hospital, Helen and Catherine sat in the emergency ward. As Helen's coworkers passed by through the morning, they gave her sympathetic or curious stares. One offered to let her department know that she couldn't work that day.

When Mrs. Russell came down the corridor, Catherine silently gripped Helen's arm. Mrs. Russell's face was pale, her eyes bloodshot, though she wasn't crying. A minister was walking with her, speaking in low, comforting tones. The woman's gaze passed over Helen and Catherine as if she didn't see them.

All Helen could think about was what Mrs. Russell might say to the authorities. How much did she really know? Before he'd died, Captain Lunenborg had said that Mr. Russell had gone to discuss the situation with his wife. But at that point, Mr. Russell hadn't seen Helen and Catherine. Helen imagined Mrs. Russell hearing more gunshots and coming out to find the bodies. She'd obviously felt like she had to call the police. Or had the sound of gunshots made someone else call?

Helen's stomach twisted with guilt and shame for thinking about their welfare when Betty was lying dead in the morgue. Tears continued to stream down her cheeks, much as she tried to staunch them with her soaked handkerchief.

Two policemen, their uniforms with shiny buttons down the front, their helmets sporting a badge, paused before entering the room where Mrs. Russell was waiting with her minister. Helen recognized the men, Constable Venn, the portly middle-aged husband of one of her fellow nurses, and Constable Hillard, a gray-haired officer past retirement who used to oversee the Guernsey Grand Hotel patrol before the war. They'd both known Betty. Everyone had.

The two men kept their heads together, talking in low, solemn voices, but Helen was able to hear some of it: references to Mrs. Russell's shock at discovering the gruesome scene, her belief that her husband must have surprised Captain Lunenborg and Betty in a rendezvous that had turned deadly. There was skepticism about why they'd meet in the Russells' gazebo. The police even brought up the recent death of Lieutenant Schafer, as if a fourth body during a war was so unusual.

At one point, they spoke about Betty as if she was the cause of it all. Helen couldn't help gaping at them, and Mr. Venn at least had the decency to blush. The men walked away.

"When this war is over," Helen whispered, her voice trembling, "I'm going to make sure everyone knows what *really* happened, how brave she was."

Catherine nodded, but she didn't seem to be able to speak and cry at the same time.

The minister left the private room and, a few minutes later, so did Mrs. Russell. She saw them still sitting there, and Helen could have sworn her look was cold, but it was gone so quickly. She, out of everyone, knew how the scene had begun between her husband and Captain Lunenborg, but Helen bet she hadn't told the truth about that.

Eventually, the hospital staff told them that the police wouldn't allow an undertaker to come for Betty's body, not that day, at least. After arranging for the hospital to coordinate with the undertaker, Helen and Catherine made the trek to Mrs. Markham's, where a neighbor lady was still sitting with her.

Mrs. Markham's pale skin now seemed the color of a gray winter sky. She barely acknowledged the two young women, just rocked herself slowly in her chair, repeating over and over that no man was worth the agony he brought on women.

Helen knew that men had done terrible things to the Markham women, but Betty had been bravely trying to find justice in the middle of the war. Not that she could tell Mrs. Markham that, nor anyone else. But when the war was over...

38

HELEN

F our months later, the Germans finally left the island in defeat, bound for PoW camps on the mainland. Helen stood in her baggy Sunday clothes near the piers along with everyone else and watched them leave. They looked dejected, bowed down, emaciated—but she did not pity them. Everyone was hungry on Guernsey—several people had died of starvation. If not for the Red Cross ship *Vega* delivering care packages several times, even more people would have died.

At least the German prisoners got to live, unlike so many, including Sergeant Doepgen. After Schafer's death, as if feeling the need to punish *someone*, the Germans had reassigned him to the Eastern Front. Catherine was told that he'd died the first day he'd arrived to cart wounded soldiers away from the battle lines. Helen had been worried about Catherine, but although her eyes had briefly looked haunted, she'd put any guilt she might have felt behind her. He'd been an enemy soldier—whereas Betty had been an innocent.

Near the pier where the Germans were leaving, a young

island woman with blond braids stood holding a little child, tears streaming down her face as the Germans passed by. One young officer reached out as he passed by and touched her hand. The baby reached for him, too, but the man was prodded up the gangplank, and he gave her one last anguished look. When she couldn't see her lover anymore, the young woman turned away and hurried through the crowd, some of whom eyed her with open disdain. But she kept her head high, her wet eyes resolute and full of hope.

Helen knew there were women who'd fallen in love with German soldiers. She only hoped the islanders would forgive them and not take out their disappointment on the innocent children.

Helen knew a little something about how love survived war. She'd received a letter from Germany two months before. She'd opened it with trepidation, telling herself that if the Germans decided to come for her, they wouldn't send a letter. But it was simply a note from the wife of her patient Lieutenant Beering, thanking her for the good care her husband had received, even though he'd been Helen's enemy. The woman must not know that her husband almost hadn't come home, and by his own hand. With the war almost over, and certainly her part in it, Helen had let go the last of her guilt regarding the lieutenant.

On VE Day just a few days before, the Germans had reluctantly let them listen to Churchill's speech as they gathered in the road outside homes where once-hidden radios now openly blared from windows; at last talks were underway for surrender.

Helen's eyes stung with sadness. Her friend Betty had not lived to see what her sacrifice had helped make happen: Allied victory, German defeat.

She felt a light squeeze on her arm and glanced up at Dr.

Patrick Coleridge, giving him a reassuring smile. When more doctors had been needed on Guernsey a few months ago, the Germans had transferred him from the island of Jersey. He was in his early thirties, with auburn hair and a perpetually cheerful face, a man who'd decided to make the best of every situation.

They'd become friends, which was all Helen would let herself contemplate. She had been the one assigned to make him familiar with the hospital and its routines. Patrick had arrived when Helen was still overcome with grief, and his obvious attempts to make her smile had been tolerated and, eventually, welcomed. He had a good heart.

"So does life just go back to normal?" Patrick asked ruefully.

She shrugged. "Will it ever?"

"Perhaps a new normal." He looked around at the harbor, bare of German ships. "It will be so good to make our own decisions without worrying about offending Germans and getting ourselves thrown in jail."

She chuckled. "I kept telling you not to contradict *Herr* Doctor, but you wouldn't listen."

"A night in jail was not a bad thing. It taught me humility."

She looked into his laughing eyes and shook her head. "And yet you didn't learn your lesson. Time after time, you came so close to disrespecting him. He was itching for a chance to put you in jail again—or perhaps send you to Germany."

"Bah, the hospital needed me too much." He eyed her with teasing speculation. "Did you worry for me, Helen?"

She actually blushed. "Of course not."

He hesitated, then said, "Why don't you come with me

later today? Some of the staff are going to inspect the underground hospital the Germans were building."

"Underground hospital?" Her voice was hoarse as memories flooded back, and with it the clutching pain of grief and loss, of everything Betty had sacrificed to keep that hospital from being used by a force invading Britain.

"The Germans are gone now," he said quietly. "They can't hurt you."

"Helen!" came a woman's voice.

Helen was glad for the distraction.

Catherine came running toward her, pushing aside the gawkers who watched the Germans depart.

Helen smiled and waved. Catherine hugged her, and Helen felt her friend's thinness—but her strength, too.

"Hello, Patrick," Catherine said, then turned to Helen with a wide grin, her eyes shining with happy tears.

Helen knew what had happened before Catherine could speak. "Your brother's home!" she cried and hugged her friend hard.

"He's home," Catherine whispered. "He surprised us at lunch. You should have heard my mother scream."

Patrick smiled. "That is the best news I've heard in a long time."

"Thank you." Catherine pulled a handkerchief out of her pocket to dab her eyes. "He says we look terribly thin. But so does he—he fit right in." Though Catherine was smiling, her tears didn't stop as she glanced at the departing German troops. "I can't believe it's finally over."

Helen started to cry, too, and they hugged again, long and hard. Patrick continued to gaze at the ship, as if trying to give them a moment's privacy. He was always so thoughtful.

Catherine stepped back and held Helen's shoulders,

looking in her eyes. "More of our soldiers came back today, dozens and dozens of them spilling out of landing craft."

"I missed it," Helen said. "I was at the hospital."

"Did Jack...." Catherine began, her voice trailing off in hope. Then she glanced at Patrick as if realizing what she'd said.

Helen knew Patrick would never be offended. She shook her head. "I've heard nothing." She beat back the rise of despair.

Catherine gave her a sympathetic glance and turned back toward the pier. "More and more soldiers will be arriving." Her voice held encouragement.

"Hmm," was all Helen said.

Patrick studied his watch intently. "Ladies, the hospital needs me. I'll see you both later." To Helen, he said, "I'll call you."

He strode off, and she waved fondly.

Catherine lowered her voice. "I think you need to write to Jack. You can't expect Patrick to wait forever."

"What?" Helen said, startled.

Catherine rolled her eyes. "You know how he feels."

"I would never put him in such a position. We have never discussed such a thing." Helen felt hot with blushing.

"Of course not, because he's a gentleman. You know he doesn't date anyone."

"I have introduced him to so many nurses who would have loved to have dinner with him!"

"Uh huh." Catherine shook her head. "You need to write to Jack."

"I—I don't know."

"I want to know what happened with Mr. Russell's note," Catherine said firmly. "We deserve the truth. And then we can take it to Mrs. Markham and tell her everything."

"We don't have to wait for that. Let's tell her now. If she talks about it to someone, it will no longer matter."

Mrs. Markham's health had slowly deteriorated since Betty's death. Sometimes she thought Betty was at school or work, and other times she remembered everything and mourned her all over again. Maybe knowing the truth at last would bring her some comfort.

But it wouldn't bring back Betty.

~oOo~

Mrs. Russell and her son were on the first ship away from the island. Not that Helen blamed them. Though Mrs. Russell had a small group of friends who professed her innocence, most islanders believed she and her husband had been collaborators, and that Mr. Russell had hardly stumbled unaware into his gazebo the night Betty died. After that, Mrs. Russell had to queue for food like the rest of the islanders, dressed in black, clutching her son's hand, her head tilted proudly.

Helen hated to judge a person without all the facts; for all she knew, Mrs. Russell had tried to talk her husband out of his German sympathies. But she'd certainly been well fed when her husband was alive, with new stockings and lipstick whenever she wanted them. Helen couldn't help wondering how many Reichsmarks Mrs. Russell was able to exchange for British sterling, with no questions asked. The British had already shown a startling propensity to ignore complaints against collaborators, claiming that without proof, nothing could be done. They didn't want to see proof, Helen thought bitterly. They wanted the war and its uglier consequences to be over.

A week passed, and the king and queen's visit briefly

stirred up the island. Helen heard nothing from Jack, and word spread that his family did not plan to return. They had been her last hope. She was beginning to fear that Jack was dead, leading her to walk through the hospital in a daze of grief. True, he'd made her no promises, and could very well have met someone else. But she *needed* to talk to him. She discovered his family's Wiltshire address from a neighbor and wrote them a letter.

One afternoon, Catherine showed up at Helen's kitchen door, out of breath from riding her bicycle too fast. She held up a creased and tattered envelope.

Helen gasped. "Is it...?"

"It's from Jack!" Catherine said with a squeal.

Helen closed her eyes and leaned heavily on the table with relief.

Catherine patted her shoulder. "A soldier friend of his came to my house and asked if I would give it to you, since he didn't have time to travel out to your cottage."

With trembling fingers, Helen took the letter and sank into a kitchen chair, looking at it for long minutes. It could be everything she'd waited so long to know. Jack wasn't dead. She should be thrilled, relieved, but...she wasn't. She'd felt that something was wrong for weeks now.

"Would you like to be alone?" Catherine asked with sympathy.

"No." She took a deep breath, slit the envelope open with a knife, and unfolded a thin sheet of paper as her heart beat rapidly.

DEAR HELEN,

I wanted you to know that I was injured after leaving the

island, and I lost my leg from infection. I'm still convalescing with my family to tend me.

HELEN FUMBLED for her handkerchief and blew her nose, imagining proud, strong Jack bedridden. Catherine stared at her, eyes wide with worry, and Helen briefly explained what had happened. She thought of how he'd scaled the Guernsey cliffs to escape the Germans, how he'd always wanted the freedom to explore the world on his own terms. Could he be that person again?

THERE'S no easy way to say this, but I won't be returning to Guernsey. I'm not the man you think I am, and I can never become him, not after everything that's happened. My actions toward you were unprofessional, and I hope someday you can forgive me.

As for the other note I've included—

DAZED, barely able to breathe from the ache that suffused her chest, she forced herself to reach back into the envelope and pull out another sheet of paper with trembling fingers. It was much creased and faded, but she recognized it at once: the note from Captain Lunenborg to Mr. Russell about the German weapon. She drew in a painful breath.

"Helen, is everything all right?" Catherine asked anxiously. "The look on your face—oh dear, it's not good."

Helen shook her head. "I can't—he won't—this is Mr. Russell's note."

Catherine blanched. "But if Jack has it, and not the government, was everything we did for nothing?"

"I—I don't know. I haven't finished reading."

"Then read!"

Helen wanted to throw the note into the fireplace, but she forced herself to read it aloud. *"I want you and Catherine to have this memento of what the three of you accomplished. I wish Betty could know, but I heard that can never be. I'm so sorry.*

"The note did arrive in time, but it didn't turn out the way I wanted. There was a mole in our government, Gilbert Riley, someone who received the schematics from Franz and was supposed to encourage production of the reconfigured German mines. Your note helped the government identify him. But instead of arresting him, they let him go, because they wanted the Germans to believe he was safe. They wanted to pass false information to the enemy, and it worked. No one can know. Make sure Catherine understands that. The government doesn't want citizens to know the true cost of winning the war—and the sometimes ugly way it had to happen. They aren't announcing that he was a traitor, but they recently let him know that his life would never be the same. I believe he killed himself, but I can never be certain.

"The government wishes it could thank you and your friends for all that you did, but they can't. It's a matter of national importance. But I wanted you to have the note, to know that everything you and the others sacrificed truly helped us to win this war. I trust you to hold onto it until the right time to reveal it, though it can't be anytime soon, since they don't know I took it. Thank you for everything you did. Sincerely, Jack."

Helen realized she was still clutching Russell's note in her hand. She set it down with great care as she took a deep breath. "So no one can know that Betty gave her life for that information."

Tears were running down Catherine's cheeks. "That's grossly unfair."

Unable to sit a moment longer, Helen got up and went outside to stand in the garden where she could listen to the sounds of the sea. It usually calmed her. Not now. She'd been living in fear for Jack for months, and now he didn't want to see her again. Did he regret everything that had happened?

She heard Catherine come up behind her. "What aren't you telling me?"

The pain of heartbreak made her gasp aloud as she lowered her head and hugged herself.

"He's not c-coming back," Helen whispered. "H-he regrets...everything."

The disappointment of betrayal made tears flood her eyes.

"Jack wrote that? *Our* Jack?"

"He says he can't be the man I n-need."

"Oh, Helen!"

Catherine hugged her hard, absorbing Helen's tears the way only close friends could.

"H-he always warned me that we couldn't have more together, b-but I refused to believe him." She hiccoughed a sob. "I thought I knew him, but if he could do *this,* I never knew him at all." Obviously, their night together had only been a moment's respite in the midst of war.

"Shouldn't you tell him the truth?" Catherine asked gently. "It might change everything."

Straightening from the embrace, Helen put her hand protectively on the small swell of her belly. "No."

"Helen—"

"If he loved me, an amputated leg wouldn't have stopped

him from coming back. I'm not going to force him to return and ruin all our lives. This baby deserves a willing father."

"But Helen—"

"I have my position at the hospital." *I hope,* she thought bleakly. "I'll get by. There have been many babies born during this occupation under questionable circumstances. What's one more?" Her voice broke.

Catherine hugged her again, and they stood together for a long moment. "I'll be here for you. My whole family will."

Helen managed a smile. "I know. Thank you." Her smile faded as she thought of the friend who could only be with her in her heart. "I'm going to talk about Betty's attempts to find out information for the war effort. I want people to know she wasn't a Jerrybag."

"We can't provide any details. The frustration might be worse."

"I'll take that chance. But I promise not to speak about the note. I will keep it safe and always know we were a part of the victory, even if it has to be a forgotten part."

"For now. Jack says we can reveal it someday."

Helen sighed. "Can we? He's obviously angry with the government. I don't want to get him in trouble—or get ourselves in trouble."

Catherine looked toward her bicycle with regret. "I have to go. My family—"

"Of course. Go be with your brother. I'll be fine." She had to be, for her child.

"Why don't you come with me!"

"No, but thank you. I can't be with people right now."

Catherine seemed to know that insisting wouldn't work. After watching her bicycle down the lane, Helen turned to stare at the cottage that always made her feel the warmth of home. Now it just seemed so lonely.

~oOo~

That evening, as Helen was washing her supper dishes, she heard a knock on her kitchen door. A stab of fear went through her, until she silently reminded herself that the Germans were gone, and no one could hurt her anymore.

No one but Jack, it seemed, she thought bleakly, and he'd hurt her in a way she'd never imagined him capable of.

She wiped her hands on a towel, went to the door, and called, "Who is it?" Years ago, she would have opened it without asking, but no more.

"It's Patrick. May I come in?"

Frowning, she opened the door and stared at him in confusion. Although they were friends, she'd never invited him to her cottage before. "Hello, Patrick. This is a surprise."

"I know." His usually cheerful face was drawn in sober, serious lines. "May we talk?"

"Of course." She stepped back, and after he stepped inside, she shut the door. "Would you like some tea?"

"Yes, thank you."

He seemed awkward and uncertain in her kitchen, words she'd never associated with him.

"Please sit down. Unless you'd rather sit in the parlor?"

"No, the kitchen is fine. We don't need to be formal with each other."

He said it in a questioning tone of voice. She smiled. "No, we don't."

He didn't say anything more as she put the kettle on to boil. She watched him in confusion, surprised and worried about his change in manner.

When at last they each had a cup before them, he took a fortifying sip and said, "Catherine came to see me an hour ago."

The air left Helen's lungs in a rush and she sat back with dismay. "What did she say?" she asked tightly.

"She told me that you're pregnant," he said, "and that the father isn't coming back."

She realized her hands were covering her belly, not with shame but with protection. "That was my story to tell. Or not."

"Did you think you could keep it a secret?" he asked, wearing a faint smile. "Or did you intend to leave?"

She sighed. "I didn't intend to leave."

"Good. This might not be what you want to hear, but I need to say it. I admire you tremendously, Helen. You are far too perceptive not to know how I've felt about you."

Her cheeks hot with embarrassment, she stammered, "I—I don't know what to say." She'd notice him watching her intently once in a while, but he'd catch himself and give her his friendly smile. She thought she was misinterpreting his interest, but Catherine had understood—and so had Helen, if she was honest with herself.

"You just need to listen," he continued. "I have been content being your friend, because I feared it might be all I ever had of you. But it seems I've been given a second chance."

"Patrick—"

"For someone who doesn't know what to say, you're determined to try."

His smile contained a tenderness that somehow made her eyes sting. She looked away, blinking. She was so emotional these days.

"Why are you here, Patrick?" she whispered. "Just say what you mean to before my eyes turn into watering pots."

"Then I'll get right to the point." He reached across the table and took her hand. "Helen, will you marry me?"

Her mouth fell open, and her tears overflowed down her cheeks. "I once dreamed of such a proposal," she said hoarsely, "but hadn't imagined it would be out of pity."

"Pity?" His eyes widened with shock then narrowed in determination. "This is not pity, and if my words don't convince you, then let my heart do so." He stood up and came around the table, dropping to one knee before taking both her hands. "I never thought I would be lucky enough to propose to you, much as in my dreams I did so many times."

"Patrick, we've only known each other for a few months!"

"I know all I need to know. I know how devoted a friend you are. I see how you give everything to your patients, regardless of the emotional cost to you. I know your courage to outlast a German occupation. And Catherine hinted to me that you're even braver than I know—not that I would press you. I want you to feel that I deserve your confidences, that I've proven myself."

"But this baby won't be yours. How will you bear that?"

"A baby I am privileged to help raise will be mine in every way that matters to me. I was adopted as an infant, so I know that love can grow and endure without a biological bond." He bent his head and kissed the knuckles on each of her hands. "I will spend each day showing how much I love you, Helen, and I hope someday that you will feel the same for me."

He wasn't asking her to declare her feelings, but he was openly sharing his own. He was a man who was unafraid to be vulnerable, to risk his heart.

Everything she and Jack had experienced together swamped her memories: the tense nights when he'd been hiding in her house and might be discovered, the unease of wondering what he was doing or when he'd be caught, the longing to be in his arms, and the last sadness and joy of finding such fulfillment and then losing it. Those crazy emotions she'd experienced with Jack were not the things one built a life on. He'd proven untrustworthy. Melancholia was like a brief caress of a past that she would put behind her.

Patrick was a man one could trust.

He searched her eyes, and she gave him a tremulous smile. "I'll marry you."

His expression was full of such joyous disbelief that she almost chuckled.

He snatched her to her feet and hugged her, before suddenly pulling away and staring at her stomach. "I could have hurt you!"

"You're a doctor—you know better."

"Well, it's different with the woman who'll be your wife." He put his hands on her shoulders. "I know we won't have the grand wedding of your dreams, but being together will be all that's important. We have so many plans to make. And if you decide you'd rather put painful memories behind you and leave Guernsey, I would do that, too. My family comes first."

Family. It was such a good word. She stood on tiptoes and kissed him, and the expression on his face was as if she'd given him the greatest gift. She would work hard to give him the loving family he deserved.

A sad chapter of her life was over. She was glad that the next one was already beginning.

39

CHELSEA

One moment, I'd been sitting in a chair next to Grandma's hospital bed, wiping my eyes over Betty, but now I was just staring at her, my stomach clenched in disbelief, my mouth so dry I didn't know if I could speak. Everything I thought I knew about myself whirled around in my head and resettled into new and unfamiliar patterns. My mind was full of childhood memories: fishing with Grandpa on a sunny day in his canoe, working with him on the little village in the middle of his train set, where he let me paint my own house any color I wanted. He came to every play, every lacrosse game, and all that time he was loving me out of the goodness of his heart—not because I was related to him.

What had it felt like to marry a woman pregnant with another man's child, wondering if she could ever love him the same way? And then they'd never had any other children. Had it mattered to him? Did he mourn in some private way?

Grandma watched me, biting her lip, eyes wide. "Talk to me, Chelsea," she said softly. "How do you feel about—"

She gestured lamely, as if trying to encompass the enormity of what she'd told me.

I let out my breath as I leaned back, away from her, clutching the chair arms. I wanted to say, *You lied to me. My whole life. My mother did, too. Am I supposed to ignore that?* Instead I murmured, "Grandpa...wasn't my grandpa."

"He *was* your grandpa," she said, her voice firm. "He married me and treated your mother as his own. At first I thought he was just being honorable and perhaps pitying me, but I came to understand that he loved me with his whole heart, and your mother was a part of me. More for him to love, he always said."

Dazed, I murmured lamely, "It was good to hear about how you met. I still miss him."

"I do, too. Every day. But it's been ten years now, and my missing him is mostly filled with the joy of our marriage, the good memories, rather than the sadness of losing him. Oh, don't cry again, my dear."

I wiped my tears with the back of my arm. Somehow I had to digest this new revelation, find a way to accept that she'd done what she had to do—just as she'd done fifty years ago. I reminded myself what it must have been like to be pregnant with the child of a man who'd abandoned her without even returning to let her down in person. Not that my biological grandfather knew the truth of what he was really losing when he made that decision. Or maybe I didn't know the whole story. "Did you ever see Jack again?"

"No. If he came to the island while I still lived there, he never visited me."

"Did you ever consider telling him about Mom?"

She sighed, plucking at the blanket repetitively. "Many times. But it was a different world then, Chelsea. He told me to forget about him, that he didn't want to be with me. So that's what I did."

Could I blame her for not tracking down a man who didn't love her?

She said, "I thought that contacting him later would have been a betrayal of your grandfather and everything he'd done for me—for us. Did I make the right decision? At the time I thought I did, and it never haunted me. But in recent years..." She let out a sigh. "I don't know. But I can't change the past."

"When did you tell Mom the truth?"

"When she was eighteen, and old enough to understand."

"And she didn't think I deserved to know when I grew up?" I reached for a tissue and blew my nose, angry at the never-ending tears. I was trying to be logical and understanding, but my emotions weren't listening.

"I wanted to be the one to tell you, and I...couldn't find the words. You worshipped your grandpa. I felt like I'd be taking those memories away from you somehow. But when I woke up after the fall down the stairs, I knew I couldn't keep the truth to myself any longer. I had to reveal...everything."

"So you never told anyone about Mr. Russell altering the German schematics?"

Grandma shook her head. "I did not, not until Karen approached me. I thought it was time the world knew the truth. But Catherine and I told people that Betty had no choice but to date Captain Lunenborg, and said she used it to good advantage by trying to spy on him. But without any kind of proof, our words were often dismissed. It was easier for them to believe what they'd always believed, rather than admit they'd misjudged a young woman."

"It's still an incredible story. Did you tell Grandpa?" I asked.

"I told him everything. When you love someone, you trust him with all your secrets. Speaking of memories..." She opened the bed table drawer, pulled out a little box, and handed it to me. "I'd like you to have this."

I opened it to see a brooch, shaped like a bouquet of flowers made of tiny jewels. "Grandma, it's beautiful."

"They're not real jewels, of course, but it was my mother's. I wore it for many years after she died as a way to keep her close to my heart." Grandma gave a soft sigh and blinked rapidly. "It is not so easy to imagine her face after more than fifty years, but I remember the essence of *her*, and how she loved me. That brooch comforted me throughout the war. I want you to have it now."

I was surprised to find my hand trembling as I lifted it out of the box. At first it had almost felt like a bribe, but then I chastised myself. That wasn't Grandma's way. I *knew* her—the truth of her story couldn't change everything about her. "Thanks so much, Grandma. It's kind of like I'll have a part of you." And I wanted that. She'd done the best she could in a terrible situation, and I could never judge her for it. I pinned it to my shirt.

She chuckled. "It's not exactly in style, I know."

"I don't care." I hesitated. "Thank you so much for trusting me with your story."

"Why wouldn't I trust you?" Her eyes narrowed thoughtfully as she regarded me.

I shrugged. "It's been hard to trust myself lately. I've been feeling like my dreams of being an actress are so pointless that I should go back to school and get on with my life."

"Dreams are never pointless, Chelsea. They're what

make us grow. My friends and I never thought we could accomplish anything during the war, but we persevered."

"You're not comparing my twenties to yours," I said lightly, even though there was a lump in my throat.

"No comparisons are necessary. Living a good life means taking chances. I'm proud that you're giving it your best. And if acting professionally is not in your future, you'll still have learned much about yourself and had fun along the way. Regrets are a terrible thing. I don't want you to have any."

I smiled at her, though my lips were trembling. But more important things were happening than my career aspirations.

"What about you?" I asked. "Someone knows you have the note, and they don't want it to come out."

"I was tempted to destroy it many times—I guess I should have. But it connected me to Betty and Catherine, to a time when our contributions meant just as much as a soldier's." Grandma patted my hand. "It's late. Let's sleep on this. I'll try to have a decision about going public by morning. And if you have any other questions about Jack, I'll do my best to answer them."

I leaned down and kissed her soft cheek. "Thank you for trusting me with the truth and letting me help. It's something I'll never forget."

Grandma kept smiling as I backed away, even as her eyes closed and her expression relaxed. As I pulled the door shut behind me, I noticed a man standing at the far end of the hallway, past the elevators. He was thin and older, with gray hair, and he looked at the window as if passing the time. I had seen him when I first arrived earlier in the day. I wondered if he was waiting for someone, or taking a break from visiting. There was something about him that seemed familiar, but I couldn't place it. When he never looked my way, I got on the elevator and put it out of my mind.

But hours later, after dinner with a high school friend I hadn't seen in a while, I thought about that man from the hallway again. He made me...curious, even uneasy. And before I knew it, I was parking near St. Vincent's hospital just after evening visiting hours. I thought it might be difficult to talk my way upstairs, but I'd been visiting enough that the desk attendant answering the phone just waved me through.

On Grandma's floor, there were nurses at the central station, but none in the hall, which was deserted now that most visitors had gone. The lights were low, and I saw only a faint light beneath Grandma's door. A shadow passed swiftly across it. Too swiftly for an old lady.

I opened the door, flipped on the overhead light, and saw a broad man dressed in scrubs bent over Grandma, his back to me. My momentary relief fled like a dousing of ice water when her legs kicked feebly and one of her hands flailed. After crossing the room in two strides, I realized he held a pillow over her face. I gave a horrified cry, and the man whirled, dark eyes wide over a scruffy beard. Grandma gasped for air as the pillow released.

"Get away from her!" I yelled.

I lunged for his arm, and he flung me sideways, where I hit my head against the wall. My vision briefly blurred, and when it cleared, I saw that another man had entered, the same one I'd seen lingering in the hallway that day.

And he had a gun.

He pointed it at the man trying to kill Grandma. The first man raised his hands away from the pillow and took a step back.

Gasping, Grandma came up on her elbow, her face pale

with strain, her eyes streaming tears as she stared at her rescuer, the lean old man with close-cropped hair, silvery gray in the light.

"Jack," she breathed.

The way she said his name, full of shock and relief and wonder, I knew this was Jack Dupuis—my grandfather. I gasped aloud, then covered my mouth with both hands. I couldn't risk distracting him.

But his eyes, so vividly blue, were my mother's eyes—my eyes.

He didn't look at either of us, but spoke to the stranger. "Move away from the bed."

The man stepped back, hands still raised.

"The woman who hired you is dead," Jack said. "This is finished."

The woman? I thought.

I saw Grandma's eyes widen in surprise as she took deep lungsful of air and trembled. I couldn't imagine how she felt, seeing the man who'd rejected her over fifty years ago, now standing in her hospital room holding a gun on a stranger.

"Come with me now," Jack said to the man. "I see no reason to make a scene that will draw the police."

"Sounds good, mate," the man answered with a London accent.

He wore a little smirk, as if he thought he'd soon take down an old man and escape.

"Jack—" Grandma began, her voice hoarse.

"We'll talk later." He didn't look at her, but motioned with his head toward the door. He put the gun in his pocket but never took his hand off it, as he limped behind the stranger.

And then they were both gone.

My head pounding, my stomach queasy, I rushed to

Grandma's side, even as she swung her legs off the bed, wincing.

"Let me help you," I said. Dizzy with anxiety and worry, I just wanted to hold her.

"I'm all right, Chelsea," she said, reaching for her dressing gown and shrugging into it.

"How can you be all right? *I'm* not all right—the man was trying to kill you!"

"I'm glad you said that because I had the strangest feeling it was all a dream. That was Jack, your grandfather. I haven't seen him in..." Her voice faded away, her gaze distracted. She stood up, and the remaining color drained out of her face.

I put my arm around her thin waist to find her trembling hard. "Sit back down, please. Want me to call a nurse?"

"No." But she sank down on the bed. "I'm too concerned about Jack, and I don't want to explain what happened. Where is he? What is he doing? I won't be able to bear it if he dies trying to help me."

"He looked pretty competent to me. I saw him out in the hall earlier today. Twice."

She gave me a sharp look. "What?"

"He's the reason I came back tonight. I was uneasy. I kept telling myself he was probably a visitor hanging out, but...I just had to come."

Maybe something about the way he carried himself, or the tilt of his head, *something*, had made me notice him in the hall when his back was to me. Had I subconsciously known we were connected?

"You could have been killed," she whispered, hugging me close.

"So could you!"

We clung together for a long time.

"We should call the police," I said, settling next to her on the edge of the bed.

"No! We can't get anyone else involved, not yet. It could put Jack in danger. I mean your grandfather. I mean—oh dear, I don't know what to call him."

"Jack's fine," I said, giving her a weak smile.

She seemed to search my face. "I never thought to see him again. But I can't imagine how you must feel, as if a ghost has come to life."

"Ghost or man, he saved your life and I'm so grateful."

Ten minutes later, a nurse came in and did a double-take on seeing me. "It's past visiting hours, young lady."

Grandma smiled. "I couldn't sleep, and I asked her to stay. It'll just be a few more minutes."

She frowned, checked something on a monitor, then put her hands on her ample hips. "Make sure you're gone before I come back."

I nodded vigorously.

When she'd gone, Grandma said, "It'll be hours before she comes back. You're fine."

A half hour later, we were still sitting side by side on the edge of the bed, my arm around her waist, when Jack stepped back into the room and shut the door. Grandma let out a whoosh of air, as if she'd been holding her breath the whole time.

I stared hard at him as he took us both in. Though his skin was lined with age, there was a vitality and alertness about him that let me know he wasn't a grandpa who sat around and watched TV.

He pulled up a chair and sat down in front of us. After a cursory glance at me, he spoke to Grandma with a dashing British accent. "Helen, are you all right?"

She nodded.

"Your breathing is rapid," he said. "You could have died." To me, he said, "Why didn't you call a doctor?"

"She wouldn't even let me call the police," I protested.

"No," Grandma said hoarsely, then cleared her throat. "Where is he? That man who..."

"You won't have to worry about him anymore."

She sagged back a bit and stared at him, as did I. I didn't think Jack meant that a killer had seen reason and left of his own accord.

"But—" Grandma began.

"Don't ask, Helen," he said. "I may be retired, but I still do things in the name of my country now and then."

My mouth sagged open. Was he saying he'd...

Jack looked directly at me for the first time, and I flinched at the probing directness of his gaze—and the strange echo of my mother's eyes in his.

"I saw you earlier today," he said. "Who are you to Helen?"

Grandma straightened a bit and said calmly, "Chelsea is my granddaughter—*your* granddaughter."

Jack stiffened, and we stared at each other. With everything I knew about him, I believed he wouldn't give way to emotions easily—he'd been a soldier and a spy, after all. Those blue eyes studied me with intensity, then widened, perhaps with shock, as if he was working his way past all his defenses and finally letting himself believe the truth.

"I just found out today, too," I said lamely.

His face went a bit florid; his eyes grew moist. And that touched me more than I could have imagined.

"It's...good to meet you." He spoke with a hesitancy that seemed foreign to him.

I smiled. "I feel the same. Thanks for tonight."

He nodded, studied me for a few more seconds, then

turned back to Grandma. For a long time, neither of them said anything, their gazes locked on each other. I thought of all the things they could be thinking, the regrets, the anger, the sadness, the disbelief, as they remembered what they'd been to each other—and how Jack had left her alone.

"I'm so sorry," he said at last, reaching for her hand, then pulling back as if he didn't have the right.

But Grandma caught his hand. "I am, too. There's so much I want to explain, but we can discuss this another time. That man...the person who hired him...was it Mrs. Russell?"

Jack hesitated and glanced at me. Would they try to send me out of the room like I was a child?

"You can speak in front of Chelsea," Grandma said. "I've told her everything. As far as I know, Mrs. Russell never had to explain herself or her husband's actions."

Jack nodded. "It was her. I've kept an eye on her through the years. A very old connection of mine in the government told me about a journalist digging into the past who'd discovered a collaborator who'd once lived on Guernsey. When the journalist ended up dead, I knew who had to be behind it."

"But why? Mrs. Russell was able to leave the island and any past German collaboration behind."

"Did you know she'd remarried?"

Grandma shook her head.

"Do you recognize the name Althea Theobald?"

"Isn't she in the House of Commons, representing a London constituency? What does she have to do with our situation?"

"She's also the long-ago Mrs. Althea Russell," he said coldly. "And do you know what position her name is being mentioned for?"

"Prime Minister." Grandma sounded stunned.

My gaze moved between them as if I was following a tennis match.

Jack continued, "And what happens when an ambitious Member of Parliament discovers that her deepest secret might come back and spoil her ultimate prize?"

"She has an innocent journalist killed," Grandma answered, "and comes after me for the proof that could reveal her past to the world."

He nodded in grim satisfaction.

It was like a James Bond movie, I thought in disbelief, but real and with such deadly consequences. That woman thought she was so above everyone that she could live in luxury during a war while others starved. She could rebuild her life, consequence-free, while others lost a leg, like Jack, or their life, like Betty. She'd built a political career while hiding the biggest secret of all, and instead of seeing it crumble when her true nature came to light, she'd doubled down on her villainy and orchestrated murder.

Grandma frowned. "You told that man that Mrs. Russell —Mrs. Theobald—was dead."

"And she is. Another suicide by a coward who didn't want to face what she'd done, especially when I told her the government planned to indict her for war crimes. I imagine it'll be in the papers today."

Jack's gaze was steady, but I wasn't certain how much of that was true. And I didn't care.

He leaned forward and put his hand on Grandma's. "You're safe, Helen."

I started feeling uncomfortably out of place. Grandma seemed to have forgotten I was there.

She looked down at his hand and back into his eyes.

"You've made a habit of rescuing me far too many times, Jack Dupuis."

He shrugged and said with serious intensity, "You rescued me, too."

Grandma was actually blushing. "I don't understand."

"The war changed me more than I wanted to admit, and losing my leg—well, I didn't feel like I was worth anything anymore. But then I saw how brave you were to go on with your life, to find happiness, and to know that Betty gave up *her* life, and all I'd done was lose a leg. I knew I had to find a purpose again, too. I created a private security firm, successful enough that sometimes the government asked me for help."

"You were a spy—again?" she said with a gasp.

"I wouldn't say that."

So self-deprecating. It really was like a James Bond movie. And he was my grandfather. I didn't even know what to think anymore. It seemed the danger to Grandma was over, and they were looking at each other in a way that made *me* blush. Frankly, it was adorable. And romantic. These last few days had shown me the woman she was, not just my grandmother, but a captive in a war who'd risked her life multiple times for what she believed in. She'd risked her life for Jack, and he'd let war and injury change how he saw himself, as if he wasn't worthy of her.

"Did you ever marry?" Grandma asked.

"I did, but we divorced after five years and never had children."

"I'm sorry to hear that."

"Don't be sorry for me, but for her. We didn't want the same things, and I didn't make her happy, though I wished I could."

"What are you doing now besides rescuing me?" she asked.

His smile was teasing. "I just bought a cottage on Guernsey."

"No!"

"Yes. I plan to spend at least winters there, or maybe the whole year."

"I can't picture you settled down."

"I don't know. It might be time. Do you think you'd come visit me?"

I saw the hope lighten his eyes—those blue eyes that connected us. I imagined his life had been a lonely one. What was he saying—or not saying?

Grandma shrugged, her expression sweetly uncertain. "I...I don't know."

"I'd like to renew our friendship," he said quietly, then glanced at me. "I'd like to get to know you, Chelsea. And your parents."

"My mom, especially," I said. "You'll really like her."

He grinned, and I saw the man Grandma had once loved.

"What do you think, Helen?" he asked.

Grandma smiled. "I did always love Guernsey in the winter."

~The End~

HELLO, dear reader!

. . .

THANK you for taking the time to read my new book! If you enjoyed it, please consider telling your friends or posting a short review. Word of mouth is an author's best friend and much appreciated.

For those who've never read my novels before, I come from the world of historical romance, where I really enjoyed the research. History has always fascinated me. About five years ago I found myself drawn to historical fiction set during the World Wars. I was reading women's stories, rather than those of battles, and I was fascinated. The more I read, the more I felt my subconscious was nudging me to try writing something different. I finally settled on Europe in World War II, but where? As I did more and more research, sometimes I felt I was hovering over Europe, looking down on all those countries, but unable to narrow my focus. Should my heroine be a Londoner surviving the Blitz? A French woman in the Resistance? I just didn't know!

And then I saw the movie *The Guernsey Literary and Potato Peel Pie Society*, set on Guernsey in the Channel Islands, right between France and England. It took place just after World War II, but with lots of flashbacks during the war. Before this movie, I'd had no idea that a part of Britain had been occupied by the Germans. It was like the proverbial lightbulb going off in my head, and that random feeling of floating over Europe zoomed right down to that little island, 9 miles by 6 miles. I read everything I could get my hands on, including many autobiographies of people who survived the occupation. I've given you a list below, in case you want to explore what happened for yourself.

Somehow, as I brainstormed this book with my critique groups (the Packeteers and the Purples, women I've known and loved for over 20 years), one heroine became four, if you include Chelsea, Helen's granddaughter. This was another new challenge for me, trying to tell so many women's stories in one book. And being a romance writer, I still wanted a romance, even if it was a minor plot. Once I read about British spies sneaking onto the island, Jack came to life.

I took some liberties with the timeline. The entire occupation lasted five years, but due to wanting to write Helen's pregnancy, I had to make the occupation seem shorter than it really was. Other than that, I tried to be historically accurate, and any mistakes are certainly mine!

I'm not sure what's next for me, although I think I'm heading back to Valentine Valley to write another contemporary romance as Emma Cane. Please sign up for my newsletter if you'd like notice when the next book will be published.

Thank you so much for reading this book! And if you like it, please leave a review wherever you purchased it. Reviews help authors find new readers!

THANKS AGAIN!
Gayle

BIBLIOGRAPHY

The Guernsey Literary and Potato Peel Pie Society, by Mary Ann Shaffer

The Model Occupation: The Channel Islands Under German Rule, 1940-1945, by Madeleine Bunting

A Child's War: The Occupation of the Channel Islands Through a Child's Eyes, by Molly Bihet

The Silent War, by Frank Falla

A Doctor's Occupation: the Dramatic True Story of Life in Nazi-Occupied Jersey, by John Lewis

How We Lived Then: History of Everyday Life During the Second World War, by Norman Longmate

BOOKS BY GAYLE CALLEN

The Daring Girls of Guernsey: a Novel of World War II

Secrets and Vows Series

You Only Marry Once

On Her Warrior's Secret Mission

The Knight Who Loved Me

The Bodyguard Who Came in from the Cold

The Brides Trilogy

Almost a Bride

Never a Bride

Suddenly a Bride

Highland Weddings Trilogy

The Wrong Bride

The Groom Wore Plaid

Love with a Scottish Outlaw

Brides of Redemption Trilogy

Return of the Viscount

Surrender to the Earl

Redemption of the Duke

The Scandalous Lady Trilogy

In Pursuit of a Scandalous Lady

A Most Scandalous Engagement

Every Scandalous Secret

Sons of Scandal Trilogy

Never Trust a Scoundrel

Never Dare a Duke

Never Marry a Stranger

Sisters of Willow Pond Trilogy

The Lord Next Door

The Duke in Disguise

The Viscount in her Bedroom

Spies and Lovers Trilogy

No Ordinary Groom

The Beauty and the Spy

A Woman's Innocence

ABOUT THE AUTHOR

After a detour through fitness instructing and computer programming, GAYLE CALLEN found the life she'd always dreamed of as a writer. This *USA Today* bestselling author has written more than twenty-five historical romances and has won the Holt Medallion, the Laurel Wreath Award, the Booksellers' Best Award, the National Readers' Choice Award, and has been a nominee for RT Book Reviews Reviewers' Choice Award. Her books have been translated into eleven different languages.

The mother of three grown children, an avid crafter, singer, and outdoor enthusiast, Gayle lives in Central New York with her dog Uma and her husband, Jim the Romance Hero. She also writes contemporary romances as Emma Cane.

Visit Gayle's website
Chat with her on Facebook
Find her on Goodreads
Sign up for Gayle's Newsletter